A CHILD MADE TO ORDER

Gripping psychological suspense

PIOTR RYCZKO

THE
BOOK
FOLKS

Paperback published by The Book Folks

London, 2017

ISBN 978-1-5207-9886-8

www.thebookfolks.com

Dear Leslie,

Thank you for dedicating your time to reading my novel.

I hope it will touch you in some way.

Piotr Rzyski

To Ewa.
This is for you.
For your support and belief.

PART ONE: Lies

Vlog, 165th entry 2.9.2014

She had made all the arrangements. This was it.

This was her last speech.

No one could know. Not even the public on her blog. Especially not her public.

What she could do right now, was share herself with them. After that, after her plan had run its course, she would long be remembered.

Her emotional overload had started long before she faced the camera. She had learnt to conserve her energy for the public, long before she went live. A necessity of her profession.

A stuttering, low-quality webcam feed appeared on the laptop screen. Murky shadows parted and revealed the contours of a face. Marianne's face. Her own face.

She barely had the courage to face the camera's lens. Not because of the public, but because she couldn't bear looking into those eyes. As she met them on the screen, she finally recognised herself. Despite her age of twenty-five, her features were that of someone twice that.

Marianne's face was covered with nose and brow-rings. She remembered now that she had first impaled her skin just after her third miscarriage. The rings were only simple tools. A means to dumb down the mental pain she had to suffer through each day. And at that time, she had needed those rings more than ever.

She had gotten used to the heaviness that pervaded her body. And it was more than apparent on the screen. It had accompanied her ever since she had learned about her disease. Or rather, the nature of its irreversibility. A death sentence for her new-borns.

But she had more important things to do now. This show was about her final message to her audience, to the community of infertile women who depended on her. And although, right now, she only felt primeval destruction inside herself, it was still genuine. And this authenticity had made all the difference for the past four years of her blog. Only she could muster this intensity, and when her eyes finally faced the viewers, the effect was magnetic in its potency. No wonder she had amassed a following, and not a small one. This kind of pain was hard to come by, even in a world soaked with suffering.

"I don't think you get it, do you? Childlessness... that's not a loss. That's a death in the family. And this death will never have a funeral, nor a proper mourning. And who would actually care about us?" She stopped for a slight moment to let the viewers meditate over the last question posed, and its absurd notion.

"Certainly not the doctors, shrinks, family, and the people in charge at *Bioteknologirådet*. Who would care about a ticking bomb with a rare genetic disease?"

When she spoke, the words seemed to float into the air. The effect was trance-like, addictive in its quality. She was convinced she was a woman with a mission, and this day would be the greatest milestone in her journey.

"Mark my words. Mitochondrial disease. Do you want a child with irreversible nervous malfunctions, muscle dystrophy, dementia? You fucking name it, and I will give it to my child. You see this face? That's who I am."

She sniffled and fell into silence. Her body was quiet, as if she was meditating. But the meditation was not about serenity, it was about holding onto her emotional sanity. And the only thing that mattered was to prevent the inner volcano from erupting.

"Do you know what makes the loneliest moment in one's life? It is having so much love to give, and then realising that it will never be yours to give. Never! Not to my little one," she all but hissed at the public. The only thing that could follow this peak was the blackness as she terminated her cam.

But she wasn't done.

It often gave her a thrill of pleasure to let the audio channel run long after the visuals had gone blank. With only her ragged breath remaining, pulsing its pain at her audience, she couldn't feel more alive.

This was high drama. Staged and constructed by her God-given talent. She was sure that it left everyone watching numb, with a black hole in their heart.

They would remember her long after that.

And this was just the beginning.

Chapter 1

Monday, 8th February 2016
Evening
They were all waiting for her downstairs, Viola knew that. They being everyone who was someone in Oslo's media circles. The occasion was a late evening cocktail party. A party held in her honour. Viola knew that in the eyes of everybody downstairs she had achieved a career milestone today, the stuff her fellows dreamed of. Syria and Middle East correspondence for the biggest newspaper in Norway, *Aftenposten*. A position many aspired to but seldom reached. At the age of 41, this was quite an accomplishment. Her intuition as an investigative watchdog had gotten her to this place, a point where everyone either adored her or simply despised her. And it was her unwavering determination that kept her there.

Except for one small detail. It was all lies.

The stuff everybody expected of her and thought about her was one thing. But in her case, the appearances never corresponded with the inner truth.

That's why she was here. Upstairs, in the bathroom. Dressed in her onyx Sherri Hill one-shoulder cocktail dress. Hiding like a wounded animal, scraping her knees against the bathroom tiles.

This was the only place where she didn't feel like she was about to lose her mind. And the only thing that took away some of the numbness, stabbing at her heart, was the scrubbing. Her hand clenched onto a piece of wiry cloth, while she did her best to remove a practically non-existent stain from the bathtub. Holding onto it, the steel fibre felt real enough, jagged enough to hurt, a necessary pain.

The screeching movement back and forth held another quality. She was convinced it would wipe away everything that had happened here. In this bathroom, in this very tub. Five years ago. And the further into the past that date drifted, the more actual weight it carried.

She needed this cloth to lighten that load. It held a potential. She wasn't naive enough to think it would remove the thing called the past. The hole in herself. It certainly wasn't an eraser of all the wrong choices she had brought upon herself. That never worked in her case. But it was, nonetheless, the best option she had.

She had to believe that.

A thought skittered along the periphery of her mind. Surely someone would notice she was missing downstairs. And would eventually knock on the door, forcing her to pick up the pieces, what was left of them anyway, and put on that unwavering mask of the hostess. And before that realisation could wreak further unease in her thoughts, a dull thud sounded against the door.

"Viola? Hon? You okay? Remember the party? Your party?" a muffled voice said. Ronny worried about her, maybe too much. Always prepared to hug her and soothe her. The way only a trusted partner would be willing to do. Most people would cherish this quality in a man. And sometimes she reminded herself this was good. She explained to herself that she was lucky.

"Sure. Perfect." She uttered the words, more preoccupied with whether he would sense the quiver in her voice than their content. But however much turmoil she might have stirred up inside herself, she had also perfected the art of self-presentation. A quality that, in her profession, translated into self-preservation. Her tone was as controlled and soft-spoken as a Buddhist monk during a retreat.

"Okay... It's just... You've been in there for over forty minutes – you okay?" Viola heard the underlying concern in his voice, which immediately grated on her nerves. Beneath his compassion, she could discern pity.

They both knew this kind of visit was far from the first one. And if there was something she couldn't stand, it was to be reminded of this very fact. That gaping hole in herself.

"Perfect. Go ahead. Will be right down." She heard his feet shuffle away, resigned, into the distance.

She slid her face closer to the tub, inspected the perfectly polished surface, and felt an inner groan spread through her body.

Her time was up. She was needed downstairs. Now.

But the stain, it was still there. Difficult to discern at this point. Tiny as it was. But barely visible didn't mean it wasn't there. She knew. It was there.

She felt it.

She felt it all over her body.

Late evening

As she made it down the stairs, Ronny watched her. He had waited in the hall for her to come down, and his face was blanketed with concern. Several unanswered questions hung in the air. How could she leave her guests for so long? What was she doing up there? Would she blow this party in some inconvenient way?

On bad days, she was scared witless of the growing intimacy between them, of feeling that something deep inside her was beginning to stir.

But she also had good days. And with them came the capacity for emotional insight, a voice that whispered to her that this man was a treasure.

Despite her erratic behaviour, he was still here, backing her more than ever. Their mutual history went back only two years, but he had made it this far with her. With the wreckages of her past relationships, the burnt bridges, the unending escape hatches, his stamina baffled her.

Yet, her moods and her fickleness, these were nothing compared to her lie. The same one that had forced her to scuttle up to the bathroom, while she should have been taking care of her guests.

She had no second thoughts about this. After all, it was for his own good, a sacrifice she had to resort to in order to keep him. Simply because if he found out the truth about her, he would leave her that very second. She was sure of that.

If she had learnt anything in the past twenty years, it was that men leave. Every single time. So, naturally, her lies were more than justified. And she would do anything to keep the status quo. Most of the time it was worth it.

She had experienced way too many relationships where the only glue that existed was the dizziness of the initial infatuation. There were guys she connected with, and men whom she respected professionally. But most of the relationships dwindled off after half a year or so. When she was the Dumped instead of being the Dumper, there were always excuses and apologies for why it didn't work out. But as she listened to them, it was more than obvious that none of them were actual reasons. Maybe because none of the men had the guts to admit, or the capacity for understanding, that the romantic love spun by society as the be-all and end-all was just a fairy tale. Yes, there was the unconditional love of a mother to her child. This she had experienced in every pore of her body. The addiction and emotional blindness of romance she could not understand.

So when the sex fizzled out, the man's interest in her went with it. Suddenly, she would go from being the number one priority on the list, to sharing the last place with all the excuses they scrambled to come up with.

Her relationships, in general, meant disillusionment. But she didn't think of this as a negative term. It was simply drawing away the illusion that was draped over her eyes during the initial romantic crush period, revealing the man's true nature, be it more or less self-absorbed.

So, it was quite unexpected, this whole thing with Ronny. Sure enough, the passion cooled off after about a year, but was replaced with a growing intimacy. Something she had never thought herself capable of. And while her past partners had looked for every reason to get off at the next stop, Ronny did everything in his power to be sure she didn't look for the same reasons. He made sure that he was there for her, that he supported her, even when it didn't fit his schedule. And when she really stopped and considered this, how many men were actually prepared to give up so much of themselves, their career and boys' time, in order to nurture a relationship? Not to mention, every day could be quite good. They fit together. This both amazed her and frightened the hell out of her, in equal measures.

Suddenly, she noticed his quirks. Like leaving the freezer door open so everything would melt inside, or tossing his clothes into the wrong drawer, mostly her drawers. She never had the calling of a housewife, but she would wash out the refrigerator without making a scene. Or even mentioning it. Then she would separate his clothes from hers. And where others would grow resentful of his habits, she found these things endearing.

As she eyed him in the hall, she knew he wanted to approach her, provide the necessary comfort, but she lifted up her hand, waved off his worries. She sent him a soft glance, a gentle reassurance that she was fine. He needn't worry because of that bathroom thing.

The look in his eyes showed his relief.

She put on a smile. The one she had practiced to perfection for the past twenty years. The one that said she felt awesome. She couldn't be any better.

And as she stepped into her living room, she was prepared to play her role pitch-perfect in what was supposed to be the greatest moment in her life.

Chapter 2

Viola was immediately greeted by twenty or so of the very finest and brightest in the journalism business in Oslo. Their glances were filled with genuine concern. But as she greeted everyone with warmth, the tension melted away and worried glances vanished.

The exhausting hours she spent with many of them certainly made them more a family than her own flesh and blood. These were the people who laid down the groundwork so her stories wouldn't fall through at the editorial. Day in, day out, they sacrificed their health to give their story, and the people in it, the justice it deserved. They stood behind her one hundred percent when the information for the story needed to be firmed up, by getting confirmations from her sources, on or off the record. And she reminded herself that their loyalty wasn't due to their fears, but out of genuine respect. Something she had won through incessant perseverance and investigative insight.

As she finished her cheek-to-cheek rounds, she had melted away all the curious glances. Her unspoken absence became a thing of the past.

And as she stood back, eyeing them all standing there, one thing struck her. Whenever she painted an overtly rosy picture of people, as she did now, she was slapped back by a reality check. Despite everything they had been through, could she be sure these smiles were genuine, or their presence here was not forced? After all, she had the tendency to forget one simple fact: She was at *Aftenposten* on separate terms than most. She was the daughter of the chief editor.

Maybe it was time to curb her gullibility.

* * *

"And as your sorriest excuse for editor-in-chief, and drunk at that, I was supposed to announce my daughter's phenomenal success – another one. That's disgusting, right! This time only as the Middle East correspondent for our smallish paper." As always, Anne had all the guests grasped in her steely grip. And her proclamation was immediately met with thunderous claps. Flashy speeches were her domain, the moments she lived for, and one of the few things able to satiate her ego. Viola had never shared this showmanship quality with her mother.

No one else in Viola's life would bring up such a storm of clashing emotions. There was the utter respect and devotion that stemmed from two decades' worth of watching the best editor-in-chief in action.

It was Anne who had shown Viola what it meant to be both the managing editor and, later on, editor-in-chief. Viola's memories about the paper went as far back as she could remember. In her wide-eyed pimply-faced stage, she spent all her free time observing reporters after school. She had done everything in order to get a summer job, just to do the most lowly work there. She remembered the exhilaration of making her first editorial pitch.

Anne and her father had played no small role in shaping post-war journalistic ethics in Norway. Her journalist family were the initiators of the "Be Cautious" manifesto, which laid out some of the most concise ethical rules a journalist working in the profession could hope for.

But as with everything, all these accolades had their murkier side. As time passed by, Anne grew more self-conscious about this family tradition. It became baggage that weighed her down. And in recent years, this weight turned into fear of showing her weaknesses and losing her grasp on the people that slaved for her. So Anne made sure that if anyone presented a threat to her position, she would pulverise them into professional non-existence. Therefore, the competition was nil, out of respect, sometimes even out of admiration, but mostly out of fear.

* * *

Viola moved up to Anne and stood beside her, as everyone cheered them on.

"Stop it, Anne! A hug would do," shrieked Viola theatrically as a response to Anne's challenge.

But Anne scoffed back at her and shook her head in playful confrontation.

"Hugs? Everybody would think I should be proud. I mean, I am not only the boss but also a mother. So maybe I should be twice as proud. Come on! What a load of BS. You want the truth?" Anne glanced over at everybody, shaking her head at all of them. Especially Viola. Then, she silenced the public with a pointed finger, demanding their complete focus.

"The only thing going through my mind right now is... Who the hell is going to replace my top watchdog and bring me in more of those shiny Gullparaplyen statuettes for only the best investigative journalism since... well, since... I did *my* rounds."

The crowd was about to erupt into cheers, but Anne stopped them as she raised up her arm.

"Because, as I've always said, great journalism is supposed to provoke anger and inspire action while it batters at our souls." As Anne delivered her grand finale, everyone exploded into cheers and wild whistles.

Everyone except Viola. She felt an inner sigh pass through her whole body as she heard the last sentence. This was Anne's most treasured quote, and heard for the first time or used sparingly, it meant all the world to Viola. But in Anne's mouth, it had turned into a rusty cliché a long time ago.

The real trouble started when things got personal. When Anne actually attempted to be a mother. This was the stuff of nightmares only Viola knew about.

Because when the curtain dropped, things got ugly. Not only did she have no regard for Viola's feelings, but Anne would use the personal stuff as leverage.

It astounded her how Anne, who had taught Viola everything about giving other writers the space to be themselves, was also the woman who needed to have the final say in all decisions in Viola's private matters. From the most important, to the most trivial ones.

Lately, Viola also realised that some part of Anne detested Viola's success. With Viola being so much more engaged in actual field work, she was able to strike on some hefty stories. And Viola could sense Anne's growing bitterness. After all, why should her daughter steal all the limelight, all the glory?

Viola's shrink advised her that if she wanted a proper life, some hope for an autonomous being, she should run. It was not too late to start living a life of her own. Anything to escape Anne's middle-of-the-night visits just to check on Viola's well-being, or her non-existent sex life. And if Viola was crazy enough to let her inside, she was barraged with a host of invasive questions, disguised as motherly worries.

So why didn't she run? Her shrink challenged her with a whole slew of questions. Was it only for the job's sake? Or the sentimental value of their mutual professional history? Or was it all just a pretext to give in to her own weakness? A way to not have to face the real world. Then maybe it was about how much Anne's professional support truly had helped Viola. Or was it just to build the family brand, another one of Anne's ego boosters?

But as Viola listened to her psychologist, she came to the conclusion that these questions were way too awkward. Maybe even inconvenient. If there were problems to begin with, and there were none, it wasn't as if she didn't want to face them. Of course not. So she let these matters be. And continued with her life in the usual manner.

Viola was drawn back to the here and now as she noticed Anne produce a tiny bronze necklace. Inside was an old nautical compass. This item epitomised everything Anne had worked for throughout her life. The three generations of the family tradition. She barely knew her grandfather, as he was one of the most aloof people she could remember. But she always imagined that if his spirit could manifest itself back into this world, this compass would be the thing that would host it.

"My grandfather. Few are aware what an obnoxious, cruel geezer he was. But he had one thing covered. A key to our profession. A small reminder of our family's journalistic tradition and a guide on what truly matters for our stories," Anne said, then draped it onto Viola's neck. And everybody responded with more claps.

As she accepted the token, Viola was humbled to silence. For once, she had done something without the support of her mother. And, for once, Anne hadn't pulled her strings. This was all Viola. She rarely felt a true sense of pride. One that didn't stem from the ego, but from dignity that came from true respect for oneself.

And she could barely contain the emotional flood.

"I remember a rookie. What... twenty years ago? Yeah. A kid dreaming of an unbiased look at the Middle East on behalf of the Norwegian people. Wow! That's a tall order! But here I stand today. And what do you know? Yeah, some dreams do come true," Viola stuttered out, barely managing to finish her sentence.

Public speeches didn't usually cause her any distress. She was way too good with pretences. Something her mother passed on to her. As she held up the necklace, though, tears graced her cheeks. Genuine moments like this, that's when her shell cracked. And she was surprised that she lost a little bit of that control.

It felt wonderful.

The Middle East correspondent position was, perhaps, the most coveted spot a journalist could hope for. Ever since Viola had set out on the same course as the rest of her family, this had been her goal.

But when Viola thought about this now, she realised she would have to be a complete lunatic to accept this position. After all, what sane person accepted a job where half of the time you wouldn't know if you would live to see another day? Or where the local public opinion, or at home, was rife with cries of wanting to lynch you, accusing you of partiality to whatever side was the most convenient for their own agenda.

Viola knew all of this. She knew half of the correspondents had broken under the excruciating pressure. And the other half who said they had made it, simply lied. She also knew there was a good chance she would too. But it was still worth it. Because if Viola wanted anything approaching a deeper meaning, she knew it existed in moments filled with injustice and cruelty.

That's where true human nature lay for her. Not because of the ferocity itself but because of what came with it, true human heart and compassion. Something that always went hand in hand with the inexplicable evils of this world.

And if she could do anything worthwhile with her life, an influence she could exert, this was it. A life well served.

The subtle cheers rang in Viola's ears for many hours.

Night

The party went from noisy to laid-back as the night drew to an end. Most people had already said goodbye or would soon be on their way out.

Viola's attention was caught by an insistent ring of the doorbell. Her mind scrambled to reach a more lucid state, trying to recollect if she had forgotten about any last-minute invitations. But nothing of the sort surfaced, and certainly not at this late hour.

As Viola threw the door open, she saw that it was Stine, a woman in her early fifties, whom Viola had known for a couple of years. With the night nearing dawn, Stine was the last person Viola would have expected. Stine had always been a simple woman, a farmer's daughter, born and raised in Skiptvet, a tiny town an hour's drive from Oslo. She was also a woman of few words, having a simpler and more direct approach few people in the city still knew anything about. But it was not Stine's timing or etiquette that threw Viola off now. It was her facial expression, which screamed a desperate urgency.

"Stine? Wow! Come in?" Viola mumbled out the first thing that came to her mind.

"Ms. Viola. We talk, Miss?" Stine spat out the words, leaving Viola trying to decide if it was a question or an order. She returned a perplexed glance, letting Stine peek inside to see the party. Hopefully this would be enough to suggest the inconvenience of the moment. The worst moment for any kind of talk.

But Stine practically trampled over Viola, obviously not prepared to listen to Viola's objections. Or anyone else's, for that matter.

Viola had met Stine three years earlier, and she still wished it could be undone. But as it went, they shared a rocky past, one that her mother and Ronny barely knew anything about.

Three years earlier, Stine's daughter, Marianne, had gone missing, and a nationwide search did little to solve the matter. Viola offered to help look for Stine's daughter. After all, Marianne was no ordinary woman. She was a public figure, a known personality in the blogosphere, but most of all, she was the voice of the many childless women out there.

For Viola, Marianne's blog was different. It was full of desperation and pain. But the way she saw it, this pain wasn't as self-absorbed as that of others in a similar life dilemma. Instead, it was pure, simple, and genuine. And Viola wasn't the only one who appreciated this young woman's intimate online shares. Marianne had gathered quite a following, her WordPress posts sparking off pages upon pages of tear-wrenching stories.

Viola was amazed at how a blog could fulfil such a healing role. Whenever she thought that the Net was dehumanising, suddenly, gems like Marianne's pages would shine through. A perfect example of true group intimacy and unconditional love shared over some bits and bytes.

"I know Miss is busy. But it's my daughter. My Marianne." Stine shouldered her way inside as she voiced the words. Viola let her in, and tried her best to cover up a heavy sigh.

"I know how hard it is with... And no trace and all. But..." Viola knew she was blabbering now, but Stine wasn't interested in Viola's inconsistency, nor in hearing her out. Instead, the older woman gripped onto Viola's shoulder.

"Miss. Miss was the only one who actually cared. Miss. I am a simple, stupid woman. No manners. Countryside, and all. Not like Miss. But. But..." Stine rushed ahead without so much as a breath.

Viola felt cornered again, and she hated people doing that to her. Demanding things from her that she couldn't possibly give them. So she did the only thing she felt she could do. While she politely nodded and smiled, she began to push Stine out the door again. But just as she had almost managed to get rid of the older woman, Stine shoved a phone into her face.

"But. But. But... The blog has been dead since she disappeared. Right? So, what is this?"

The first thing the police had done was make sure to very closely monitor the place where Marianne had spent most of her life. But when she had disappeared, the case got such a heavy-handed treatment from the press that nobody dared post a single comment on it. Unless that person wanted to become the prime suspect in an ongoing nationwide investigation.

Stine pressed her finger at a snippet of text from Marianne's blog. A fresh comment read: "Don't let the bed bugs get under your undies. – Anon." The comment on the blog was dated the day before. But Viola only shrugged this away.

"Doesn't mean anything. Could be from anyone. Most probably a prank," Viola responded, but even before she said the words, another possibility began to dawn on her. An option she had long ago given up on.

"These are my words, Miss! I sang them when I put her to sleep." Stine shoved the phone screen right into Viola's face.

"Don't you see? My baby..." Stine fumed at Viola's face.

"She is alive." Stine's eyes drilled themselves into Viola. And there was something unsettling hiding behind them. They weren't those of an older woman in search of advice, nor were they of a pleading beggar.

Stine's eyes were filled with a determination, but one that bordered on insanity.

Late night
Viola shut the door after Stine's retreating figure. And just as she turned around, her glance met her mother's inquisitive eyes. The disapproving glare could be felt across the room; it stiffened her neck and shuddered her body.

20

How long had Anne been watching them? Any other day, this would have been the beginning of a conflict between them, but this time Viola tore her eyes away from Anne, turned her back on her, and shuffled away from the guests.

Was this a vanished woman's call for help? And if so, why this way, why the blog, and why a message with exactly this content? A message that only her mother would understand. If it was meant for Stine, why didn't she simply contact her mother directly? Or at least the police? Was someone preventing her from reaching out? And why after two years? This didn't make sense. Any of it.

She should know by now, this was useless. Marianne's disappearance had never led to any concrete answers. And if it did, the single answer led only to a dozen new questions. She should stop this right now. It was a clear dead end. She had her guests, and she had her own life to live. She should get back to them, take care of them. And she should prepare to leave for Syria. Do what was expected of her.

But her legs wouldn't listen, and instead carried her away from the people, and their laughter. Her body seemed to switch to autopilot.

For two years, she had tried to shove all of this into some murky recess of her mind. A place where it wouldn't ever come out again. But however much she tried, however much she reasoned with herself, all that could change now.

She felt herself disconnect from the faint murmurings of the conversations around her apartment as a flood of thoughts overwhelmed her mind. If Stine's message turned out to be true, she knew what this meant for her. And she wasn't sure she would be able to handle it this time around. If Marianne was indeed still alive, this changed everything.

Chapter 3

As Viola froze the stream from Marianne's blog on her laptop, she eyed Marianne's frustrated face. Viola's body quivered with a junkie's exhilaration. She realised she was out of control. And knew it was bad for her.

That's why she hadn't opened this video for over two years. But after Stine's visit, there was no way around it. Marianne's confessions were like extinguishing a forest fire gone amok. However much she wanted to escape from the whole thing, some part of her was fuelled by the blogger's pain. After so many years of hosting her own demons, this was the thing her mind and body responded to best. Marianne's pain was simply a sounding bell that found the exact same frequency, the exact same tune to play.

And she needed more.

But before she could restart the blog stream, she felt someone behind her. A mildly-confused Ronny watched Viola amidst the clothes strewn all over her room. She had completely forgotten her packing. Her plane was leaving for Syria in two days.

"All set, I see, huh? The trip, you know?" he started off with a good dose of caution.

She threw a glance at the mess, then just sighed. Ronny knew almost nothing about Marianne. Just a few scraps of information, here and there, something she had shared over two years ago. Everything concerning Marianne was way too close to home for comfort. And she had learned the hard way that this kind of stuff was best left alone. Because this was what people, even good people, used against you sooner or later.

So she waved away the mess with an innocent grin.

And as he eyed her, he responded by throwing an envelope into her lap. She ripped it open and revealed a flight ticket to Damascus. What was this, another pair of tickets? Her mother's secretary had already taken care of her ticket. Paid by the paper and ready to go.

Then it struck her. This wasn't about her.

This idea had been so remote to her from the beginning that she never spoke to Ronny about it. But now that she saw the ticket in her lap, her mind flashed with an uneasy thought.

Even before Ronny spoke it out loud, she knew he would ask to go with her. But this was not some two-week vacation. This was a rest-of-your-life kind of proposition. And just this very idea sent her mind into panic mode.

"Is this for me?" she asked, referring to the ticket. "I mean, we've been together for what? Two years? I just..."

How could she even think of saying yes to this adorable and trustworthy guy? After all, their relationship was based on her lies. And this piece of paper was the decisive kick in the gut.

No.

This was the perfect time to come clean. She had to tell him the truth. Get it over with. He would never forgive her, and she would lose him forever, but at least she would regain some decency.

"For you? Come on! Don't flatter yourself." He attempted to recover his dignity by chuckling it away.

"Do you have any idea how much cash a medical practice in Damascus can bring in?" He grinned back while he searched her face for a reaction, anything that would make this moment less humiliating.

But his joke was only met with even more silence. She knew she had to break this off. She couldn't just keep standing there.

She realised this was it. Everything in her screamed for some courage to be truthful. He deserved it after two amazing years that had been everything she had longed for. She would ask him to sit down for a moment, and then she would apologise to him for not telling him the truth about her long-standing problem. Then she would fall into his arms and cry. It would be a genuine tear-jerker. Prime-time drama, maybe even ending in her redemption.

And however much she had convinced herself he would leave, there was the remote chance he would actually stay. However minuscule that chance was, it was worth the risk. For the sake of their relationship and a fresh start.

She raised her eyes and braced herself for what she had to do.

The truth.

But then something in her skipped a beat.

And instead, she just jumped into his arms and screamed out in joy.

"Is that a yes?" He eyed her, flustered. She sensed his body let go of the worst tension. After all, they were inches away from their whole future falling apart.

"Shut up. And reserve a seat number beside me," she said as she struggled to cover up her racing thoughts.

Finally, he loosened up and responded with an intense hug. But the moment she was in his arms, her eyes were drawn back to Marianne's contorted face on her laptop.

* * *

She dug through the cupboards after something. But before she got halfway, she had already forgotten what she was looking for. As she eyed her bags, trousers, makeup, lingerie, and shoes littered all over the room, her mind churned away on what had just happened.

She had just committed Ronny, the man whom she was supposed to love, to resigning from one of the most promising careers as a general physician in the city. He had more than enough patients and a fair share of respect amongst his fellows. Things he had worked for half his life. And Ronny wasn't just a steady workhorse, he was unrelenting, energetic and, most of all, he cared. That's why his patients loved him.

But not until one particular night did Viola fully realise what it meant for Ronny to be a doctor. Early on, she had noticed that he slept badly. He often spoke in his sleep, tossing and turning. But this night he screamed himself awake. He was drenched in sweat and disoriented. And then he began to cry. When she held him, wrapping her arms protectively around him, he confessed how much he worried. He stressed that he might miss a life-threatening diagnosis or he might commit a fatal technical error.

At first, she thought his fear was grounded in the danger of being sued for malpractice. And she would understand that. But then she realised it stemmed from his deeply embedded core values. From the key to his profession: "First, do no harm". This was more important to him than anything else, she had learnt. And no matter how hard he tried to distance himself in a professional manner, he still suffered. Just because he cared so much.

This had been a turning point for her internally. As she realised what kind of a man he was, an uncanny respect for him blossomed within her. And if she could name what it meant to be in love, this was it for her.

As she thought about this now, her mind struggled with the fact that after two passionate years, Ronny was now prepared to flush his career down the drain. Just for her. How valiant, romantic.

And utterly stupid.

But who was she to judge anyone? After all, she was the one with a pack of deceits. Wasn't Ronny doing all of that based on some fairy tale she had woven around him? A piece of literary fiction based on someone loosely tied to her. But with a huge copyright disclaimer at the end of the titles. One he might not have noticed.

She wanted to shriek at herself. Slap herself hard enough so she would wake up from this bad dream called Viola Voss. But instead she just sighed, allowing herself a moment of remorse. Then she continued to search her cupboards, for something she still couldn't remember.

And at that moment, her fingers brushed against something buried away in a wrapper. She uncovered two wooden picture frames. A golden autumn of a three-year-old boy kissing and hugging her. Despite the tangible carelessness and intimacy in them, they felt like ancient times. Way too distant to be real.

How the hell did it get there?

She had been through the apartment seven times. Or maybe even eight. This number was important. Necessary. The frequency was to make sure Markus had not only been cleansed from her past, but evaporated.

So how did this frame end up in that cupboard? Could it be Ronny who put it there? Just to test her, to see if she would go crazy? A cruel, freakish test.

Or maybe it was her mother. Did she have any keys? If she did, this would be exactly the kind of thing Anne was capable of.

Then it struck her. A touch of lucidity. There was probably no one to blame. Her mother couldn't have been inside her apartment. She couldn't have put that frame in the cupboard. Her partner was the most sensitive and caring person she had ever met in her life. Benign, compassionate. He would never do such a thing.

26

So, this left her with only one possibility.

Her worst enemy had left it there.

Herself.

And however much she pushed that away, it could be the only solution. Not only did she leave the frame there herself, but she also found it at the worst possible time. A time when Marianne's mother suddenly turned up out of nowhere, claiming her daughter was still alive. A blogger whose pain struck more than a chord in Viola: something she had desperately attempted to push away for years.

Her history and Marianne's past crashed in on her simultaneously. This time around, she knew she had it all under control. But how long would that last? Maybe all the more reason to find her answers.

And there was only one person who could give them to her.

Morning

When Ronny glanced back inside Viola's room, the mess was still there. Only more pronounced.

As his eyes flitted over the chaos, doubts began to creep in on him. This ticket, the trip, it was nothing short of a revolution in his life. And he kept telling himself it was going to be a good thing. It was supposed to change things. For the better. So why did everything inside him hurt so much? Why were his feelings in such a jumbled disarray?

He knew he was making a sacrifice. Stretching himself farther than he needed to. Or maybe, was able to. And he was also aware this was a one-way road. All the groundwork he had laid into building a practice, all the clients and trust he had built up, gone in one fell swoop. He had to be crazy to even consider this. Yet here he was. Tickets ready, her yes obtained, a practice to be shut down, and his life to be irretrievably transformed.

He didn't want to go into the details with her. The problems he had experienced along the way. The apartment he couldn't rent out and had to sell, the favours he had to cash in with his professional peers in order not to abandon his patients with no medical care available. If he had told her the truth about what this move meant to him professionally, how much of a chance he stood at a career in Damascus, she would never agree to his proposition.

So he delivered the sugar-coated version, the one without problems, without the burnt bridges. And most of all, without the stuff that might break his future.

No. He was not the one to dish out his problems to anyone. Especially not to her. And one thing was certain, there was always some baggage left unpacked. He had stepped into this relationship with his fair share. But he had quickly decided it would be for the best to leave that out of his life with Viola.

It was Kristin, his last partner. At one point, late in their relationship, maybe just before the end, Kristin had been fighting with her tumour, something that had taken all her strength. And before he had known it, he had found himself leaving her. Or maybe he had escaped her. For reasons that had baffled him. Or rather, none that he had understood at that point. However, he had presented this to Kristin, whatever excuses he had procured, be it some vague personal problems, or a burnout at work, the simple fact was that he had abandoned her. He had left her when she had needed him the most. It had taken him the better part of a month before he had realised what he had done. He had returned to her, but it had already been too late. Not too late for her, because the tumour had turned out to be benign. But too late for them. This had been the last time they had ever spoken.

His past had shown him what happened when he failed people. And if he promised himself anything in this life, it would be to never repeat the same mistake again. This time, there would be no excuses. No matter what, he would be there for Viola.

With a heavy sigh, Ronny was about to leave when he eyed the wooden frame. He approached it, turned it over, and his eyes took in a glowing Viola. With her Markus cuddled into her.

He had never met him. If he hadn't seen a picture at Anne's place, he would have only been able to guess this was her son. It was a wonder it still existed in this place. She made it explicitly clear, even repeated several times that she had cleaned up the apartment. Seven or eight times, that's what she had said.

Then there were the constant bathroom trips. He felt it was connected to Markus, but what had happened there, what lay behind it, that remained a secret. But with time, it got harder to overlook, as her stays got longer and more frequent.

Yet, he had also learnt there was no use pushing her for the details. The last time he had done that, she had treated him to a week-long silence. She had blamed it on her period, but he knew that it was not time for it. After this incident, he didn't want to visit that territory again. So he left this, and so much more, unspoken.

This didn't bring them closer together. On the contrary, they drifted apart, as he felt Viola raising a wall between them. At one point, he thought about leaving her, but then he quickly corrected himself. It dawned on him this was a test. The same one he flunked with Kristin. So he stayed and fought on for them without questioning the rights and wrongs.

He eyed the Syria tickets on the table. Maybe this move would be good. A chance to get away from things, to start afresh. A way to straighten out his personal stuff. But most of all, to build a family, which he longed for so much. He never pushed her for kids, as he felt her gushing wound after Markus. And he was willing to accept that, even to disregard his own desires. As long as she was happy. Correction. As long as *they* were happy.

Besides, his own problems, his needs, were nothing to talk about. Especially not to her. So, yes, things would change. Despite the fact that he doubted he would ever have this woman's heart completely, things would improve.

He put the picture frame down and approached her cupboard. Then he started to open her drawers. One by one, he started to go through them.

Chapter 4

Noon

Pål had always been rock solid. A stalwart in his profession and his community. That's how Viola remembered him.

So, it was with an uneasy surprise that Viola greeted the man at the door, who was unshaven and stank. His eyes were sunken, his body malnourished, and his face puffed up from way too much drinking.

And now, as Viola sat on his dirty sofa, she cast an unnerving eye at his apartment. The place was trashed, dust, litter, and clothes intermingled in a perfect harmony. What the hell happened? Was Pål divorced? Where was his son, Tommy? Whatever the situation, glancing at Pål's condition, Viola knew better than to push the matter.

He glanced at Viola's laptop and the comment from Marianne. And soon enough, he chuckled, a moment of authenticity flashing across his face. The old mockery. Apparently, hard times didn't erase everything.

"I don't get it." Pål eyed Viola. It was clear he was struggling with the piece of evidence Stine had discovered the previous day. Viola knew it, he knew it. But she had no other choice than to shrug it away, pretend she had no clue what he was talking about.

"Surely you are able to tell the difference between the substantial and the trivial?" He scolded her as if she were a child, then pointed to her laptop.

This side of him was also familiar. Being no more than eight years older, Viola could never grasp how this always gave him the right to be paternal, especially towards the opposite sex. And even more so if you gave him a reason to tear you apart, like this half-assed evidence.

Hearing his reproof, Viola breathed out in relief. Despite the demolished apartment and Pål's sorry state, maybe there was still hope. Maybe there was someone in there. And maybe she had a chance, as long as she managed to engage him.

"You don't get it, do you? Who she was. And what her fight was all about. No other public person did so much for childless women. And if that isn't clear enough for you, that means women with no options." She launched this at him, hoping the attack would scratch away some of his callousness.

But Pål just froze, then followed it with an arranged smirk, which probably was supposed to communicate his contempt.

"You are damned right. I don't get it. And you know why? These times, they..." He was about to charge into one of his old tirades about how anything of value had deteriorated in recent times. He always started with the justice system's recent fall, but mostly ended up with the pizza delivery guy being late. She had to shut that door. And quickly at that. Get him focused on this matter instead of self-resentment.

"No, I don't know," she said, cutting him off. "Listen, Pål. The supposed struggle. The supposed kidnapper's traces. The supposed break-in. The whole goddamned kidnapping had *supposed* written all over it." This was an age-old argument between them. Or at least since they met each other on this case. And it never got resolved. There

32

were a ton of clues that motivated this kind of thinking. Inconsistencies that deserved more attention.

Marianne's laptop was found in a river nearby, trashed and mangled beyond any recovery. Everything pointed to an assault, and was stamped as one. But two months later, after Viola hired an IT-specialist to sift through half a year's worth of data from Marianne's Net provider, it turned out the girl had done an extensive number of searches with keywords like 'How to destroy a hard drive beyond repair' and 'How to fry a hard drive'.

And it didn't stop there.

Not far from the laptop, several pieces of clothing were found. After a thorough DNA analysis of the torn-up pieces, the fibres were traced back to Marianne, due to some skin fragments. All in all, there were three pieces found in the vicinity of the crime scene. Parts of a glove, scraps of a winter jacket, and the remains of a wool hat. Again, everything implied a struggle spread out over a contained area.

But when Viola had gone through a mountain of Marianne's Visa statements, she had found the winter jacket, the wool hat, and the gloves bought on the same day, two weeks prior to Marianne's disappearance. This in itself wasn't suspicious. But shortly thereafter, Viola had visited the H&M store where Marianne had bought her clothes. After some arduous searching, she had found the salesperson Marianne had bought these clothes from. And it had turned out Marianne had been obsessed with finding materials that would tear easily.

Then there was something much more unnerving than any other clues. Marianne's video posts had never been about a formula. Viola always saw them as emotionally free-form, dependent on the content, and the blogger's inner necessity to communicate.

But about a month before her disappearance, all that changed in a subtle manner. The raw emotionality was still there, unchanged, but there was something else. What struck Viola was that they all now had the same length. And what's more, they felt... off. At first, Viola couldn't grasp what it was. But then it slowly dawned on her. They were all choreographed. And done so with a lethal precision. Viola soon arrived at the conclusion that they had been prepared, and recorded ahead of time. Maybe in anticipation of the blogger's disappearance.

When Viola had confronted Pål about all of this, at first, he had been eager to go down this line of investigation, but as time had gone by, and nothing concrete had turned up, everyone had grown weary, and more than prepared to put a stop to the torment of the family. Soon enough, everyone thought it best to shut the case down. And even Pål's incessant motivation had burnt itself out. He had told her then that way too many cases had some inconsistencies, some things that never added up. She had to accept that.

What crap, Viola had thought at that time. And her attitude was no different now. If anything, she was even more convinced they had let something slip by. Correction: *she* had let that happen.

"I've appreciated your input during the case. But facts are facts. She was taken against her will in her apartment. Then *poofed* into air. So, let's leave it at the poof." He replaced the smirk with a grin.

Viola had what she called a quirk, a habit of entertaining catastrophic situations. The kind where people died a horrible death. The more torturous, the better. And there was no better situation than in moments like these, when stupidity and cruelty surfaced hand in hand from people. With a well-placed upper right hook, followed by a kick in the groin, she sent him plunging out of his seventh-floor balcony. And it gave her some much-needed relief.

It felt good.

At least until her mind snapped back and realised he sat in front of her and still hadn't wiped away that grin.

Viola had expected several possible outcomes from this conversation. One of them would be a simple 'no, this one is not for me', or simply 'I don't have time'. It would be a failure on her part. But she didn't expect this. Not a man who had lost his sense of the ground floor, the stuff that mattered.

No. This wasn't the same person who had spent countless sleepless hours with her, slouched over some meaningless scraps of evidence, never prepared to give up.

"You know what scares me the most? It's not all the discrepancies and inconsistencies. What frightens me is that the person I thought really cared, doesn't give a shit anymore."

He eyed her, thought about it for a moment, then croaked his reply.

"Because I *don't*... care. Especially when you bring me this... crap."

Viola grabbed onto the only thing she had now. Her breath. She became her breath. In. Out. Damn. In these kind of situations, distancing herself was the only thing that worked. That was the theory, at least.

She had come here to shake this man's life up. Mobilise him towards better things. But, instead, she found herself barely sitting on the edge of the sofa, shaking.

She grasped at the past and their investigation. Maybe she could appeal to his ego. She remembered clearly how much he enjoyed a simple compliment. Especially when it came down to his line of case reasoning. His mind was heavily polished from all these years of police work. Viola thought it part truth, part his ego trip. Yet, at this moment, she was prepared to sell it as his wishful thinking.

"Please. You remember your theory? I remember you checked the surrogate mother arrangements, adoptions, local and foreign fertility clinics. Maybe she disappeared because she found the right answers to her problems. And your theory. Brilliant, if you ask me." But even before she finished, she felt herself sigh. Few liked their egos whisked as much as this man. This much she remembered clearly. She couldn't have been more clumsy with the delivery, though. Bordering on inane.

He paused, just to make space for the same thoughts they were both thinking now.

And Viola knew that whatever help she could get from that man, that opportunity was gone now. Pål's tone fell back to that of a reserved drone.

"I am glad you enjoyed my theory. But it is exactly what you said, a theory. And those leads you are talking about... All dead." He fell silent.

It wouldn't be the first time he had gutted her open. As if to confirm this, his tone changed from a distant drone to a caring comment. A father instructing his daughter on the hardships of life.

"Viola. Dear. We've been through this countless times. Listen. The poof in the air is easier to handle. For everybody. And it's certainly a lot less paperwork."

Her eyes shot around the mess in his apartment as if this could help her decipher what lay behind this behaviour. But no clues sparked any conclusion.

She had come here because she trusted him. At least as much as she was capable of trust.

"At least I have my priorities sorted out. What about you?" he lashed out at her, out of nowhere.

"Meaning?"

"You tell me. Because I've watched you beat this horse with a sledgehammer. To a pulp. For how many years? And why? Why do you care? Listen, Viola, you want help? Want a missing woman? I can find you one a lot less... complicated."

Viola got up and began to walk out of his apartment. She had already been a basket case before she walked in there. She had hoped to find some allegiance, but instead found someone in worse shape than her.

"I would settle for a man who cares." She spat the words out at him. She was about to slam the door open

36

when he extended his foot to prevent the door from opening any further. That got her attention, all right. And frightened the hell out of her.

"Wrong time and address," he said.

"Sorry. Had you mistaken for someone else."

Then she ripped the door open and raced outside. And as she whirred down the endless flight of stairs, her mind attempted, in vain, to regain its bearings.

Chapter 5

Afternoon

The subway was full. Viola's breathing grew more desperate by the second. She knew she couldn't go on like this for much longer. She couldn't stand these people, or her situation.

The last two years had been so by the book. Under control, just as she expected of her life. After her breakdown, shortly after Markus, she had done some grim therapy sessions. The luxurious retreat had cost way more than she could afford at the time. But her mother was more than happy to pay for her daughter's well-being. After all, it was either that or be forced to reveal a failure in the family.

And Anne didn't accept anything less than success in her life. So, Viola spent two months outside of Tromsø in the northern part of Norway, cut off from pretty much everything that made her happy, just to make her mum happy. And as a side-effect, she pleased everyone else, especially the doctors. The breakdown was just a coincidence. A sudden blip on the radar that would never show up again. Anne was happy that Viola seemed stable.

Or at least could fool the experts into thinking this was the case.

Still, the retreat had not been all that bad. It helped her to regain some much-needed distance from herself. It had also taught her some basic meditation techniques. She was never much into spirituality or New Age thinking. Her mind was way too pragmatic to even consider going down that road. But the basic meditations had done wonders for her. And ever since then, she had used five minutes each morning to slow down, be fully present, and focus on her breath. Simple everyday mindfulness.

Now, as she stood in the cramped subway, choking on the lack of air, she attempted again to focus on her breathing. And what usually worked wonders, did nothing for her. On the contrary, she got even more agitated, bordering on delirious.

When she was finally prepared to push herself towards a premature exit, something caught her eye. A boy's profile standing sideways to her. Perfectly curly blond hair and that nice rounded chin.

It looked just like him.

Markus.

Viola blinked once, twice. And the more closely she looked at him, the more she became mesmerised by every single detail of his features.

Viola began to push herself towards him. Shouldering everybody in order to reach the boy. And he was just standing there, all by himself. All alone.

Maybe it was Markus.

After all, it would make sense. He could have gotten lost. And, somehow, he was taking this subway, maybe he was even looking for her. Hoping to find his mother again.

She pressed on, elbowed her way through, and when she finally reached him, he spun around towards her. A flash of recognition passed through her body. His ethereal face looked right into her eyes.

Of course.

It was Markus.

It all made sense now. Him being here, finding him, a miracle. And everything that followed was just joy. The feeling of the boy's soft hand against her callous palm. The trustful exchange of glances between them. And she realised all this suffering she'd had to endure wasn't for nothing. No. It was just so she could find him. Right here, right now. As their eyes met, she understood he was just as alone and lost as she had been.

But at this moment, nothing would ever come between them again. And nothing would force her to let go of his hand.

As she drew him out of the subway, Viola suddenly felt a woman's hand lash at her back. The woman's fingers wrenched at her coat, and her eyes glared with a blistering accusation.

Viola thought the subway stations gathered all kinds of crazies. And this woman had to be one of them. So, she shielded her Markus, and decided to make a run for it. She had to get him to safety.

But she had barely made it across the platform when words finally pierced through her clouded mind.

"What the fuck, Lady! What the hell are you doing with my son?" the woman shrieked at Viola. And this time she ripped the boy away from Viola's hand. Viola peered into the kid's face.

Not Markus.

Not Markus.

Other accusations followed. Lots of nasty words were thrown at her. Unintelligible, toxic threats of police and other grim consequences. Stuff she knew she couldn't deal with.

So, she made a run for it. And as she escaped, her senses were covered by a dense fog.

Chapter 6

Late Afternoon

Viola barely had the time to connect to *Aftenposten's* news server before Anne came running for her. She had expected to face her mother as soon as she walked into the offices, but she didn't expect her to show up with such urgency.

Anne had always been a pedantic control freak. But Viola couldn't decide if this was an ability necessary to survive as the chief editor or simply bad leadership.

Few remembered it more clearly than Silje Bredtvet, who had voiced her opinion clearly on several things concerning *Aftenposten's* runnings. And why shouldn't she, she had been the managing editor at that time. Everyday operations had been her sole responsibility. And although she answered to Anne only, Silje had a much clearer idea of *Aftenposten's* mechanics than Anne did.

Silje had worked almost as long as Anne in the business. And she thought she had the clout to have an opinion of her own. Especially since she was Anne's best friend and most trusted confidant for close to twenty years. And at that time, she fought for something worth fighting for. Silje's concerns were mostly legitimate, with

41

some precise solutions for updating the paper technologically, moving into the next decade. Only Anne didn't see it as an opportunity, but as a power move to dethrone her.

No one was really sure what happened afterward, but Silje resigned a week later. The reason given was serious health issues. Maybe the story would have been somewhat credible, if not for the fact that Silje applied to several other papers shortly after this. But for some unexplained reason she was unanimously turned down. Her career finished a couple of years before retirement. And Silje never recovered after this.

Viola had a good relationship with Silje, whom she had always respected deeply. She even visited her once, after everything cooled off. But the broken woman Viola saw that day made it unbearable to keep returning to her. No matter how much Viola thought of herself as a person fighting the good cause, when she got near Silje she realised she could just as easily end up like her.

Mother or no mother, Anne was more than capable of doing this to her own daughter. Viola knew that, and so did everyone else. And as an addendum to the whole story, a few years later, Anne made all the changes to the paper Silje had suggested, but dressed them up as her own ideas.

"I see you are prepared for the trip." Anne's words were tinged with sarcasm as she eyed Viola's messy desk. This was Anne's default modus operandi. Nothing out of the ordinary or to be scared of. So why did Viola's knees suddenly feel weak?

All would have been fine. Viola would have been packed and ready to go to the Middle East. She loved her job, and she was prepared to do anything for the paper. But that was two days ago. And now she felt as if some invisible force had begun to rearrange her neurons into some new configuration.

She felt every inch of her body telling her she should speak to her mother about this. Voice her doubts. Yes.

This time she would talk to her. Despite the past, this maddening family-professional relationship, and despite what Anne had done to Silje.

Viola glanced at her mother and touched her arm gently. She was not quite sure why she did it.

"Cleared your desk, dear?" Anne's tongue pressed hard at the word 'dear'.

"Can we talk?" Viola immediately sensed she might just as well have said she was not going to Damascus.

"Talk? Now? We can. Sure. When you get there. On the phone." Viola knew that if she didn't speak up about her feelings now, things would only get worse. Her only hope left was to appeal to the business side of their relationship.

"That's exactly what I wanted to talk about. For the good of the paper?" she said, but Anne's reaction was exactly the opposite of Viola's intention. She sensed this appeal was like hanging up a big red sign that read: *I am in trouble*.

Anne eyed her daughter, her calculative mind speeding through the possible worst-case scenarios.

"It's that Stine woman from yesterday, isn't it?" whispered Anne. Viola knew that however self-focused Anne was, her mother had a very firm grasp on reality. So, this insight came as no surprise.

"Come on! Of course not."

"Listen, girl, the only thing you have to worry about is that I won't be paying for yet another retreat to get you back in shape. Like the last time, huh? That was a one-time deal only. Right?" Anne closed in on her daughter, not out of considerate intimacy, but like a predator hunting its prey.

"Since when did my mental condition become a topic?"

"Since you dropped out of the most expensive two-month rehab after Markus's death," Anne spat out at her, and it amazed Viola how this woman could so completely crush another person with simple words and still maintain her own peace of mind.

"Which you have nothing to do with. Understand?"

"Which I have *everything* to do with," Anne insisted, but then she hesitated over her next line of attack. And this could only spell trouble.

"Especially since you've been lying to your partner about your... condition."

Viola's forehead exploded with heat, and her vision blurred. With her heart racing like mad, and her knees popping under the stress, she scrambled to regain some kind of composure.

Anne had crossed an unspoken line. One that Viola had been sure would never be broken. Especially not by her own mother. Viola's condition was her own. She had made that clear fifteen years ago. And if one thing was understood in their relationship, it was that Viola's disease was never mentioned.

"Well... I... Do you even have the faintest idea...? You realise how hard it is to tell someone that you will..."

Cripple his children.

"Cripple his children." That's what Viola meant to say. But these words failed her. Instead, they reverberated back and forth in her head, as if in some maddening echo chamber.

Viola glanced at her mother. Defenceless and numb, she fell silent.

"So, you've found the perfect solution? Moving with him to the other side of the world? Leading him on about a family? That's going to make things better?"

Viola had sensed Anne's building resentment for quite a long time. She hated the choices Viola had made in her life. She just never had the right opportunity to voice it. Until now.

"The least the poor guy deserves is the truth about Markus, and your..." Anne suddenly stopped short, perhaps that little remaining part of her that still cared

44

about her daughter was rearing its head. Even she knew this might be too much.

"My...? My what! You *fucking* dare say it," Viola blew up in Anne's face. She hadn't spoken to her mother like that for a long time. If ever.

Viola searched desperately for any justification that would excuse her mother. Some misunderstanding, the job at stake, too much stress, or even a bad day. But no matter how she looked at this, however much she tried to find a reason to forgive Anne, there was only one conclusion: her mother was a heartless bitch.

"Never. *Ever.* Mention Markus or my condition again. Not to Ronny. Or anyone fucking else. Clear?"

Anne saw Viola's surface was cracking.

"Sorry. I am sorry. Please..." Anne whispered the words. And in some kind of unexplained gesture, she gripped Viola's shoulders. Then, she hugged Viola to herself.

But the only thing going through Viola's mind was that Anne never hugged. Certainly not at work. A big part of her wanted to scream at Anne. Had her motherly instincts finally woken up after twenty years?

Anne did her best to calm Viola down by stroking her hair, then slid close to her ear.

"Listen, hon, you do your part. Okay? Which means no rehabs. But an amazing performance in the Middle East. Right? And I think what you and Ronny have is way too precious, huh? Would be a shame to involve him any further. Yes?" Anne delivered her message and locked gazes with Viola.

Had she heard her mother wrong, or was that an outright threat? Viola's mind reeled from the words. Her eyes darted around the room in horror. She wanted to shriek. She wanted to flail at her mother. She was prepared to gut-punch her own flesh and blood.

But instead, she did the only thing she could.
She nodded submissively.

Viola's feet still carried her along the rain-splashed sidewalk, long after what she thought was physically possible.

She had known this day would come. But she never realised it would come in such a brutal manner. The day her mother used Viola's condition against her.

Ever since her disease became known to her mother, they'd had a truce. Despite all that Anne was, Viola thought her mother cared enough about her to respect this boundary. It was never spoken out loud. Simply a sign of respect, a family understanding. So, when it happened today, something broke in her. In their relationship.

Viola had found out about her mitochondrial disease when she was in her mid-twenties. But it had taken the doctors almost a decade to pinpoint this as the root cause of everything. By that time, she was already a nervous wreck and on all kinds of pills. Every benzodiazepine, antidepressant, and beta-blocker became game. If there was anything to try, she would do it.

During those ten years, she had gone through countless doctors, specialists, and a living hell of misdiagnoses.

The real story started in her early twenties, after a sudden miscarriage. At that time, she barely understood the implications this would have on her life. In those days, she was a fountain of optimism, bursting with life and ready to take on everything that came her way. A miscarriage was a shock. Painful as hell. But bad things never happened to her. This was a one-time thing. She would get back on her feet in no time.

But she never did.

After half a year of stuffing Clomid, a fertility drug, down her throat, with CNC machined precision for intercourse, and then intrauterine inseminations, she had no further success. The only thing that seemed to be growing were the side effects of blurred vision, head-splitting migraines, and vivid nightmares; her follicles were not.

Suddenly, she realised artificial insemination was the only option she had. Fortunately, three rounds would be covered by the Norwegian Health Service. Surely this extraordinary gift would save her from financial ruin.

But after six gruelling IVF procedures, three of the cycles paid for out of her own pocket, she was not only emotionally ruined but was also in serious debt. Something that would take her the next decade to repay. As the years went by, everything was turned inside out in her emotional life. Not only did she lose her partner, who couldn't deal with her condition, but everyone in her circle slowly pulled away from her.

Or was she the one who pulled away from them? That detail remained quite fuzzy. Nevertheless, the outcome was a socially barren life. And that had suited her just fine. It still did.

Her attitude towards life had turned from a careless bystander to a drowning victim. In no less than seven years. But that was far from the end of the story. Despite her unpaid mortgage and her overdrawn credit cards, she went from specialist to specialist in the hope of finding some new procedure that would give her hope again.

And what did she get in return? She got a brutal kick by fate right in the gut. She won the damned lottery. She learned she was 1 in 15,000 who had one of the rarest diseases in existence. Mitochondrial disease.

The bitter irony of it all was that with this disease, every procedure she had been through had been utter nonsense. Even if she could conceive, the chances the baby would be healthy were close to nil. She learned from the same experts who had put her in financial debt that the IVF procedures were actually the last thing she should be doing.

In her condition, playing Russian roulette was a far safer option.

She never could imagine herself adopting. She detested the idea, worrying that, for her, it would only be a bitter reminder that she had given up. She had lost the battle with her own body. Lost the last vestige of her womanhood. No. She would never go this far.

But as her options dwindled into dust, her world turned upside down, and suddenly this alternative seemed far from unacceptable. And for every day that went by, the thought grew on her. Until it blossomed into a full-blown fountain of desire. All of a sudden, she felt reborn, ready to start a new life, with her adopted child by her side.

That was the idea, anyway.

But the reality proved to be something else. There was the inevitable needle eye of the *Bufetaten,* the Norwegian child adoption council. The men in charge performed psychological profiles and scored every woman with half a dream. The points were only points, stupid numbers, yet these numbers mattered. They decided her future.

And everyone else's.

So, she did everything she could to paint the picture-perfect future mother. But the *Bufetaten's* Orwellian-like prying eyes dissected her persona into bits and bytes. Found out about her long-standing depression diagnosis, her bad drinking habits, and even her anger problems. She wanted to gut their beer bellies wide open, wrench their eyes out from their sockets. But then she reminded herself she was past that, her heavy emotional baggage melted away by the way of the heart. Breathe in. Breathe out. Right.

And maybe she would have had a chance. Or so they told her. But the simple fact she didn't have a partner, that was unacceptable. She might as well forget it.

As if childless women didn't have enough of a struggle, why not build a catch-22 into this whole wanna-have-a-baby-badly-but-don't-have-a-partner thing? Set up an even bigger hurdle for them, one that they will surely not even consider jumping. They all needed a partner, but many men just didn't want to be with women who couldn't give them kids. And Viola couldn't blame them. You don't pamper a horse with a broken leg, in some vain hope it will win more races.

You shoot it in the head.

But it didn't stop there. The hard fall came only after that. The changes started off subtly, not all at once, rather in small, almost imperceptible ways. But, this time, her reality warped into some evil twin version of the world of Oz.

The habits were the first to go. She stopped shopping at malls, especially during the holiday season. And by that time, malls meant incessantly shrieking kids, ugly, loud, howling babies with heads that were way too big. They were there in all kinds of nasty forms and variations, the stuff that made her queasy. She had to do everything to avoid this. Naturally.

Then there were the holidays. Viola put up a list on her fridge. It was a long checklist of her love-to-dos. The list was the only thing that kept away the sinister shadows of her own mind gone awry.

Even worse than holidays, was spending them with both close and distant relatives. Fortunately, her family was small, and way too career-obsessed to bother with children.

Still, there were some exceptions to this rule. Distant cousins who loved to smother her with their new-born babies. After a weekend of stomach-wrenching, nauseating baby diapers, she had to take a week's sick leave. After a few of those, she did the only thing she could. She avoided them all. But when pushed further by recurring invitations, she finally cut off ties with everyone who either had kids, or was planning on having them.

The few friends she had left suggested vacations. They would surely alleviate some of her loneliness. Maybe she would even meet someone.

Yeah, sure.

The holidays were another black hole of inner traumas and silent disasters. Wherever she attempted to travel, she was attacked by hordes of toddlers. Perfectly happy families with perfectly carefree kids made for perfectly grisly holidays. She attempted to adjust her trips according to her needs, book places where there would be no teensie-weensie, itsy-bitsy, eensie-weensie thrown her way. But the simple truth was that it was hard. No. It was impossible to find places devoid of that smothering happiness. After a few more attempts, she gave the idea up altogether. If she wanted torment, she could just as well stay at home and drink herself into a stupor.

Two decades flowed by, and for every year that passed, her checklist of love-to-dos shrank. No more ski weekends, no more baby showers, no more christenings, no more children-focused news pieces, no more beers with baby-obsessed colleagues, no more personal talks during work, just in case kids were mentioned.

Then one day, she realised as she gaped at her checklist that there were no bullet points left on it. And she was alone, right in the middle of a Christmas evening.

Finally, Viola stopped in a deserted street, as her mind snapped back from the past.

She eyed herself in some window filled with baby clothes. She saw a face mirrored back to her.

It wasn't her.

This was some alien woman standing, moping at her. Some bystander on the sidewalk, watching her life from afar. That woman's face was numb, and it wanted something from her. With its needy eyes, it expected something of her. Only she didn't know what anymore.

Once that woman's desire had been to experience the greatest gift life can give. Something as uncanny as unconditional love. Yet who had she become instead, with her crippling disease?

A child murderer.

Chapter 7

Night

It was the middle of the night, but she was still in her coat and shoes. Viola sat on her bed and watched Ronny as he slept.

After the meeting with her mother, Viola had less than five hours to decide what to do next. And the longer she thought about it, the further she seemed from an actual answer.

She glanced at his face, which was covered with an inner stillness. Given her life situation, this guy may as well have been from another world. A constant reminder that another life path was possible. A promise of intimacy and true kinship. Just thinking about it carved an aching hole in her.

Here was a man prepared to give her everything. His time, his tenderness, himself completely. Everything she had wanted for the past twenty years. And now that she was here, why was she about to blow it all?

Then doubt crept in, like it usually did, and covered her senses. Would she be able to give him the kind of closeness that he longed for? Would she be able to fulfil some of his needs? But it struck her it was best to shy away from questions she already knew the answer to.

So, she touched his hand gently and Ronny woke up. He eyed her quizzically, seeing her clothes, her shoes, and the time of night. But she interrupted him before he could ask her anything.

"Remember the Marianne girl? The one with the mitochondrial disease?"

"Yeah?"

"Stine, her mother, was here during the party," she said quietly and shied away from his eyes.

Ronny sat up in the bed.

"Yeah. I didn't want to bother you. But you know what? She found something on her daughter's blog. She is reliving the past, I guess. Marianne blamed herself for wrecking every relationship she had because of her disease. And then she met this great guy. Prepared to do everything for her. And this time, she decided to lie. Lie about her condition. Her struggle. Her desire for kids. Everything." She said all of this. And for every word, she felt a little bit lighter. She doubted that he sensed what lay behind these words, what sort of truth she had actually uttered.

"And him? Did he want kids?" Ronny asked. Viola felt that although they were talking about people he had never met, Ronny was still able to offer them his full empathy. She saw it in his eyes.

"Badly. And she tried to tell him. But I guess she was just too damned terrified of losing him," she whispered, weighing her words carefully. One wrong step and she could say too much, damaging what they had together beyond any repair.

"Damn." Ronny mulled this over. "I guess it was his right, wasn't it? To know, I mean."

"A deal-breaker, huh?" she finally said, presenting the question she longed to ask. She had never before had the guts to talk to him about this. Not in her situation. On the contrary, she avoided it like the plague. She felt her body begin to tremble. Too subtle to be noticed. But enough to hurt. How did he feel about children?

He eyed her. Then threw up his arms. And laughed. Disarmed the bomb that ticked inside her.

"Come on! What's up with you women? Maybe a little too much in your own head? Do you realise there are actually guys in this world who can settle down without kids? Guys more, like, traditional. You know, beer and rough sex only. Like me." He let out a chuckle.

She snickered back. Ronny was the last guy on earth to touch beer. And that rough sex was more talk than anything else.

"Yeah. That would be you." She continued to laugh, the colour returning to her cheeks. Then she brushed her hand along his cheek, and got up to exit. This sudden exit was necessary. The only way she could hide the truth as tears began to flow down her face. She had to flee.

"Hey, Lady! What's with the story? No ending, or what? Did she summon the courage to tell him?" he yelled after her.

"I... I wish that for her," Viola whispered to herself and scurried out of the room.

Chapter 8

For the first time in three days, Viola had woken up feeling good about herself. After she had talked to Ronny the day before, the black hole inside her had somehow lost a little power over her. She felt like she could breathe again and had the strength to get into her car. Make her way to Stine.

She had some bad news for the woman. The kind of news she would rather deliver in person.

Viola peeked at the wintery Oslo landscape sliding behind the windshield. She was approaching the Skiptvet community where Stine lived. Soon the typical Norwegian treehouses were replaced by single houses. And then, even more separated farmhouses. This was Skiptvet, where both Marianne and Stine had grown up and lived. With a population of just two hundred people, it was a flourishing farming community, but still an hour's drive away from the heart of Oslo. It was a different world from the one Anne and Viola came from. A simpler place, devoid of the pretences of the city. A place with all the time in the world.

The Voss family came from a different area, more central in Oslo, the suburban area named Østkanten, and more specifically, Bogerud. Viola had moved from Bogerud to the centre of Oslo.

But she hadn't done this because of the so-called 'Whites-Escape', when the native Norwegians fled from the multi-ethnic population that was streaming into Oslo.

Rather, she moved right into the heart of the melting pot of the Norwegian capital, Grønland. Despite Anne's violent disapproval, Viola prided herself on the fact that success for her was not measured in the apartment's location or how few Pakistani neighbours she had, but in how early she could go out into the street and grab a cappuccino on the sidewalk or buy the most exotic Thai food. A flurry of social classes, languages, customs, and just plain contact with people who had such a wildly different outlook than her – all this suited her perfectly. And as a bonus, she was a bicycle trip away from the *Aftenposten's* offices.

* * *

Viola eyed Stine's austere house. When Marianne first disappeared, Viola had practically moved in here. At that time, she was prepared to do everything she could to locate the missing girl.

So, she spent endless nights slaving away over every shred of evidence she could find in this house. Despite Stine's intense intrusions into Viola's life, she still felt her heart ache when she remembered Stine's desperation. An obsessive, all-encompassing need to find her daughter.

This unbearable desperation had a familiar ring for Viola. If she could feel a connection with Stine, it certainly was this black pit. So Viola practically threw away her duties, her own life, while searching for the young woman.

Somehow she had explained to herself that if she found the young woman, if she fulfilled Stine's wishes, then maybe her wounds might also be healed. But it wasn't only some kind of redemption Viola saw in Marianne.

Viola became more and more convinced the young woman held some unforeseen key to Viola's own search.

Every night, she lulled herself to sleep with the conviction that Marianne had found an answer to her mitochondrial disease. And every night Viola would fall asleep with a silent prayer concealed somewhere deep in her mind. There had to be something that would help her locate the young woman. And then, only then, would Marianne tell her exactly what she needed to do. In order to be happy again.

She knew she was mad to entertain this thought. It was more than ludicrous, considering everything she had been through. And she caught herself in this constantly. Was this the only way to be happy? Was this a prayer, or simply a toxic attachment?

Someone told her that an attachment was a belief that without a specific thing one wouldn't ever be happy. This helped her get things in perspective. But then she woke up the next day and felt her mind was rearranged again. And her prayer was renewed. With even more vigour.

But gradually she realised that no one listened to her prayer. It was never answered. Stine never found her daughter. And Viola's Markus died. So, if anything was to be learned, Viola was always confronted with the sad irony of life. The more intensely her prayer grew, the less likely it was to be answered.

Or maybe it was because she never believed she deserved an answer? She couldn't decide.

Viola stepped towards the door and was about to knock when she felt someone behind her. Stine came around the back in an apron, smeared in blood. The woman carried a headless chicken, which was still wiggling its feet. The bloody spectacle seemed natural for Stine. Nothing could be more appropriate for her.

"Come in, Miss. I have some wonderful stew for you." Stine glowed as she practically pushed Viola inside.

"Sorry... Can't. Dropped by just to tell you... Well... I can't be of any further help, you see." This case was never easy, and turning the poor woman down was even harder.

Viola hated herself for this. She could have done this on the phone to make it easier on herself, but she simply didn't have the heart. Not in this case.

And now that she glanced into Stine's eyes, Viola understood she had made a fatal mistake. Her physical presence and the intense disappointment in Stine's eyes just made it worse.

Seeing this caused an immediate panic to surge within her. She had made it all the way out here, with good intentions, but she didn't need this guilt trip. She swerved her body to leave.

But Stine was quicker and moved to block her exit.

"No!" Stine spat out firmly. "Please... Miss. I have proof. Real this time," Stine whispered, but her attempt at submission felt even more awkward.

"Stine, I just can't undo my life and career based on some prank comment on the blog. You see that, don't you?" She had to make the old woman understand. After all, it was so obvious.

But as Viola glanced into Stine's eyes, she could see that the clarity of the matter escaped the old woman.

"But, Miss. I know Miss is from a better family. In Miss's eyes, I am not much. But Miss Viola knows how it is to be Marianne."

"No! I know nothing of what it is to be like her." Viola made sure there was no doubt this time. She should get away from this woman as fast as possible, while she still had the strength. But Stine thrust herself into Viola's face.

"Miss knows exactly how it is to be like her." There was just something strangely odd about this old woman's stare, maybe even a touch of psychosis.

"Because Miss Viola is broken. Loss broken. Broken over little ones? I know. But Miss Viola fought for a little one, didn't she? And when Miss finally had it? What happened? Something even worse happened? Didn't it?" Stine whispered the words.

"How do you...? My mother had no right." Viola did everything to pull herself together, but the damage had already been done. And the planned escape was now impossible. She was as defenceless as a new-born.

"Your mother? No. I don't need anyone's stories. People talk lies," Stine scoffed at Viola's suggestion. Then she burned her gaze into Viola's face.

"But eyes tell the truth. Huh, Miss?" she whispered in a hoarse voice. At this point Viola just couldn't handle it anymore. The weight of Anne's earlier words crushed her.

And then, without any notice, Stine suddenly loosened up, stepped back, and glowed towards Viola as if nothing had happened.

"Now, Miss. Let's go eat my stew. And watch the new evidence." Viola was yet again reminded of the black hole inside her. If someone wanted to wreak havoc in her life, Markus was the place to do it. A place where she couldn't tell up from down, or right from wrong. How long would it be like that? Pain ground into the fabric of her soul. Or maybe that was not the right question. Maybe she should be asking if it would ever pass.

Viola eyed her car. It was still not too late. She made up her mind to make her way towards it.

Instead, she felt her body move inside Stine's house. Some unknown force pushed her into an inevitable chain of events.

* * *

The images from Stine's video danced before Viola's eyes. She pressed the mouse instinctively and rewound the whole thing. Then she pressed play once again. How many times had she done that? She had lost count, and by now, she didn't care.

Viola had told herself that Stine's talk was some kind of delusion. Brought on by way too many years of grief. This conviction was more straightforward. And certainly more convenient.

"Miss?" Stine said.

Viola was prepared to deny what she had just perceived on the screen. Maybe even try to convince the old woman she was crazy. But that would be lying. After what she had just seen, she just couldn't.

At this point, she knew that everything she was hoping to avoid would come to pass.

Noon

Viola wrenched her body into her car as she attempted to start the engine. For some unexplained reason, the brand-new leased Audi failed her miserably.

Her hands shook as she hit the dashboard. As Viola's inner frenzy flooded her body, her gaze stumbled upon Stine's piercing eyes. The old woman moved towards her. Held out something in her hand.

But Viola was done. Done thinking. Done talking. The last thing she needed was to stay here. And as everything in her screamed escape, she pummelled at the dashboard again. And, somehow, the engine finally started. Relief spread through her body, as the car spun out of Stine's yard.

As Viola drove away, she threw a glance at the old woman in the rear-view mirror. Was she holding something in her hand? Was that Viola's purse Stine had been attempting to give her?

No matter. She would deal with this when she got home.

Chapter 9

Evening

When Ronny got home he found Viola sitting in the hallway. Perhaps sitting was the wrong word. She was somewhere halfway between taking off her shoes and her winter jacket. And her clothes still lay strewn all over the floor, nothing packed. It seemed as if Viola had forgotten she had arrived home. Or that she had stuff to do.

When he slid closer to her, he noticed an emptiness about her. She just sat there. Transfixed.

"What's going on?" Her only answer was an even deeper silence.

His questions were mostly met with an answer. A positive candour. Sometimes on a superficial level, when she was at her busiest, but he was prepared to forgive her for those occurrences. Especially since she had her ways to make him laugh, to engage his mind, and sometimes even to warm his heart.

Yet this time, there was nothing but an impenetrable wall. A blankness he had never seen before.

"Hon?"

When she finally surfaced from some deep crevice, her eyes spoke volumes. A flash of pain resonated in his body as he glanced at her.

Then, without a single word, she grabbed his hand and led him into her work room.

* * *

The video was blurry, recorded in a hurry and maybe even in great distress. It was caught through a phone that had been placed temporarily on the night table in some nondescript place. It could be a hospital, maybe a clinic. But in the background, the windows were covered with iron bars that resembled a prison more than a medical institution. The lighting was sparse. But maybe that was the whole point. It was probably done in secrecy, and maybe even at great risk.

A woman's hand stuffed her phone onto the night table and the lens immediately framed a child. The boy was about two years old, and with his barely open eyes and weary body, he struggled against being woken up at this late hour.

"Puhleeeze stop. Sleep..." he mumbled. The woman hushed him into silence. She whipped her head around and checked if anyone was coming. When no one appeared, she sat down beside him.

By now Viola had watched this video countless times. At first she was jolted with enthusiasm, but as she replayed the scene, time and time again, her mind began to batter her with questions.

Was there something strangely artificial about the whole act? Or was she just imagining this? No. She should listen to her gut feeling. The whole thing felt a little awkward. Maybe even forced. As if it was staged. Made up for the camera. And, somehow, the kid sensed this as well.

Viola had trouble deciding if this was due to the late hour, or maybe the inherent danger. But the woman had no time for niceties. She was way too preoccupied with the recording.

"Who am I, hon?" she asked as she came up to the child's face. It was a peculiar question.

The kid began to weep silently. She tried to hush him, then she caressed him, not to soothe him but to coax him into silence. And the tenderness came off sounding tense and skewed in an imposed way.

"Please, who am I? Hon?" This time it was more a request than anything. And the kid's sobbing began to be clearly audible. The woman glanced around herself. She was panicked.

"Please just say it, Pumpkin. Who am I? Please, hon!" she repeated, as if she was running out of time.

"Mummy. You are Mummy. I want home." The kid began to cry out loud. The woman kissed him and thanked him for the help.

Then she turned her face towards the lens. Viola knew that this move was supposed to leave no doubt as to the woman's identity. Reveal who she was for the world.

When Viola saw this for the first time, she had felt a pang of recognition. This woman had a few more wrinkles, and her expression revealed she was terrified, but there was no doubt who she was.

Marianne.

But when Viola watched this stream, time and time again, at each consecutive pass, murky doubts crept into her mind.

The space was dark and unlit. The woman's face was barely visible. The video compression deteriorated the quality even further. Everything about the recording was questionable. And as she watched it now, Viola felt at a loss, not really sure of anything any longer.

* * *

Viola felt a mess brewing inside herself as she stopped the recording from her laptop.

And Ronny just glanced at her.

"I know what you are thinking, but don't! You don't want to go there. Okay?" He struggled with the words because she saw right through him. Even if Ronny didn't know the whole truth about her, he knew about her breakdown, and that it was somehow connected to the woman they had just watched. What he didn't know, Anne had probably filled in. His eyes told the whole story. He was afraid for her. Worried she would do something rash.

Still, she couldn't help it. Something inside her screamed she should stop this right now. But then another part pushed her in the opposite direction, a place where she would find answers. No matter the consequences. And at this point, even if this was semi-substantial proof at best, Viola had to convince Ronny to help her.

But she also knew that even before this argument had started, Ronny had already lost it. And it was not because she had a better plate of arguments, but simply because she was Viola.

She never forced him into anything. But she knew she held an eerie power over him. If push came to shove, what were his limits? What would he do for her? These thoughts scared her; how easily he had assumed this role.

Her shrink claimed that love could only exist if it was properly cultivated, and not dominated. He also claimed that her personal borders should be dynamic, changing according to the situation and the relationship at hand. She listened to him and appreciated his words for what they were.

A simple delusion.

Simply because she knew better.

Her life had carved it into her, taught her that to be submissive was to be taken advantage of. And if she could prevent anything, it was exactly this kind of bullshit. She didn't like the sound of the word compromise. It really never existed in her vocabulary. This was the good stuff, breastfed from year zero by her mother. And as the years went by, maybe she had grown a little bit softer and more malleable.

But a front was still a front.

Her shrink suggested in a subtle manner that this might be the root of her suffering. This unrelenting control she kept firmly draped over her true self. And maybe that was the reason she never knew what love was. Maybe it was time to let go. She nodded repeatedly and congratulated him on the precise dissection. But even before she left his office, the only words grinding away in her mind were, *Screw you*.

Viola's thoughts were whipped back to Ronny and the task at hand. And this time, she decided not to force herself on him. It was worth a try anyway, despite the obvious front.

"This woman's mitochondrial disease, and this boy, Ron. You realise that... it just can't be..." She tried a soft argument with him. The most reasonable one.

Ronny nodded. He knew all the facts about the disease. But she saw it in his face. This time, he was not going to give in that easily. And at first this grated her nerves. But then it hit her.

She realised this sudden newfound stubbornness surfaced only because he cared for her. Didn't she have enough proof of that from yesterday, when he offered to come with her to Syria?

"But how can you even be sure this child is hers? Based on this video, it's conjecture at best. Drop this!" He shook his head in dismay as he issued the outright order. She realised this was the first time he had ever done anything like that.

Late evening

"For God's sake, Viol! That's twenty years! You've worked your ass off to get that Middle East job. And you are gonna throw it all away?"

The quarrel had blown way out of proportion. She expected resistance, but not all-out war. Not with a man who had been the epitome of compassionate silence for the last two years.

However she tried to explain it to him, he turned it against her. If it had been at some other time, in some other context, she might have found it sexy. If there was something about him that ticked her off, it was his malleable nature. Way too plastic for her taste. But now, this newfound defiance just exhausted her.

"It will wait," she snapped back.

"Wait? Anne wait? You kidding me? She will drag your ass through the mud. All in the name of the family's reputation."

She fell silent. He couldn't be more accurate in this assessment. Her mother would not only drag her ass through the mud, but would see to it that everybody knew about it. She didn't need to go further than Silje to confirm her worst suspicions.

But this was not the time to agree with her partner. She needed his understanding. No. She needed more. She needed his help, because a plan had already begun to form in her mind.

Maybe diplomacy wasn't the right way to go about this. This softness began to grate on her nerves anyway.

"Ron! That's enough. Look at her! It's not a question of *if*. I simply *have* to." She pointed at Marianne's terrified face, then locked gazes with him.

"So, what are you saying?" He leaned back. As if to ready himself for the coming impact.

"I wasn't asking for your permission." There. She had said it. It certainly felt more right. More truthful to herself. She didn't feel good about it.

She knew there would be repercussions, or some other yada about how relationships weren't built on this kind of communication, but all of this was just what her ex-shrink would have told her.

It was her life to screw up, anyway.

And the moment she uttered the words, all the power drained from Ronny. Well, almost.

65

"Based on this thing... You will never find her." He scrambled with the last attempt to stop her, as he pointed at the recording.

Night

Viola ached at the sight of Ronny's exhausted face. Her brilliant idea had turned out to be mediocre.

It was the middle of the night, and they had been up for six hours straight, trying to find any clues in the video material. Anything that would help them locate Marianne.

The surroundings in the recording turned up nothing. There were no signs, text, clothes with logos, or any other clues that could give them any kind of hint where Marianne might actually be.

She saw the inevitable doubt creeping into his face. Six hours ago, she had to force him to help her. Rarely had she been such a stubborn bitch. Yet, in spite of this, he didn't air any of the hesitation he was feeling once they got started. Not even once.

She had been through most of the material at highly magnified resolutions, but the recording had been compressed for Net streaming, turning it into a pixelated sea of ambivalence.

She was so close to finding her. Viola let go of the trackpad and let out a crushing sigh.

Ronny looked across at her. She knew he wanted her to succeed. He wanted her to find Marianne. Powerless to do any more, he came up behind her, kissed her cheek, and began to massage her neck. His hands felt great, and right in that moment she could have fallen over from exhaustion. But her mind churned, crunching away at a possible solution. This couldn't be right. If this was Marianne, and it was a message, she was way too smart not to think about leaving a clue.

Viola jolted up. She magnified the captured QuickTime stream in her window. Then zoomed in on the image behind Marianne's kid. She pointed behind the iron bars in the window.

"See? There! The helix?" Her eyes lit up.

Ronny sat up and leaned into the screen. He squinted his eye, then the other, but finally just shook his head.

"Viol, there is nothing there. Just some stuff. Blurry stuff..." he whispered with all the reservation he could muster.

"Stuff! That's a sign. A helix sign. You know, like the DNA. Can't you see that?" She was on the verge of screaming. But the words weren't hostile or aggressive. For the first time in six hours, she was bursting with excitement.

She realised one needed a bucket load of imagination to see it was a sign, but she smelt victory nonetheless. She disregarded his doubts with a smirk, then captured the screen. Zoomed in, sharpened, cropped. Then inspected the area behind the iron bars. After some fast Photoshop work, the image was beginning to show some potential.

The helix sign materialised into an actual sign – sort of.

Ronny straightened up. He was impressed.

Meanwhile, she uploaded the image to Google's image recognition software. Immediately, a myriad of images followed. The result of her search. Ronny's eyes flashed up at the results.

"God. This hurts my overgrown ego."

"What?" She was way too preoccupied with scanning the pictures to catch onto his meaning.

"You being way smarter than me," he finished with a groan. She chuckled, but then stopped abruptly.

"Damn. Look at this!" she whispered and nodded Ronny to the screen.

"A casual family selfie on the street. See what's behind them?" She pointed to the building far behind the family members.

And there it was. The same logo that was in Marianne's video. A shiny symbol on a modernist building in the background.

Viola inspected the metadata of the picture. Then threw the geo-location into Google maps. The result flashed up a small town named Gjøvik. Located about a hundred kilometres from Oslo, the city had about 20,000 inhabitants.

When she zoomed in closer on the geo-location, she landed on the outskirts of the city. And there it was. A clinic. The medical facility appeared under the name InviNordica. And from the first glance at their web page, she learned their main business was treating infertility through in vitro.

"Gotcha!" She scribbled down the address, then threw herself at Ronny and slobbered him with a slew of wet kisses.

Before she knew it, the chair cracked under her excitement, and they found themselves on the floor. As her hands tugged at his shirt, her breath pulsed against his mouth. She couldn't remember the last time she had wanted him this bad.

Sex, to Viola, was mostly a necessary evil. It was done for him, because it was an item on the to-do list, most often the last one. Only because she had to, and rarely out of a genuine want. It served a purpose. A necessary glue for their relationship.

And if anyone ever told her there was something wrong with her sex drive, she would tell this person to shove the twenty-years-of-infertility up where there was less light.

Yet now, her body pulsed with lust. She felt electrified as she clawed at his chest. But then he held her back.

"Hey. Do you really think I will let you anywhere near this place? Forget it. Not without some police protection."

She eyed him, considering whether she should take this argument further.

Making her decision, she wrestled loose from his grip, and ripped open his shirt. As she swayed hard against his chest, she heard no more protests from him.

Rene

She had to be patient with him, she knew that all too well. But where there should have been progress, she was met with only hurdles. And where she had been promised great things, there was only disappointment. Rene had to lower her expectations, lower the bar even more.

Rene hunched even closer to Trond and stared into his eyes. She reminded herself that her proximity assured him he was safe. At least, that's what the doctors said. And she had to listen to them. It was the only assurance she got.

He was barely four, and although his face was full of bursting radiance, she had to push away that gnawing feeling she had inside herself. There was something inherently off about his face, something she attempted to forget each time he twinkled at her. Yet this time, as his grin widened, she was struck by the subtle misalignment of his features. The nose just a little bit too low, the eyes unevenly spaced, and the brows just a little too big. But she pushed away these facts and reminded herself that no one paid attention to these things. It was way too vague to be noticed, anyway. And the eeriness that prodded at her and reminded her that he was different, those were only her feelings betraying her.

After all, he was her son.

She slid even closer to him and looked over at his hand, which was scribbling away on a few paper sheets.

"Concentrate, Pumpkin. Please, concentrate," she whispered to him and glanced down at the drawing. On the paper were countless mathematical fractions, divisions, radians, and degrees.

"But, Mum, can I play?" he pleaded with her, eager to get up. But Rene caught him by his collar and gently pressed him back onto the bench. Then she reminded herself one more time she had to be patient. She had to make it worth his time, motivate him, inspire him.

"Oh, sweetie. Didn't you want to be a mathematician when you grow up? Remember our goal? My... your dream?" she said and beamed at him as she shoved the paper back into his lap.

Lately, he had learnt a new trick. He expressed enthusiasm where he had none, and as soon as she let him off the hook, he was gone, off to play somewhere else, or even worse, doing stuff that had nothing to do with their common dream.

As she gazed into his eyes, she saw right through him. He was avoiding their homework. She felt a sting of impatience at the boy's lack of involvement in this important matter. Why couldn't he see what she was doing for him?

She punched a few numbers into her calculator and locked eyes with him.

"What is 0.0434 divided by 0.0109?" She jabbed at him with her finger, demanding an answer straightaway.

"I don't know," he whispered under his breath, exasperation filling his face. She felt another sigh pass through her. Had all these years gone to waste?

She swivelled her head closer to him and pointed to his head.

"It's all in here. Remember that!" She said the words slowly, one by one. Making sure he got every syllable. And as she locked gazes with him, Trond responded with a barely audible sniffle.

"You are hurting my arm," he whimpered and glanced at her hand, which was clenched onto his shoulder.

Rene loosened her hand and retreated. In that moment, it began to dawn on her. The futility of it all. She wanted a better life for him. She had come here just to have him. She did everything they had asked of her. All by the book.

She took all the hormonal treatments that left her body in ruins. She had prolonged her stay there, on several occasions, until the word "indefinitely" began to have an abstract sound to it. And all of it was done because the staff recommended it. Only the best for Trond was good enough.

And they were right, it was all done so he could have a future. To give him a head start in this infested rat race. Something her parents were never able to give her. But despite all of this, he still wouldn't listen. He shied away from her pleas. He ran away from his math training. He refused the clinic's diagnostics, flailed at the staff, and spat out his medication.

Ungrateful little brat.

Why couldn't he see the obvious? In this world, there was no place for runner-ups, and much less for the last one in the line. Besides, after what she had done for him, he owed her this much. To make her finally happy.

And she had to admit, there were times when everything in her just gave in, and she boiled over. Then she simply stared into his eyes and asked him if he wanted to be just like all the others? Did he really want to be a nobody?

But inside herself, she knew that he risked even more, because a nobody faded away into obscurity and was simply forgotten. But her boy would be ridiculed. He would be made a laughingstock just for being different.

"It's 3.98165." Rene heard the words uttered behind her back. She whipped her head around and eyed her son.

Had she heard him right? Had he given her the correct answer? No. It had to be her mind playing some trick on her. This was just a coincidence. Or even worse, maybe he was cheating. She inspected his face closer, then scanned around him. No, there was no way he could have seen the read-out on her calculator.

"What did you say?"

"It's 3.98165," he moaned out the words between tears.

Normally she would have given him a hug, anything to hush the boy down. But this was far more important; this might even be a breakthrough. She grabbed onto her calculator.

And as Trond burst into tears from the cold shoulder treatment, she inspected the display. Immediately, her eyes sizzled with excitement.

The display read: 3.98165.

Chapter 10

She was half-running towards the flat complex where Pål lived. It was a bunch of filthy blocks, a relic of the fifties when the Norwegian economy was still down on its face. Times when barely anyone had heard about the magical kingdom of oil.

Viola was about to enter when she was interrupted by a barrage of messages on her cell phone.

She grabbed a peek and heaved an involuntary sigh. Only her mother sent messages at the frequency of a machine gun shootout. And if this proved anything, it was that the only person Anne was interested in listening to was herself.

Where the hell are you, gal? Call me asap, Anne demanded of her daughter in the first message.

You've let me down big time! Anne's second message followed five seconds later. This woman wasn't about to give Viola the chance to respond.

You are a fucking bitch! Anne blasted at Viola in another message. *Sorry...* Anne rolled an apology and regret into one.

You still haven't told me where you are. She followed this by yet another reminder why this conversation started in the first place.

Dear? You know I love you, was the big finale. As predictable as ever.

This was business as usual. And it struck Viola how numb she felt lately. These messages, they did nothing to her. She felt nothing.

The mere thought made her panic. She scrambled inside herself. Was she about to become just as numb as her mother, her emotions ground to dust by the constant everyday assault?

Then it struck her. This nothing, it wasn't exactly a nothing. She still felt something. This nothingness had a foul smell to it. It reeked of Anne's emotional garbage.

This was good. This cheered her up. Things weren't as bad with her as she initially thought.

She crammed the phone into her purse, slashed a smirk onto her face, and raced inside.

* * *

She covered her ears and prepared for an assault as Pål's head protruded from his door.

He certainly had a right to take it out on her. Not only had she badgered him the last time she had come, now she landed at his place in the middle of the night. She had brushed up on her twenty-second speech to perfection, and was now prepared to deliver it in ten. Which would be about how long she would have before he slammed the door in her face.

Viola knew she had burned her bridges with him during her last visit. But at this point, she wasn't going to beat herself up over minor details. After all, the man she respected was long gone. Replaced by some spineless phantom.

How did that happen to people so quickly? Despite their professional relationship, she had spent enough time with him to become fond of his obnoxious quirks. His pedantic attention to people's darker traits bordered on genius and served a purpose at his work. But his social misalignment did nothing other than get him into trouble.

And seeing him like this, she was afraid to dig deeper. Because she sensed Pål had a gaping hole where his heart should have been. She didn't care for these kinds of truths. The ones that broke men and women. She fancied even less the thought that he might share his story. A tale that might well highlight that the two of them had way too much in common.

"Pål! I am so sorry. And you were so right the last time. But just give me thirty seconds. I have some key evidence. Please? Okay. Great!" She moved towards him aggressively, leaving no chance for second thoughts.

"Actually... I wanted to talk to you," he said in an overtly cautious manner.

"What do you mean?" she croaked, almost under her breath.

"I am in," he announced without any bravado, as if this was the most obvious thing in the world.

"In? You mean *in*, as in you will help me?" She tried to get a grip on what was going on. What had happened to him? Had someone threatened him? Or even worse, had he had a sudden bout of conscience? Decided to change for the better? But as she tested that idea, it just felt off.

However she analysed it, there were no clear-cut answers. And if she asked, he would surely not be inclined to give them to her.

"I don't get it. Don't you want to look at my evidence?" she probed, searching for some trace of true motivation.

His front remained unperturbed, a closed book. So here she was, and she had gotten everything she wanted before she even stepped inside his flat. But certainly not in the way she expected it.

Was she prepared to take a chance on a wild card like this?

How many people were willing or able to help her at this moment? She didn't see a queue. No. Pål was the only one. And this was the only help she would be getting.

Maybe Marianne was at that clinic now. But would she be there tomorrow, or the day after? How much time did she really have? Given the time window she had to work in, with or without a hidden agenda, Pål was it. He was her only shot at finding Marianne.

And as he nodded her in with his twitchy smile, it was with an even bigger reluctance that she finally stepped in.

Chapter 11

Morning

She had been standing in an obscure corner of the *Aftenposten* office for far too long. She was staring like a stupid little girl at the supposed epitome of her family's heritage, the necklace from her mother.

As sure as she was of her goal while at Pål's place, at this moment, hesitation crept up on her, prickling her skin. She knew that Anne was preparing some kind of farewell party at the offices for all the people who hadn't been invited to her home. This made the whole situation more than delicate.

Viola was sure her mother would blow up if she heard her intentions. But this time, she wouldn't use the escape hatch. She would stand up to her mother proudly and sell the bad news without the neatly-packaged lies.

This meant convincing Anne that she was in perfect control of the situation. And she had to find Marianne, no matter what.

Viola remembered little of her father as he had passed away when she was young. But she heard two kinds of stories about him. One kind was from her mother. And the other was from everyone else. She didn't even make it past twelve before she made up her mind which kind she wanted to believe in. And she remembered that moment of realisation. How could she not? A green-eyed teenager, crushed by the fact that her mother had her own somewhat warped take on reality.

This would reverberate in everything she did in her life. Not only that, but she used Anne, the most toxic relationship in her life, as an example, a role model. And if there was anything to learn, it was how to get ahead in life using her personal take on reality. Even though life was still tough, lies made everything somewhat more manageable. Lies about her condition, lies about her relationships, but mostly, lies to herself. After all, why shouldn't she?

Her suffering justified every lie she told.

Before she realised it, she had managed to arrange her life in a maddening configuration. One where the only truth was the work she did, the only place where she refrained from this alternate reality.

So now, as she stood not far from Anne's office, this was the beginning of a new phase. A turning point. A new beginning. One where she would stand on her own. Where the lies would stop. Where she would dictate her own terms and be truthful to herself.

She inhaled deeply; she was pumped up and ready. Then she plunged into the chief editor's office.

* * *

Anne's mouth tested the bitter words. Viola had just broken the news as softly as she could. She had paid extra attention to repeat the word "postponement" enough times to ensure it would drill itself into her mother's subconscious. But even with her pep talk, and all the stakes at hand, Viola watched as her mother grappled with what she had just been told.

"A postponement? Of your position in the Middle East?" Anne repeated the words one more time.

"A week?" Viola did her best to fill her smile with as much sugar as she could manage.

"What do you think this position is, a fucking last-minute takeaway at McDonald's?" Anne said. "Postponement. Delays. Rescheduling. Cut the crap, girl. What's going on? Really?"

This was her chance, as she adequately put it in her own words, for a new beginning. She took a big breath and prepared herself as she jumped out into nothing.

"I... I could... I want..." But that was as far as she got.

"What did you say, girl?" Anne hurled an impatient glance at Viola.

"Nothing," Viola whispered. She was losing it completely. Curling up on herself like a terrified little rabbit. What the hell happened to that woman just outside of the office? She had to get out of here before she folded completely under Anne's steel grasp.

And as Anne barely heard Viola's whisper, her mother smirked at Viola's helplessness, then pointed behind her.

"Nothing? Well, tell that to them." Viola cast a glance behind her and realised the whole newspaper staff was lined up neatly in a row. This was a siege, and she wouldn't be getting out of here alive. Unless she decided to come clean or bend under Anne's rule.

It was obvious Anne was sure of her own victory. And as Viola's eyes swept over her audience, she realised her mother was right. If she had any doubts about going to Syria, and couldn't express herself in front of Anne, was it going to be any easier to spill it in front of fifty industry professionals?

* * *

Anne's left hand massaged Viola's neck as she thrusted her out of her office and in front of the packed crowd. Anne's prized trophy daughter was about to give a victory speech. And if there was one thing Anne loved more than her own speeches, it was Viola's. Not because she was proud of Viola, but because it made the chief editor look great.

And with nothing less than this expectation, they exited the office in front of five dozen people, everyone ready to burst into thundering applause. But the only thing Viola could think of was how to contain the volcano of adrenaline about to burst within her. Her shaky hands were cramping all over, so she did the only thing she could: she hid them behind her back. For every second she prolonged this situation, her mental condition inevitably deteriorated. She knew she had to say something before it was too late. Anything would do. Still, she came up a blank. She had zero idea where to start or how to break the news.

And before she could utter a word, the crowd erupted into a standing ovation. By the time the clapping had died down, Viola was a mess. These were the people whom she had worked with for the last fifteen years. A staff that respected her and trusted in her judgement.

However well she phrased it, she knew these people would sense trouble a mile away. You didn't just postpone this kind of assignment. Just as you didn't postpone being appointed to the presidency because you had more pressing matters to attend to.

"I... I umm... am not going," she managed to blurt out, though the words were barely intelligible. But it was enough. Everyone got the message. And the only thing that followed was a collective gasp, which passed through the room, while all eyes remained riveted on her. Everyone tried to reconcile the words Viola uttered with the unequivocal watchdog success that they were all familiar with.

And everyone came up short.

Anne had always been a master of disguise yet, this time, her face simply short-circuited – even she had trouble concealing that it would be hard to undo Viola's announcement.

Noon

Viola was crushed against a wall in a cramped cleaning supply room, the most secluded corner of the newspaper. Probably the only place where Anne could murder her and dispose of the body. And as Viola glanced into her mother's eyes, she could see Anne was more than prepared to rip her daughter to shreds. For Anne, this was a public disgrace, as the last thing she had counted on was for Viola to undermine her position and dish out disobedience in front of the staff.

"This was a mistake, right? Your postponement, you can have it. Even now. But we are talking two days. Maximum." Viola had never seen her mother like this. Ever. She had expected anger, some heavy pressure, and maybe even long-lasting resentment. But right now, she realised how important this was to Anne. To the chief editor.

For the first time, Viola sensed Anne's words were tainted with fear. It wasn't every day that Anne had to deal with situations beyond her control. And things didn't get more out of whack than her own family jumping ship at a key moment in the growth of her media dynasty.

And as Viola glanced into her mother's unnerved eyes, she began to feel sorry for her. Well, almost. But despite her conscience jarring inside her, there was one thing that came even more naturally than compassion. She put the squeeze on Anne.

"Actually, I need more time."

Immediately, Viola saw Anne's inner struggle. The older woman attempted to put some serious brakes on her emotions.

"What's this? It's that Stine stuff, huh? It has to be her. Right?" Anne grasped at anything she could.

And her intuition was right. It was all about Stine. But Viola enjoyed seeing her mother squirm way too much to confirm it. She just shook her head in denial.

But this didn't stop Anne from barging forward.

"You are losing it. I knew it. Exactly like the last time that woman was in your life. Right? I did everything to get you back on that horse. Only, after Markus, you never did. Not in your head. And I am supposed to treat you as a professional peer?" Anne spat out and pointed to Viola's head, as if mere pointing would prove something was wrong with it.

"Leave my son out of this. Are you forgetting the awards I brought to the paper? How does that count for publicity? And sales? And the Middle East job? No thanks to you." But even before Viola could finish her sentence, Anne made a sneering gesture. This in itself felt off, as her mother never expended such emotions. Not that overblown, never that crude. Viola sensed this couldn't be good.

"You want the truth? The other candidates for the position were a helluva lot stronger than you." Anne said.

"Including that kid Jon? What is he? Barely twenty-five? I bet he was willing to do so much more than just say thank you for that job?" Viola bit back, knowing all too well the emotional configuration going on behind the scenes there.

Anne scoffed. Then she slid right up to her daughter's face.

"No. The truth is that I didn't only pull some strings. I whipped everyone into submission. That's how you got the fucking job," she hissed at her daughter.

Viola wished for her mother to be a liar now, a con-woman delivering her ultimate trick. But she could see it in Anne's eyes. She wasn't lying. Not this time.

Viola felt her stomach explode as an invisible force wrenched at everything inside her. She needed to get out of here, before she lost it. But as she made her move, Anne slid over to block her way. And from the look of it, she was far from finished.

"Now. Get your shit together. And your ass on that next plane. That's three days."

But the only thing that raced through Viola's mind was what she had done. Their relationship had always had a serious limp. But as she looked into Anne's face, she realised they had reached a tipping point. Damage was dealt, and it might never be undone.

But at this moment, Viola wasn't sure she would want to try anyway.

Late afternoon

Viola scuttled out of the newspaper office like a wounded animal. Her eyes were slaloming past everybody's glances as she attempted to make it out in one piece. Still, she felt everybody's raised eyebrows, imperceptible coughs, and silent laughs. The fact that she didn't see them, didn't mean they weren't there. She could sense every one of them, drilling into her spine, weighing her body down until she could barely make it out of the building.

Yet for every step that she made out of this office, she was closer to disconnecting from this place. And as she threw the door open, her past came crushing back at her.

She remembered hearing about the childless and their stories. All the narratives that promised her that her own story would have a blissful ending. One where she would reach the promised light at the end of the murky tunnel. Find the procedure that was just right for her body. One that actually worked and didn't maim her hormonal system.

But after ten years of trials and torment, she realised she never heard about the other kind of stories.

The stories about the people who had finally arrived at the conclusion that not only were they physically disabled, but their lives were worthless and meaningless. So, they might just as well give up.

Those were the true stories.

As she burst through the last door, she left all the confused glances behind her. And it struck her more clearly than ever, her life was this kind of story.

The true story.

PART TWO: Deceit

Vlog 1st entry 13.3.2010

"Hello Dolly, to all you girls out there! I am Marianne, and this is my first post."

Nervousness pervaded her body all morning. She had all sorts of doubts. Would she be heard? Would people believe her story was genuine? And would anyone care? She knew she could blow it. All of it. After all, it was the very first time.

Then she pushed away all the doubts and summoned her courage as she turned on the webcam. And in that moment, she saw her green eyes gaze back at her.

This was her big moment of truth.

"I am here for a reason. Because of one single moment in my life. The most defining one, you could say. And those of you who have been through that moment, you will know what I am talking about. It is the moment I realised my body won't ever know the feeling of having morning sickness, of being pregnant, of giving birth. That exact point in time that crushed all meaning from my life." She uttered the words, and felt her body reverberate with a painful groan. These life-defining thoughts were the DNA of her body; this moment influenced all her convictions. The same convictions which now led her to rip herself open for the public.

"What provokes me is that single women get stamped as 'insufficient'. You know what I am talking about. Just because they don't have a partner. The Norwegian government and the *Bioteknologirådet*, the Norwegian Biotech Council, think that single women don't have the same rights to children as couples do. What the hell is wrong with this picture? They claim it is for the best of the child to have two parents. Who the fuck came up with the idea that single women are insufficient? That a child will have an identity crisis because it doesn't have a father? Or that I won't be able to support it? It terrifies me. We haven't gotten further in this country? Come on, folks! It's the fucking twenty-first century, isn't it? Just look at Denmark and their fertility regulations. What do we have to do? Go out on the town and get a random fuck, in some vain hope a child will be the result? I know many of us do. At least those who can get pregnant. But I want to be the first one to know, from your experience, your story, if a one-night stand equals a responsible father, a proper family. You tell me! Or maybe better tell that to the Bioteknologirådet. The wise men with their fat asses, stubby fingers that push the buttons, deciding our future." She was inflamed, and finally let out her breath. Her mind felt crushed just thinking about this, much less talking about it. Yet this didn't sap her energy like the last seven years had. This didn't drain her like another IVF cycle. No. This was something else. A new quality and meaning. She could feel it.

"Don't they see that being a mother is not just some random act committed on a whim? It takes perseverance, courage, your whole emotional core, to even make the decision. It's a long and arduous process of preparation and planning, a carefully thought out process. All you girls know what I am talking about. Only you would understand what it is like to be excluded, shunned and isolated in what is supposed to be the most democratic country in the world. I admire your courage, and hope that those of you who have the courage to go to Denmark for IVF will get your wish fulfilled." Adrenaline pumped through her veins, she was primed, ready to take on the world.

"This is not just a first post. But a new beginning. Do you know why I speak up? Because this country needs our voice. A country full of hurt three-legged rabbits, hiding in shadowy corners, and impotent men deciding our future. So, I propose a new path, and not for my healing, but for all of you out there. You see, Hello Dolly is not just a random plugin in my blogger's toolbox. For many, it symbolised the hope and enthusiasm of an entire generation. These very words were sung by Louis Armstrong. For me, they are my manifesto! The message I bring to you because we all need it! Hang in there! Don't give up! Hello Dolly to all you single, childless girls!"

She finished and clicked off the cam.

Everything would change. Everyone would hear her.

In four years' time.

Chapter 12

Pål eyed Viola with apprehension. In his hands were two minuscule items. A microphone and a receiver.

"You are not serious? You are serious." She cringed at the sight. These methods were exactly the thing she detested the most. Although the Norwegian law stated that sound recordings were admissible as evidence in court, as a professional journalist she had to participate in the conversation. But this wasn't what smelt of rotten journalist ethics for her. What did, was that she went into this place as a private person, and with the intention to provoke and possibly steer the staff into illegal activities. Although some of her peers would disagree, in her mind, this was walking the razor's edge, and she wouldn't be the first one to end up in court, sued to hell and back for malpractice.

She took a hard-line stance towards similar matters, and some time ago, even ran a story on her peers, called Story Forgery. She didn't hesitate to lash out at their ethics when they took editorial liberty in their work that left out crucial facts. The reality they presented skewed the public perception of a real person. Her story caused a stir and legal proceedings. Her peers were ostracised, and the event was later labelled as a black chapter in Norwegian journalism.

Yet, despite this, there were always respected journalists, from even more respected papers, who dared to push the limits. People who saw no other means than to forge their identities in order to provoke illegal actions, just so they could subsequently expose them to the public. In many cases it worked, sometimes the end even justified the means, but she wasn't looking for attention, and certainly not to paint this all over the national media.

She only wanted to find one person. And the answers that came along with her.

"No. No. Forget it. I came here for protection. As in official protection. This won't make things better." If she was prepared to use these methods, she wouldn't have come to him. This was stuff anyone could get off the shelf. And she could just go inside the clinic, collect the recordings as evidence, and use it as proof to get a warrant.

"You have an alternate plan, don't you?" she prodded him. Pål peeked at her with clear disappointment, which told Viola everything.

No plan B.

It was bad enough she was putting her career on the line, but now she had a respected police officer suggesting they both pull this stunt.

She glanced at Pål, searching his features for answers. Something she failed to notice before. From the very first moment she entered his apartment, there was something off with this man. A warped state, one he tried to cover up from the beginning. She had seen something similar in junkies, alcoholics. But it clung to him, like a murky, invisible cloak.

Desperation.

It was there. In plain sight. She was about to gamble her safety on a man who was willing to do anything. Put him in a squeezer, and what would he do? What was he capable of?

"Do you see any other way to get a proper warrant to this place? That's our only shot at evidence," he whispered with a growing impatience, reminding Viola who came to whom in the first place.

"And the official channels?" Viola tried the obvious one more time.

"If you want to help her any time this year, forget it."

Viola's eyes went to the micro-chip mike. Hesitated even more. She knew this would garner a lot of aggravation. After all, he was willing to help her.

But there had to be another way. If she got caught with this... Yes, that would be hard to explain. And what's worse, considering she had no official assignment from *Aftenposten*, there would be no backup from there.

Add to that the small matter of how she is now perceived by her fellow professionals after her Story Forgery piece, and it would make her a hypocrite in their eyes. The woman who made a public crusade against these kind of methods, now using them?

No.

There had to be a different path. Some middle road. One that wouldn't burn all the bridges behind her. And also set her on fire.

"Can I think about it?" she asked. Pål eyed her and threw up his arms.

She saw it in his eyes. An accusation. What was this sudden bullshit thinly dressed up as journalist ethics? Fear was making the decisions for her right now. And Marianne was certainly worth more than that.

She wrenched her eyes away from his gaze because she knew he was right. And it struck her. She didn't know anymore what she was doing here. Why did she come here in the first place? What had she put first? Her own skin, or Marianne's well-being?

Noon

Viola paced back and forth in her room. Her whole body was tied in some freakish knot. After countless phone calls and dead ends, she had finally reached the nearest thing one could call authority in this clinic.

"Yes. Marianne Olsen... I understand that information is confidential... But, yes... so you told me, please." Despite that she wasn't face-to-face with the person, she could smell the irritation. She knew she had to be quick.

"Yes, but next of kin? Would the clinic make the information available then?" She fired away what seemed to be her best, and last, shot.

But she knew the exact answers she would be getting. The private clinics had a fool-proof privacy armour. Or at least the respectable ones did. They prided themselves in keeping their sensitive customer data safe from such amateurish hacks as her.

Still, she had to hang on to her delusions. Anything. As long as she didn't have to wear that microphone into that place.

"Come on, I am talking about her mother. Doesn't she have a right to know?" She may as well be talking to the air, she knew that. The only thing for her to do now was to wait for the obvious.

Still, when she heard it, she felt her stomach sink.

But she wasn't done. She had one more shot.

Evening

Viola glowed with a smile at a female Constable's desk in the main police station at Grønlandsleiret. She expected an immediate bureaucratic road block, which would cut off her chance at any kind of official investigation.

Instead, she was treated warmly by a young woman named Dina, who was open, and even a little gullible. And suddenly Viola began to see hope.

The Constable behaved as if this was her very first day at work. And with every hook Viola laid out, she realised it might actually be the case. So, Viola made sure she drew out some crucial information about her, which wasn't all that difficult.

In ten minutes, she learned Dina had been happily engaged. She had two award-winning poodles, which she loved more than anything. But, most of all, she revealed her despair that her soon-to-be-husband didn't share her love of the poodles. When he put his foot down and told her she needed to check her priorities, pleading that she treat him better than her damned dogs, she cried and apologised to him. Then she took the dogs under her arm, went out and never returned.

This off-the-record gossip led Viola to one conclusion. Maybe there was a way to kick-start this without the key element of any investigation: solid evidence. Any half-experienced police officer would throw her out of the police station at the mere suggestion. But maybe Viola didn't have a regular police officer in front of her. Maybe she just needed to connect.

"So, then, let's sum it up: we have all the paperwork done. And I can expect this thing to start any day now?" she prodded Dina.

"Miss! No. No. With all the new regulations, it would be more like a month or two of waiting time," the young woman replied with an overflowing grin. Viola sank in on herself. That may as well be ten years. Viola needed to move on this. But Dina needed the right incentive.

"Did you know that *Aftenposten* is running a long form story on the social impact of miniature poodles and how they will be forming part of the psychological framework of every urban household of the future? Brilliant, huh? We have the concept, but we are still looking for the household. By the way, your dogs, are those the miniature ones?" Viola let the ludicrous hook hang in the air. But it took only half a second for the young police officer's eyes to spark.

"I might be able to actually push this case to the less loaded detectives. Just for you, Miss Voss..."

"Please, dear, just Viola." She stressed this. With this woman and some poodle talk, the impossible would become possible. Her plan had worked. And without some questionable half-assed solutions provided by Pål.

The Constable returned her bursting energy and grabbed Viola's card. Viola straightened and was about to get up, but was interrupted by a cough from Dina.

"Umm, I think we forgot one detail. I will just need you to fill out these files. You know, to procure any evidence you might have at your disposal. Anything that would help our investigation. Is that okay... Viola?" The lieutenant sent her a warm grin as she finally allowed herself to connect on a personal level with Viola. Then, she handed all the standard paperwork out to Viola.

Viola felt a deep sting in her chest. There was no way around it. She knew what she would have to do next.

Late evening

Pål didn't ask a single question when she came back. And even if he had, she would never tell him what happened.

But the subtle I-told-you-so smirk spoke volumes. Frankly, she was sick of him. Every time she glanced at his face, his self-righteous grin would get more pronounced. No, she wasn't sick of him. She wanted to beat him to a pulp.

Meanwhile, Pål used tweezers to push the micro-chip mike inside Viola's necklace. The chip had a whole electronic circuit inside it and included a microphone, all contained in something the size of a grain of rice.

"This thing has Wi-Fi built in and will log on to any nearby network. Then it will record and stream audio in

93

real time over the Net to my I.P. address. I will be right outside the clinic with this." He pointed to his laptop, then fired up an app on it. It allowed him to log on to the sound source from the mike. A quick sound check confirmed everything was okay.

But Viola's mind was already elsewhere. The only thing that concerned her was whether Ronny would hear any of this. And when she saw Pål's laptop, she knew that might be beyond her control.

If they ran any tests on her while she was inside the clinic, Ronny was bound to hear the truth. She had come this far with him, and wasn't going to blow the whole thing by revealing the truth about her condition. There had to be a way to make sure Ronny never heard the recording.

Meanwhile, she realised that Pål had stopped fiddling with his laptop. Her hesitation must have been painted all over her face since Pål's attention was now focused on her.

"What?" she asked self-consciously. Pål shook his head.

"Even if they catch you, do you think they will locate this thing? This is not some military operation, okay? Relax, Viol." Viola's hands began to twitch.

She was committing herself to an illegal action devised by a working cop. And on top of that, she was risking the finest romantic relationship she's had for ten years. No. She wasn't risking it. She was using Ronny, she reminded herself.

"What you hear, through this... will you be using headphones?" The words stumbled out of her, as she gestured to the laptop.

Pål glanced at her for a moment, then just burst into a chuckle. Viola wanted to hurl something at him. Anything would do, as long as it would hurt enough to make him stop. What the hell was this man thinking, making jokes at her suffering?

"You meant to say, will your partner be able to hear it?" He pierced right at the truth.

"That's not what I said…" Viola tried to backtrack, unwilling to share anything more with him. And certainly not this sensitive.

"That's exactly what you said. Relax, Viola. The secret of your mitochondrial disease is safe with me." He spoke with a childish carelessness. In a way that only someone who had never been through that nightmare could do.

What was a plain fact for the cop was like a sledgehammer for Viola. How the hell could this man know? Yes, they had spent a lot of time together on Marianne's investigation. They had even shared some private stuff over a beer. Out of necessity. Only to get further with the investigation.

She had not even remotely been anywhere near revealing her secret. And now, this washed-out loser had dissected her to pieces and made fun of it. How long had he known? Had he told anyone else?

"Come on. What else could be the reason?" he said. She wanted to bash in his purplish alcoholic's face, shriek at him at the top of her lungs. But the words remained as impotent as ever. And her anger dissipated into silent agony.

"Do you plan on telling him?" He was making an attempt to reach out to her, to put her at ease, she could feel that. But Viola didn't want a confessional, and even if she did, not with this man.

"Relax, he won't hear a thing."

The damage was done. Her senses folded in on her as she hurried to raise the necessary walls around herself.

She had always thought she would be able to tell Ronny the truth at some point in time. But right now, it had become obvious she never would.

And it was not because she was afraid he would find out her secret. It was also not because she would panic if he left her. Although that was highly probable. It was because her pain was hers to suffer. This pain strengthened her, motivated her. Made her into what she was now. It made her angry. And that gave her power. It built up an inner resolve, and a drive to push herself beyond exhaustion. To abuse herself and others, if needed. It made her a success.

Most of all, it erected the armour she needed to survive. The only way she would be safe.

No.

She would never share. With anyone.

She yanked her necklace from Pål's fingers and wrapped it over her neck.

Screw it.

Chapter 13

The closer she got to the clinic, the more her stomach clenched into a knot. They had driven for two hours straight to reach the tiny town of Gjøvik.

When they arrived, Viola was greeted with a ghost town. It would be hard to find a more private place than this. Perfect for any business that wanted to keep its affairs somewhat discreet.

Pål's ubiquitous presence in the car had a strange effect on Ronny. Rarely did her partner have any problem with people. His medical practice called for a lot of patience and, above all, heart. After having his own practice for close to fifteen years, he had displayed both of those qualities in bucket loads. So why did Viola's senses scream that the two of them wanted to trash each other at first sight?

This was the first time she had seen Ronny give off such a vibe. Was it because of the circumstances and the danger she was putting everybody in? Or was there something else that she was missing and Ronny's sensitivity detected?

By the time they had arrived at their destination, Viola was certain that given just a little more time together, these two guys would maim each other. And not a single word spoken.

When they got out of the car, Ronny grabbed Viola by the arm, then dragged her aside.

"Viol. Did you smell his breath today? Is that vodka?" he whispered to her while watching Pål. Viola realised it was even worse than she initially thought. Ronny's eyes were flooded with angst. But whether Pål was drunk or not was actually irrelevant at this moment.

"Now you are imagining things. Pål is a pro." Her feeble attempt to defend Pål didn't carry much weight. But the truth was that she was prepared to go into that place even if Pål was too wasted to open his laptop.

"Pro? Your pro protection back there is half drunk. It's bad enough you threw away your chance at the Middle East. You want to do time as well?" He stressed the last words, as if that would finally knock some sense into her.

So she stopped and assessed how nervous Ronny was. She realised that if she was going inside that place, she would need support. From both of these men. That meant Ronny had to accept this.

"Hon. Please. This will be okay. Trust me," she whispered in order to calm him down. But even this backfired. Ronny just shook his head in dismay and threw another glance at Pål, who returned one of his twitchy smiles. Viola noticed their exchange and immediately felt Ronny's trust evaporate even further.

"Viol. You know how I feel about all of this… But this surveillance thing? Is that even legal? Are you sure about this?" He voiced his gnawing concern.

She succumbed to guilt once again. She knew how far he had stretched himself, just so she could be here. He had done this without questioning her motives or the real danger of this operation. This was a huge debt she would need to settle. If she got out of this thing in one piece, that is.

She knew further words were useless, they would only aggravate. So instead of offering empty assurances, she slid closer to him, then hugged into his chest. Soothed his nerves with her quiet breath.

He quickly fell silent.

Morning

Viola had prepared herself mentally. She had seen way too many strange fertility clinics. Including one straight from a Dickensian novel. So she had reduced her expectations to a minimum, especially her imagination which could easily procure some flight of a nightmare.

But as they approached the clinic, she winced at the unexpected sight of the facade. Her humblest expectations were pulverised as she eyed a grey and dirty complex of flats that had been transformed into a structure that screamed anonymity. These buildings had been built for middle-class families in Norway during the sixties and seventies, but since then, had been largely abandoned or simply torn down. And from the looks of this place, it just begged to receive this treatment. It was the last sort of place one would go to make a baby.

As they entered the premises, things went from bad to tragic. They were greeted by the clinic's waiting room.

Viola was all too familiar with IVF waiting rooms. The best ones she had attended had clearly taken the patients' experience into consideration in their designs. The walls had been built with everyone's privacy in mind, either curved or shielded. Given that there was always a lot of waiting involved, it made the whole experience so much nicer and intimate.

But the space in this clinic was as stifling as a Hitchcock movie. Every couple was crammed together, practically on top of each other. The chairs were facing each other, so there was nowhere else to look than into each other's eyes. You simply had no other choice than to wallow in the desperation of the couples opposite you.

Viola's train of thought was interrupted by an older grey-haired woman. She scuttled out to greet a couple just entering the waiting room. The older woman was clearly a member of staff from the clinic, dressed in a white medical gown.

The couple went with the doctor. But the thing that really struck Viola was how the woman was playing all her emotional strings to make them feel at home. With their Armani and Valentino branded clothes, and their native English, they were treated by the greying doctor as if they were A-list celebrities. Then the doctor pampered and wooed them through one of the doors and into the room behind it.

And that's when Viola heard the receptionist yell at the top of her lungs.

"Miss Viola Voss, Miss... Voss?" Every couple turned their heads towards the receptionist who was shrieking out Viola's name. Everyone's eyes scattered towards her.

Her whole body froze in shock. She couldn't feel more exposed. What happened to calling out only the first initial of the surname to preserve privacy?

Viola threw a glance at Ronny, who stood beside her.

Chapter 14

Viola looked over at the CEO of InviNordica, Magda Thorsten, as the woman toured them around the facilities. This was the same grey-haired doctor she had seen in the waiting room.

Now that Viola had the chance to inspect Magda closer, her impression was even less favourable. The woman was in her late fifties, but Viola could immediately tell Magda did everything she could to stop that clock. Nose job, cheek job, brow job, any kind of job. All done tastefully, so they wouldn't draw undue attention to themselves.

Viola sensed this woman was multifaceted, but however much she tried to look below the surface, she couldn't find any one of those facets to be genuine. Just like the surgical incisions dealt to her body, Magda's character seemed to be a front. An attractive front, but a pretence all the same.

Magda did her best to smile, and with an alarming frequency. But her lavish grin resembled more a rehearsed tic than a genuine feeling, something that challenged her smoothed-out wrinkles into an action they just couldn't handle.

The woman had used the better part of an hour giving Viola and Ronny a tour around the clinic. And by now Viola felt worn, as Magda had carried on incessantly about the company's philosophy and goals.

"Our focus is on infertility treatments, which, naturally, carry great responsibility towards future parents. Our success stories speak for themselves. Where other clinics offer IVF at a thirty-five percent success rate, we stretch up to fifty-five percent." She flashed her grin one more time, just to make sure her last words reached them. And just as quick as it appeared, it vanished behind another one of Magda's masks.

"Plus, as an added bonus, we throw in a PGD, that's Pre-Implantation Diagnosis, for 256 hereditary diseases. Add to that the bonus of the all-inclusive package, and we double that amount to over 500 diseases. I mean... Now... Be truthful to yourselves." Magda stopped and eyed Ronny and Viola, just to see if they were laser-focused on her.

"Can you put a price tag on your child's health?" She rounded off her grand finale with a compassionate glance meant to underline the preciousness of the company's goals.

If Viola ever heard a sales pitch, this was it. She just couldn't understand how this woman could reduce this place – what they did here – to numbers and statistics. How could Magda think of the women here like that? Every one of them cherished hopes beyond anything that could be reasonably measured. Many of them were willing to give up their lives to have a shot at just one successful IVF cycle ending in a childbirth.

If this place was capable of delivering on their promises, they had a duty towards these women. But what did they get instead? A street pimp pushing the hottest wares.

* * *

"Come on. She is a car saleswoman! And you are her next big sale." He summed it all up as he faced her with alarmed eyes.

Viola and Ronny stood alone in the hall.

She knew he was right, dead on in his assessment, because he was voicing all of her own doubts. She had tried her best to find something positive about the place, or the woman in charge, but she came up empty. This place existed solely to lure wealthy and gullible suckers with unfulfilled dreams into plunking some of their hard-earned cash into a wishing well.

But even if she shared Ronny's hesitation, this wasn't the time to voice that out loud.

"I think you are way off base on this, Ron. I think she is doing what she believes in. Believe me, I've seen a lot of hustlers in my work, but I am a hundred and ten percent sure that woman is the genuine article." Viola said this with such conviction, Ronny's face flattened with shock. It was obvious he was trying to figure out if Viola was lying, or was simply out of her mind.

But before he could respond, Magda came running towards them.

"Ready for the tests?" She sent them both a warm smile and waved them towards the diagnostics room.

She tried to wave away his concern, simply because she knew she needed her answers. More than anything. But did she need them more than their relationship? More than the man who loved her? Her mind raced for a compromise. Anything that would ease her conscience.

"Ron, you are right. It wouldn't be right of me. You go," she whispered to him softly enough so Magda wouldn't hear her.

"Me go? What about you?" Viola saw he wanted to yell at her, shake some sense into her but, instead, he tempered his voice.

"I gotta stay." She stated this as a simple fact. Something that could not be overruled in any way.

Magda eyed them, trying to decipher what was going on. Finally, Ronny just sighed and nodded to Viola.

"If you are staying, I am staying," she heard him say, and the words resonated for quite some time in her heart.

Chapter 15

Noon

They had explained to her in great detail that counting the number of follicles and measuring their size was important. At least that's what they had told her during the ultrasound of the uterus. Despite this, it had been quick. Way too quick.

And now, as she sat in the adjacent room, the psychological profile dragged on way past the two-hour mark. She couldn't fathom how the ultrasound, supposedly the staple of any IVF treatment, got barely ten minutes, yet now she was being grilled, assessed, norm-referenced, cross-checked with never-ending checklists, tests and surveys. Viola didn't feel like a woman considering IVF; she felt like a child who had a brain disorder.

The questions were endless. What was she attached to most? What would be the easiest thing to give up in her life? Was she prepared to stay away from home for long periods of time? How long? Did she miss her family? What were her ties with the outside world? What did her friends circle look like? How far would she go with the treatment? Was she prepared for compromises, medical trade-offs, unforeseen side effects? And was she ready for a life that they referred to, rather cryptically, as the middle ground? Everything about this woman jarred Viola. And it struck her, this wasn't a psychological assessment. This was a carefully prepared checklist to see if she fit the bill.

However jarred she felt, she had more urgent things to take care of. She had not seen a trace of Marianne anywhere. And this conversation was leading her nowhere.

So, Viola thought it appropriate to put on some more blatant lies about her past. Including her knowledge about the treatment.

"Childlessness is easily curable nowadays, isn't it? Does your in vitro come with a sixty-eight percent success rate, or is that someplace else?" Viola planted her hooks and put on a stupid grin, then waited for a response. Maybe this rare amount of ignorance would draw out some hard facts about this place. Maybe even about Marianne.

But from the look of the shrink's face, all it did was gather pity.

Still, Viola wouldn't be deterred so easily. She threw everything at the older woman. The dumber and more outrageous, the better.

"You see, I've heard it's a walk in the park, a twenty-minute treatment, right? Right! And you have, like, all these guarantees, don't you?"

But the questions didn't stick. The older woman wouldn't reveal anything about the clinic, or whom they treated. Instead, her pity was turning into annoyance.

Viola realised she needed to up her tactics, bring out the heavy ammunition. And what better way than to give the female doctor exactly what she wanted?

"You know... if fulfilment is a kid's unconditional love for me, how would I feel about not ever receiving any of that? And how do the other women, you know, handle this, get through this?" Viola whispered in a subdued tone. Maybe this would do.

The psychologist flinched at Viola's exposure, sensing she was finally getting through to her.

"With the right help, anything is possible, Miss Voss."

The woman glowed with comfort, not even remotely sensing that Viola's hook had worked. Viola saw the opening immediately and prepared the knock-out. This would need way more skilful acting. But who was she fooling? She didn't need to act. It just so happened she was telling the truth.

"You know, after I lost my second one – I am ashamed now – but I really felt an inner... bleeding. I couldn't stop it. It filled all of me. Everything inside me. And I considered, you know, hurting myself. After that, I said fu... sorry. From then on, I was kinda prepared to do anything. Anything it takes!" She blurted everything out in one go. And could hardly contain herself as she uttered these words. Her body began to quiver, spasm itself to that pain, and her eyes blurred into tears.

Maybe the intention was to lie, to fool that woman into some answers, or so Viola told herself. But emotions seeped out from her pores, clawed at her mind, just as if Markus had passed away yesterday.

"And now? How do you feel now?" the shrink whispered under her nose, fully engaged by the truth on display.

"Now... I don't know. Maybe even more so?" She could hardly contain her tears.

And as her eyes met the shrink's, their connection was on a whole new level. The older woman moved closer to Viola, intent on listening, then glanced into Viola's bleary eyes. By now, she was all vested in Viola, ready to comfort her in any way she possibly could. And maybe even share a secret or two.

"Hon, I know exactly how you feel. With the right dedication, anything is possible, my dear."

"You know. I am afraid my body won't listen. And it shames me to such an extent, I feel... well, worthless. What if your IVF won't work? Would you still be able to help me?" Viola pushed in for the final reveal. If she would get anything from this woman, this was her best option.

And as the psychologist heard the last words, something must have blared off an alarm signal, because she pulled back her body, and with it the trust she had placed in Viola.

"Miss Voss, we treat only infertility here. Nothing else." The older woman punched something in on her tablet, and reapplied that familiar grin onto her face.

"Thank you. We are done!"

* * *

Was it all in vain? Viola's eyes darted around the halls, as she tried to get a glimpse of Marianne. She had never met the blogger in person, and maybe that was why, after such an arduous search, the whole thing had grown way out of proportion. Marianne had become an apparition, a hallucination that had seeped through Viola's thoughts, day and night, for the last three years. And just like a wraith, her presence was most tangible for Viola, beneath her skin and within her mind, yet Viola was sure she would never look into her eyes, touch her fingers, or simply say hi.

Had she done all of this for nothing?

No. She had to stop thinking like this. She had to remember Marianne's words. The woman had drilled into her public on several occasions that she was past thirty-two and the quality of her eggs was dropping off like crazy. Her time was running out. She was on the threshold of a cliff with her fertility. And no one in their sane mind would tell her she had real options.

This pervaded the blogger's mind. Would Marianne do everything to change that? Viola kept telling herself that she would.

One thing was certain, if this place had the technology necessary to help this desperate woman, she would have found it. Not only that, but she would have accepted any terms she was given. However absurd or expensive they were. Maybe the question was not *if* she was here, but how much Marianne was willing to accept, and what she was prepared to sacrifice in the process.

As Viola's eyes scanned farther down the hall, she twisted her body around and crashed into a teenage boy in a wheelchair.

"Sorry, I was just about to... hmm." She was about to apologise and continue her search, but when she locked gazes with him, she froze in astonishment.

The boy's eyes were burning red, and the rest of his gaunt, contorted body had a malnourished cast to it. An albino. His hands pushed with quivering jerks at his wheels with what seemed like a huge effort. Viola immediately noticed that this struggle did not only exhaust him but also maddened him beyond reproach. His mouth skewed in a spitting posture, pissed off at his own feebleness and inadequacy.

As he noticed her, he ground to a halt, then inspected her with his tiny swinish pupils. Suddenly he made a poking gesture at something on her body.

At first, her mind and body refused to listen to her. Her reactions seemed caught in some alternate timeline, transfixed by his gaze. She had to pinch herself to react.

Viola's eyes ran up her own body, only to realise her compass necklace had opened up. And the contents were now in plain sight. Her gut clenched in panic as she scrambled to clasp the necklace shut.

But when she glanced back at the boy, she realised the hallway was now empty.

Chapter 16

Magda raced down the corridor towards Viola and Ronny. With a burning urgency written all over her face, she barely collected her breath before she spat out the words.

"Miss Voss! It's of utmost importance we speak. Immediately!" Magda addressed Viola only. Hearing this, Ronny's face flushed. Magda noticed the intrusion and a barely visible grimace crossed her face, but this woman knew better than to be impolite.

"This is too sensitive. Family only, I am afraid," she explained.

Viola's back straightened at this remark. If she had a family now, no one qualified more than this man. There was no one else she could depend on more. Ronny's words were never empty, and always followed by action.

"He is family... practically." Viola pressed the words intensely between her tongue. Enough so Magda would see how important this was for her.

"Technically, no. Sorry. House rules. It's not for me, but for our customer's privacy," Magda whispered with an underlying apologetic tone.

"Privacy! Lady! Are we talking about the same place here? Have you seen your Producing Room, with cum splattered all over the floor? Or your waiting room with your receptionist yelling out names all over the place? Is that your idea of privacy?" Ronny unloaded on Magda, but before he could continue, Viola interrupted him with pleading eyes. He exchanged glances with her, and wanted to barge on.

"Ron. Calm down. Magda's concern is legitimate. Apologise, please?" Viola whispered to him, but even before she voiced it, she hated herself for doing this.

This time he stopped, bent under Viola's request, and almost broke. But the requested apology was too much for his crushed pride to bear.

Viola saw it in his eyes, a hurt she had never noticed before. She realised she needed to take the words back. But the damage had been done, and disappointment already coursed through Ronny's veins.

When she asked him to accompany her, it was done for two reasons. A couple burdened by infertility made the whole IVF paperwork process quicker, less painful to get through at most clinics. But even more so, her choice to bring him along was that she would feel safer with Ronny nearby, aware of what was going on with her at any given time. And all of this seemed good at first. Reasonable. Except right now, the very same thinking had landed her in this tight corner, with her mitochondrial disease diagnosis which might be exposed at any moment. Right in front of Ronny.

She noticed as he backed off, his gnawing aggression was now subdued below the surface with force.

Late afternoon
Viola glanced over the doctor's shoulder as she attempted to get a better peek at the computer screens the woman was initiating.

Viola expected Magda would tell her about her mitochondrial disease. But what surprised her was the absence of a whole team of specialists. A neonatologist, a

111

genetic counsellor, not to mention a psychologist – they would all be present with such a serious diagnosis

But instead, Viola faced only Magda.

To make the matter even more unnerving, Magda's professional barrier had melted away. The plastic sales pitches had been dispensed with, replaced by a Magda who simply cared.

But even if this clinic's methods caught her off guard, she realised she still had to keep up the act.

"I don't get it. You are telling me I have a rare genetic disease? And it's incurable?" Viola said. And Magda was more than willing to accept her act. So, Viola continued to go through all the motions.

"Patience, my dear," Magda whispered, then swiped her mouse and initiated a simulation titled: Viola Voss X453 – Mitochondrial disease.

"Every doctor on this planet would say that your condition is incurable with today's science," Magda continued.

Meanwhile, Viola tried her best to focus on her goal. How could she get Magda to talk?

"But you don't?" Viola prodded.

"I am not every doctor," Magda scoffed.

"How can you help?" Viola implored. But as Magda peered into her eyes, Viola could sense the hesitation.

"Would you care to stay here for one more day? Run more tests?" Magda said.

"Come on, Doctor. This is my body. I need to trust you. How exactly can you help me?" Viola prodded even harder.

The older woman smirked at Viola's demands. Both knew Viola had some hefty leverage.

Magda moved her mouse and fired up an application named Real Time Human Embryo Simulator.

The whole screen lit up with binary fireworks as Magda pointed at the screen, and text drifted lazily onto it.

Initiating DNA chain scan – Scan confirmed – Sampling the DNA genome database. Growing embryological database, appeared on one of the screens.

"This simulation is sampled directly from your DNA. It shows us exactly what would happen if you performed the incision and removal of the gene causing the mitochondrial disease," Magda continued, giving out the clinical information, but for every word Viola heard, she was even more assured that Magda wasn't speaking about some random technology. She spoke about her own brain-child, something kindled by a life-long passion.

"Simulation initiated. GENE THERAPY X3235, CRISPR DNA incision initiated. Growing embryological database. Starting simulation."

On the screen an embryo coalesced into view, and began to grow at staggering speeds. Magda gestured at the screen and let the embryo unfold in a seven hundred-fold time-lapse. In just mere seconds, it blossomed into a living and breathing form.

And as it cried out for the first time at birth, it opened its eyes. Then continued to structure, grow, and undulate into a digital dance of life.

Finally, Viola peered into a set of eyes. She felt as if someone had gutted her open.

It was a child. Something alive. Or maybe true to life.

Despite its awakened state, she kept telling herself this was bits and bytes. Despite the perfection, this was just binary code. But why did she feel so shaken? It couldn't be because of the simulation.

And then she staggered back as she realised the obvious. Her mind had seemingly locked off that possibility. But as the boy's tiny face turned towards her, a flash of recognition passed through her.

Some primal instinct told her to run. But the only thing she managed was to barely shuffle her feet.

She realised she was looking into the eyes of something that resembled her son.

113

Her eyes couldn't cope with what was in front of her.

For the first time in three years, she stood right in front of the opening to some chasm. This was the place she had thrown away the key to. For good. But here she stood, and there was the opening. And it was ready to swallow her.

"Off! Turn this off! Now," she mumbled as tears blurred her vision.

Magda closed the app. Blackness followed.

Chapter 17

Evening

She felt worn like an old rag. Her stomach twisted in convulsions, and she shivered and sweated alternately. For the last thirty minutes, she had shuffled around the clinic's wards and attempted to get her bearings.

She was prepared for the neonatologist to inform her of the different set of potential treatments available to her. She was also prepared to be advised about the preimplantation technique and how they function. And she would have expected some information from the geneticist, who was supposed to paint a realistic picture of the probability of the mitochondrial disease's occurrence in her case.

The simulation was something she never would have expected, and it pulled at her heartstrings in a way she never could have prepared for. It forced her into making an immediate decision, the only right decision. Or at least, that's what the simulation had led her to believe.

But this medical institution's unethical pressure on its clients wasn't the biggest jolt for her. After all, Viola had seen from the first moment what kind of place this was. Instead, what made her throat feel dried up and useless was another realisation. For the last five years, she had done everything to put the past behind her. In her case, the erase button turned out to be the most painful thing she had ever performed. On herself.

She had thrown out every single belonging, every piece of clothing, anything that could and would remind her of Markus. It was not just a purification process, but an exorcism of evil. An occult rite to get her life back on track.

But even this was not sufficient. There was still one more thing she had no control over. One more thing she could cut loose. So she ripped off the ties to the people who connected her to Markus. This was certainly the most painful of all her actions, but also the one that was the most necessary.

As she looked into this simulation's eyes, the boy's eyes that were so remarkably like Markus's, she realised it had all been for nothing. The pain remained, ingrained in her more than ever. And it took only a moment, a single glance at an artificial image, to scorch her mind with Markus.

Maybe she was expecting way too much of herself? Doing things that continued to tear her apart? On the one hand, she was trying to lay the past behind herself, to erase Markus from her life, but on the other hand, she was trying to find Marianne. Wasn't she like a quivering junkie, fighting for her life in rehab, and was now being dealt out freebie shots?

And just when she felt she was lost in the corridors, a pair of familiar eyes appeared.

Ronny reached out his hand.

Late evening
She hated every drop of the juice, but she continued to sip it. It was at least something to grab onto, to keep her hands busy. Her eyes focused on anything, as long as it

wasn't Ronny's gaze. She knew better than to implore his eyes. Not with the news she had to share with him soon.

They faced each other in the canteen. Things had been like that for the last hour. Their conversation at a standstill.

She always felt as if he had developed a sixth sense about her moods and unspoken wishes. Especially to keep the necessary silence. She was grateful he hadn't pushed her for the last half an hour, but as she finally met his gaze, it was plain to see that his patience was shredded to bits. His eyes were pleading for some kind of explanation.

And what could she expect? She had dragged him here against his will, used him for her own goals, even humiliated him in front of Magda, then abandoned him.

"I tried my best to get anything out of her. But no... my best shot is to stay here one more day." She uttered the words, but they were riddled with anxiety, anticipating his reaction. He returned her gaze calmly.

"If I fight you on this, will it make any difference?" he said.

But his eyes drew to the envelope that lay beside her. She had forgotten about it. The test results, given to her by Magda.

"Can I look at them?" he asked.

Her throat felt as if it had been wrung inside out. She eyed the envelope and realised her lies rested inside.

She had gone over this a thousand times, at least in her head. About voicing the truth to Ronny about her condition. But this was not how she imagined it. Not the moment, not the place, and certainly not the circumstances. As panic began to flood her mind, and she grasped at simple words, anything that would make some sense.

"They are okay... okay," she blurted out.

"Something wrong with them?" He eyed her quizzically. She responded with forced laughter.

She slid the envelope over to him. Exposing herself. She knew their relationship was as solid as she could wish for. But certain things were not meant to be forgiven. And this was to be one of them.

Ronny held the envelope. But then hesitated. There was something else going on. It wasn't the suspicion. It was something else, maybe more personal than she imagined at first. Ronny swallowed hard on some fleeting thoughts.

"My mum. She fell ill and was taken to the hospital. Pneumonia. You know. Nothing serious. Out in two weeks. But she never made it past the first week. Stage 4 cancer. I never learned the truth. Until the last moment, that is." He whispered the words and never met her eyes. For a moment he tensed, then just slid the envelope back to her.

As she heard his words, the ice inside her melted. He had never spoken with such intimacy. Never shared this much of himself. She knew his mum had passed away some time ago but she had told herself she wouldn't push him for the circumstances.

"Why didn't you share this with me?" Viola said.

"You serious? And this is coming from Miss Transparency, huh?" he said.

His words stung her but also brought on a moment of lucidity. She had always said she would respect his boundaries and aloofness. And now, as her eyes moistened, it struck her. There might be another reason for this wall between them. Maybe he had never built it. Maybe he had only reacted to her own emotional retreat. Her impregnable defences.

A reflex.

As usual, she just saw the whole thing inside out in a distorted mirror that was her own self.

"I am sorry." Was the only thing she could whisper back. She leaned into him, hugged him, and she heard him utter through a runny nose.

"Go find her."

Chapter 18

Ronny jumped into the car beside Pål. The cop was hunched at his laptop, logged onto his surveillance app, attempting to avoid calling attention to himself and people passing by.

His expression was laser-focused on the task at hand, but Ronny figured it was a good thing. He wasn't prepared to do any talking. He was hoping the cop felt exactly the same way.

Then Pål eyed Ronny, while still listening in.

"You love her, don't you?" he whispered.

Ronny heaved an almost silent sigh. This was exactly what he wanted to avoid. Ronny wasn't about to share intimate details with this guy. He threw him a look, suggesting the headphones would be a far better option. But this didn't hit home. On the contrary, Ronny immediately noticed that it piqued Pål's interest even more. The cop wasn't about to leave it alone.

"You know what, Pål? I've always thought of myself as a stable, regular guy. One with a solid enough character, good income, and a not too shabby future. I was alone, unattached, doing just fine on my own. I wasn't looking for anyone either. Things were great. No. Not great. They were amazing! Well, that was until about two years ago. But then, I stumbled upon this woman. The moment I met her, I realised a gunshot to the head would probably be better for me. She made a fuss about the stupidest things. If there was anything to quarrel about, she would dig that up and use it against you. She would always want to win an argument; after all, she was superior, intellectually, spiritually, ethically, and whatnot. And the arguments that were the most victorious for her, were the ones when she knew she was wrong. Oh! She loved those. She was a mess, if you ask me. A walking disaster area. Sometimes I sat down and decided to find a redeeming quality about her, something that would logically explain any of this. Our relationship." He paused for a breather and checked Pål. The cop stared at him, transfixed.

"And you know what? There wasn't one single thing. Nothing positive came to my mind. I mean, this is the person who will remember all your mistakes, and remind you of them. At the worst possible moment. This is the woman who never listens to reason, because she thinks she has the patent to the only moral compass in existence. The list goes on and on. Do you want more?" Ronny finished with barely any breath left. He was never the one to talk. Actually, he hated talking. But if it meant Pål would shut up, it would be worth it.

The cop was left with an unanswered question.

"I... I just don't get it. So why... you know, why are you with her in the first place?" He prodded Ronny carefully, as if he was afraid to reveal what impact Ronny's story had on him.

"Because against all reason, the sheer scale of our incompatibility, and the overwhelming odds, I can't be without her. And you know what the best part is? I have no idea why that is," Ronny whispered.

Pål wanted to say something but finally just shook his head, then scrambled to put his headphones back on as quickly as he could.

* * *

Viola sat outside the operating room and prepared herself mentally.

She had been given an anonymous survey. Nothing serious, they said. Supposedly for all patients prior to the egg retrieval process.

So she crossed it off diligently and added up all the points. *On a scale from one to ten, to what extent have you experienced any of the following as a result of infertility?*

"Tearfulness, Low Confidence, Low Concentration, Depression, Isolation, Stress, Lack of Support, Frustration, Feeling out of control, Fears and Worries, Anger, Inadequacy, Guilt/Shame, Loss of Sex Drive, Sadness, Helplessness, Despair, Suicidal Thoughts."

She glanced at the result. She'd hit the jackpot. When she thought about it in such loose terms as depression, anger, and so on, her high score was nothing shocking or revelatory. On the contrary, she felt proud of her screwed-up perfection.

Her face loosened up into a smirk for the first time since she had come here. Her last twenty years of suffering reduced to a few numbers, an innocent fast-food survey. Surely there was nothing more to it.

She crumpled it up, and threw it in the dustbin.

* * *

Ronny was more than happy for the next half hour. He had achieved what he wanted. Pål wasn't even remotely interested in initiating further talk. Instead, he refocused on the task at hand, keeping Viola safe. Just what Ronny wanted.

The men's temporary truce was quickly interrupted by Pål's fumbling at his laptop. It started off rather innocently, with twitchy pounding at the keyboard, but soon escalated into feverish tapping on his headphones.

Ronny couldn't avoid casting several glances at him. As their eyes met, he was struck at what that look meant. It had all the fickleness of a situation gone sour. When it

121

was followed by Pål's twitchy grin, Ronny knew this was even worse than he initially thought.

"Batteries. Out of juice soon. In less than an hour." Pål referred to the equipment, while trying to maintain the smile. Ronny didn't know it was possible to beam this wide and still be able to talk.

"Is that a problem? Want me to get them?" Ronny threw out the suggestion, hoping this would be helpful. But it was met with an even more perplexed reaction.

"Umm. Not possible. The thing is from HQ," Pål barely managed to sputter out.

"So? I'll go get them now." He pointed out the obvious way to resolve this. Pål just smirked back at him. Was that in the same category as the fake grin? No. It was worse because it also tried to reassure him everything was ok.

"Without permission..." Pål added the slightly inconvenient detail about his story. Ronny coughed hard at this. He prodded at the facts in his mind, then quickly arrived at the conclusion.

"You mean taken as in *stolen...?*"

Pål eyed Ronny sheepishly. The silence that followed was an adequate confirmation.

Not only had Ronny risked Viola's life with this stunt, but he was doing it with a half-drunk cop. And now the same cop admitted he had stolen equipment from HQ. How much worse could this get?

"I've had it with this shit. I am going back in there to get her." Ronny scrambled out of the car and raced towards the clinic. But Pål rushed right behind him. Yanking at Ronny's jacket, he sent him a pleading glance.

"Ease off, man. I can hear her now. As long as she doesn't take any anaesthesia and remains conscious... She... She will be just fine." Pål whispered the words in as subdued a tone as he could, as if the tone would help soothe Ronny's nerves.

Pål nodded Ronny back towards the car. Despite the fact that every inch of Ronny's intuition was telling him he was about to make a huge mistake, he finally gave in and returned to the vehicle.

* * *

She heard them utter some words, mostly nonsensical mumbles, but she still smiled, listened, and nodded to everything. They shared some technical facts about her follicle size, about maximising in vitro success, about different ovarian stimulation medication protocols that are used to "pump up" her ovaries, and so on, and so on.

Her mind had long gone into some twilight zone, in search of an alternate, more manageable reality. As an intense nausea washed over her, she tried to breathe in all the words, accept them in some way, but her mind pushed them out again, refused to register any more medical facts dealt out by the staff.

She had been here eight times. She knew all too well this was far more than she should have done. And one would have thought that each time her neurosis would lessen. But it didn't. The worst time was the first fourteen days. This was the time to see if the eggs stayed in place. And this always brought on a flood of mental flogging. Would she get pregnant or not? Would this be a new beginning? Would she be given another chance? Was this all a mistake?

According to the *Bioteknologirådet*, the cap was at three times. A healthy number for the body and the soul, or so they said. But what did those impotent men know about having a baby?

Still, she could handle fat old men and their rules. But what she couldn't bear was the silence of the baby. The one that was like a dark pre-shadowing of an apocalypse. That could only spell death. And it often did. Whatever happened in her stomach, she adored it, it was a good sign. The kicks, the burps, the movement, the caresses, and the tickles. Sometimes intense, yet also euphoric in their

123

beauty. Pure flow of life. But the sudden quiet, the lack of activity from inside, that was the stuff of nightmares. Where there should have been joy and happiness, there were only worries and death. They were all just around the corner.

What did the men at *Bioteknologirådet* know about going through a miscarriage, ectopic, or pregnancy loss?

Had they been through the dull pains in the abdomen, the lower back, the bleeding? And worst of all, the constant reassuring from the doctors that this didn't have to mean a miscarriage. This didn't have to turn out badly. Despite her dark attitude.

Yet she didn't listen to them. Because inside herself, she felt it had gone wrong. Simple mother's intuition. And if that wasn't enough, the scan always confirmed it. For God's sake! She had bled like a pig all over the carpet and they still needed to confirm the obvious?

So, she went to the hospital and they hooked her up, scanned her, and sure enough, there was only stillness. No heartbeat.

Yet here she was. At another clinic. And she felt no different this time. Yet another casual visit to the nearest car dealer. As if she were simply discussing what kind of additional equipment she wanted for her new Audi A6 S-Line.

And now they were removing a part of her body. Something that wasn't a something but a *Someone*. With stubby, cute, fragile fingers. Someone beyond body and flesh. An uncanny spark of life, the atom of a soul. How could these people around her not see the obvious?

Her mind was torn back into the real world when she eyed an older member of the staff standing over her. Smiling at her with beady eyes, he prepared some equipment that screamed anaesthesia.

"Hey, what's this?" Viola glanced at the older man, who was more than prepared to put her under.

"Please, Miss Voss. Relax. Monitored anaesthesia is required during the retrieval. Just a small dosage of Remifentanil." He minced the words with his tiny mouth and underlined them with a fake warm glow. The intention was to assure her this would not only be safe, but she would enjoy it. Quite a lot in fact.

Instead, Viola's stomach wrenched into a tightening knot. She was sure that Pål mentioned something about precautionary rules. She was also quite certain that one of them had been about anaesthesia. But her mind was muddy, tainted with way too much fear. She couldn't, for the life of her, recollect what the rule was. Or how she was supposed to act now.

"No. No. No. Forget it," she spat out. This was a border she was not going to cross. After all, doing so meant she would give up anything resembling control. She wouldn't give herself up to these people. Not now, and not at any price. She had no idea where she would wake up or what they would do to her.

She was trying to locate a missing woman. Not become one.

"Miss? We can't proceed without your consent." The anaesthesiologist's face flashed with a perplexed glance.

She felt her hand clutching onto the necklace with the microphone inside it. She surely had no guarantee they wouldn't find the mike. That very thought sent her reeling into an even bigger panic.

"Do you want me to cancel?" The man glanced at her, then looked at the rest of the staff.

Now she was getting attention from everyone in the room. Time was up, and unless she made a decision right now, any kind of decision, she would torpedo her own agenda.

Viola's insides seemed to shrink. This choice might very well be the last one she ever made. She felt her body flood with adrenaline, and her head exploded with an energy made possible only when faced with death itself.

"Do you want me to cancel?" the beady-eyed man repeated. This time with less patience.

Finally, she shook her head. No.

* * *

Pål's headphones screamed urgency. He knew his face would give him away, practically telling the whole story, so he twisted his body into a knot in the corner of the car. Anywhere so that the unstable boyfriend would have trouble deciphering what was going on.

But he felt immediately that his contorted body only aroused more suspicion.

Why the hell did Viola go along with such a decision? Didn't she listen to his precautions? Couldn't she just say no?

He was prepared to gather evidence. He was even ready to sit there for a couple of days. But he wasn't prepared for this. He had no idea what to do now.

* * *

Viola felt her consciousness slip away into some murky void. This was suddenly interrupted by a bodily sensation. A caress gently fondled her body. Only it wasn't a tender caress of a nurse, but rather an intrusive groping. Fingers slid along her hospital gown. It yanked her foggy mind back to the surface.

Her bleary eyes darted toward the sensation, but already now, she was struggling to keep focus. Her world, her senses drowned in an alternate reality where she was defenceless and at the utter mercy of those around her.

Then she felt the fingers again, slithering along her chest. Only now did she become aware of what was going on. This wasn't some member of the medical staff carrying out their job.

She was being strip-searched. Did this person presume she was already out? Or maybe noticed she was still conscious but just didn't care? She felt it as the fingers yanked at her body. Needy, inquisitive as they searched for something.

Viola's eyes darted downwards again in panic. She fought against the anaesthetic, battled her fading consciousness. She had to swim up to the surface. She forced herself, but it was no use.

For a moment, her involuntary jerks must have alerted the person searching her, because everything stopped. Only to be replaced by a stinging needle. Another set of hands that applied more drugs.

In an instant, she felt her mind accelerate into the unavoidable nothingness. She heard some unintelligible words. She struggled to separate the syllables. Were they syllables? Or just her mind losing its grip?

She couldn't make out the source. The meaning. Nothing. But then, the words began to glide into focus.

"H...elp..." She attempted to focus again. Who was calling her? Was someone trying to help her?

She summoned all the will she had left. That resilient fighting spirit in her. Her eyes jerked from side to side. She would locate the source of the words.

But then she began to lose control of her vision. Still, the words came rushing at her. Tormented her till the very end.

"H...e....lp."

And finally, she realised where they were coming from.

They were coming from her. Her own mouth was gagging on what she had left of fear.

Blackness slithered all over her.

* * *

"Help." A barely audible whisper rustled through Pål's headphones.

Despite Ronny's proximity, Pål was sure Viola's partner hadn't registered her cry for help.

Pål caught a peek of Ronny's inquisitive face. *Was the man trying to speak to him?* Only then did he realise that Ronny was repeating a vague phrase. Over and over again.

"What? What? What!"

Pål felt an immediate pang of compassion as he understood what a nightmare Ronny was going through. The cop's mind searched for a way to break this to Viola's partner gently. But no solution came to his mind.

They wouldn't lessen the trouble Viola was in now, but they would dampen the panic attack Ronny was going through. And that was exactly what he needed right now.

He was about to launch into an argument, when Ronny ripped the headphones away from him. He clutched at them with trembling palms and listened in. But he instantly realised the line was dead. Ronny gazed at Pål with fever exploding in his face.

"The batteries, remember? Nothing to worry about. I suggest we go... and get them. Actually, uh... maybe you should go," Pål whispered and prayed to God his imposed subdued tone would be mistaken for calmness.

"The batteries? What fucking batteries? You said we were okay. What the fuck is that supposed to mean?" Ronny thrashed at Pål's collar and wrung at his neck.

Pål realised he was out of options. He had no way to contain Ronny's emotions.

And this would probably have ended in a brawl, if not for the police car driving by.

"Thank God," Ronny screamed with exhilaration and began to scramble out of the car.

Pål's eyes flashed with panic. The already disastrous situation had now become fatal. He pulled on Ronny's shirt and threw himself in his face.

"No. No. No! Don't you see..." Pål had less than three seconds to formulate his long overdue brilliant lie. But his creativity wasn't exactly in full swing after the morning vodka shots.

"What? It's perfect," Ronny spat out at Pål, far from prepared to listen to anything the cop had to say.

"I promise you one thing: if you stop them, your lady in there, she will never make it out." Ronny understood exactly what Pål was saying to him. Yet he still began to step back, his mind in denial.

"It's her life we are talking about. Trust me," Pål voiced himself as truthfully as he could.

But Ronny's face clearly showed he battled with doubt.

At some other time, in a less stressful moment, Ronny might actually have listened to Pål. But this was not the time, and certainly not the moment.

Ronny swerved his body and practically charged towards the police car. Pål knew that the two bored cops, with too much spare time on their hands, were about to make their lives a lot more complicated.

He also realised that the moment they stopped them, he would have to answer questions. And that for some of these questions, he had no appropriate lies, even the lousy kind.

Void

It started with some distorted sounds that washed through the ubiquitous blackness. She couldn't identify what this was, but as its grating structure became more prevalent, it pierced itself through her consciousness.

As the drilling noise became even more encompassing, she finally tore her eyes open and became aware she was in her bed, at home. And it was the middle of the night. She whipped her head around and realised the pervading sound was her baby crying. She eyed Markus's tiny contorted face and immediately tried to get her bearings. Was there something wrong with him? Was his stuffy nose running, or maybe he had a fever?

"Liiiyo, reddiee... Leeeego!" Markus wailed and reached out with his hand towards her. And as it dawned on her why he was crying, she breathed out a sigh of relief. He must have woken up in the middle of the night and needed his red Lego piece. And when it wasn't nearby to grasp, his world must have fallen apart, something he was

129

making sure she understood right now. After all, what could be more important than his Lego at this hour?

She reached out for one of the Lego pieces and placed it in Markus's hands. This eased his biggest drama, and his fit slowly receded. She cuddled him into herself and rocked him gently.

She knew that motherhood was about these nights, unexpected Lego dramas, and even more serious accidents. Unforeseen illnesses and abrupt changes in routine. But with him, she wasn't sure if his slightest runny nose or way too many sneezes were just that, or something much more.

That's why she braced her whole body in dread. For that something more. After all, she knew the exact terms Markus arrived in this world under. And so she readied herself for anything. She often caught herself thinking more about what bad stuff could happen to him than the good moments that still popped up from time to time. At least in this way, no bad things could surprise her. As long as she was constantly focused on the worst-case scenarios, she would be prepared. For anything.

She sensed these nights were getting more common, and his reactions more pronounced, sometimes even violent. At first it was in the small things, like this Lego piece, but gradually, it wasn't so much about the toys or his humours but that he was uncomfortable. Was he getting worse? Was his condition progressing? Unavoidably deteriorating? And if so, how long did he have?

In these situations of doubt, she reminded herself of a few words she had heard somewhere: "In motherhood, the hard moments sometimes outnumber the beautiful moments, but the beautiful moments always outweigh the hard moments." The simple beauty of this message gave her some hope, especially on nights when she could barely get up and rock his wails into stillness.

And as Viola watched him with his Lego in his chubby fingers, he glanced up at her, sent her a sleepy glance, and smirked with his puffy cheeks as he cuddled into her.

Viola glowed at this moment, soaked in everything. She felt his weight against her forehead, listened to his faint heartbeat, and smelt the perfection of his skin. She grabbed onto this moment with everything she had, savoured it, then tucked it deep inside herself.

* * *

Pål watched as the two policemen cast suspicious glances at their driver's licenses. He knew the irreversible damage had already been done. His only hope was that Ronny wouldn't make the situation terminal. The only thing Ronny had to do was shut up.

It soon became apparent that Ronny wasn't used to the level of indifference that was the norm for Norwegian police patrols. And these guys were no exception, as their nonchalance was already driving Ronny mad.

"I should be inside there... helping her, you see?" Ronny was reaching a peak as he tried to explain his situation. But the chaotic nature of the recollection only managed to get him into even deeper trouble.

"Inside where? And who is that she? Could you repeat that, sir?" One of the cops threw the usual line of questioning, in order to put even more stress on a balloon that was about to burst.

"Pål! Tell them about the clinic. Viola. Aren't they your buddies! Aren't they?" Ronny demanded the very thing Pål couldn't give him. At this moment, every word was another shovel in their grave.

"Enough, sir! Calm down." One of the cops stabbed at Ronny with his finger, emphasising the need for him to stay calm.

"I am. Fucking. Calm." He repeated the words to himself.

Meanwhile, the other police officer was punching in their names on his tablet. And as the results drifted onto his screen, his face passed from evening boredom into keen interest.

Pål hoped this had nothing to do with him, but his stomach twisted and churned.

"Mister Skarbom. You were on the force. Suspended? A year ago?" the officer said, glancing up from his tablet. Pål knew these were only facts and what lay behind them was so much more precarious. And judging from the self-righteous smirk on the cop's face, he had just connected the dots, the facts with what lay behind them – the word of mouth.

But Pål knew better than to answer the question. If there was one thing he could still do in this mess, it was to keep his silence.

"What's going on, Pål?" Ronny's rage was now re-channelled back at Pål.

"Give me some answers, goddammit!" Ronny yelled, while he hurled himself at Pål. Before he could do any serious damage, the first cop rushed in between them, grabbed Ronny's shirt, bent his arm, forced him to his knees, then punched him in the kneecap, grinding Ronny's jaw into the concrete.

"That's enough, sir. Calm down!" he whispered into Ronny's ear with an assuring tone. And this time, Ronny didn't think of further resistance.

The second cop took a look inside Pål's car. Immediately, he was struck by the sight of the app recording on the laptop, property of police HQ at Grønlandsleiret.

"Sir, would you care to explain this? Police property? And your suspension?" He spelled out the words one by one with an overbearing clarity.

"Actually... it's... fuzzy?" were the first words uttered by Pål since the two cops arrived. For some reason, which was unknown, maybe even to Pål, he phrased them as a question. Whether it was because he wanted to initiate a dialogue, or simply that he wanted confirmation that his ludicrous question would be sufficient at this moment, the two cops responded with a quick nod to themselves.

The rest flashed away with clinical precision. Before Ronny and Pål could blink, they were already in handcuffs, and being pushed towards the police vehicle.

Chapter 19

A wall of shimmering light barraged her senses. Her breath stuck somewhere in her throat, she gulped for even more air. Was this what it felt like when she was born? A crushing, involuntary passage. The light burning away at her corneas, and the air pummelling for the first time at her throat.

But there was something else. Not a sensation, but a feeling accompanied by a realisation.

She was back, and immediately she felt an inner sigh pass through her mind and cascade down her body. A realisation flashed through her mind. She knew what lay hidden behind that sigh.

Disappointment.

Regret that she had made it back. However much her animal instinct of simple survival was still intact, she felt less strength to bear another round of this punishment called the world.

As the light gradually receded, so did the smothering grip on her mind. Soon, her eyes took in a sparse room in the clinic, half of it separated by opaque drapes. A woman

134

sat on the bed. Beside her rested a laptop. Going by her apron, she was one of the patients. As Viola laid eyes on her, she radiated back with unequivocal enthusiasm. The woman may have been in her early thirties, but the iridescent glow she had about her could easily shave off ten years.

But suddenly Viola's throat tightened, and she began to cough violently.

"Easy, Viola, easy. Those drugs mess with your head, huh? You wanna talk about it? By the way, I am Ingrid." She clapped Viola on the back and whispered softly to her, as if anything louder would hurt Viola's senses.

But Viola was irritated. She had way too many questions, far too few answers, and even less time. She was certainly not prepared to share her anaesthetic nightmares.

"Where am I? Who are you?" Viola rasped at Ingrid.

"Ingrid, silly. The one who placed the video on Marianne's blog. Don't you recognise me?" Ingrid announced, unperturbed by Viola's harsh tone.

Viola just shook her head in denial. She wasn't going to say it outright, but this woman was lying to her.

"Don't you remember me silly?" She twisted her laptop around and pointed at the browser, which was loaded up with Marianne's blog.

She pressed play, and the video played pretty much the same as the last time Viola had seen it.

Viola squeezed her eyes even closer to the screen, looking for any clues that might give away this scam. But she couldn't find a single detail.

Her eyes searched the room. For the first time since she derailed her life into this unknown territory, she felt a pang of doubt creeping in. Had Marianne been the woman she had seen in that clip? Or was it some twisted subconscious desire that had manifested itself? Had her incessant need to find the blogger warped her senses, forcing her to believe in something that wasn't there?

"What for? I mean, why did you place the video there in the first place? I don't get it," she prodded Ingrid.

"Things got a little out of hand, didn't they?" She chuckled at the very thought.

"Those messages. They weren't for you. They were for her. For Marianne. Don't you see? Do you have any idea how much I would give to know what happened to her? I was trying to contact her. I've got what she has. You know, mitochondrial disease. I wanted to help her. Let her know about this place." Ingrid pointed to her perfectly healthy kid on the video and let the words sink in. Viola was jolted, her mind trying to adjust to what she had just heard.

Had she been so way off about Marianne? Was Ingrid telling the truth about her miracle? And did she hear the woman right? Mitochondrial disease?

"And this thing they did with me. Drugged. Stripped. That's like normal medical procedure at a medical institution?" Viola spat out, further resisting Ingrid's story.

"Ohh... Sorry about that. But they did a background check on you. Then they discovered the recent blog comment I made on Marianne's page. Magda must have connected the dots."

Then Viola instinctively checked if she was still wearing the necklace with the mike.

She gasped out when she realised it was gone.

She whipped her head around, and heard a rustle behind the drapes. Someone was behind them, eavesdropping on their conversation from the very beginning. She grabbed at the bed railings, faltered out of the bed, then ripped away the curtain.

She had no illusions about what kind of people these were. If she got in the way of their agenda, they would hurt her. But as the curtain fell to the side, Viola laid her eyes on Magda, reclined casually in one of the chairs.

Except that the woman wasn't alone. She was preoccupied with a small boy draped across her chest. An angel slumbering. Magda cast a comforting glance at Viola, while she was stroking him to sleep.

"Want to say hi to Ingrid's boy?" she whispered so as not to wake up the kid.

Viola's mind froze, her determination crushed at the sight.

Right in front of her was the boy she had seen in the video. The same boy she had believed to be Marianne's.

Chapter 20

Noon

Viola sat inside a small playground that was harmoniously carved into the clinic's interior. She had not noticed a play area outside while entering. Or anything else that would suggest the presence of children.

But now, as she glimpsed this artificially arranged play field, she realised how far the people in charge had gone to make sure they did not call attention to themselves. Everything from sandboxes to swings had been installed inside the clinic's four walls.

As Viola looked closer, she could see that the equipment was barely used. Were Ingrid's kids the only ones here? Another peculiar thing was that the playground had been created for children up to four, maybe even five years old. Viola thought this was a rather strange thing to do. After all, this was a fertility clinic, dealing with new-borns only. Did the kids and their mothers stay here for longer, and if they did, then for how long, and why?

Viola cast an eye at Ingrid's kid. However unsure she was about Ingrid, the woman's story and her own recollection of it, one thing was certain. Ingrid was now playing with her perfectly healthy kid, claiming she had done the impossible. She had borne a healthy boy, despite her mitochondrial disease. Everything inside Viola began to act up again, as she realised she didn't know where the truth ended and the lies began.

Viola's thoughts were interrupted by Magda, who approached her. She searched Magda's face for anything below the surface. After all, Viola was in possession of some crucial information about this place. An inside look into a well-kept secret.

Viola was also a journalist, and this wasn't just some story. This was earth-shaking news. And that was just one aspect of it. The other one, which was just as obvious, was the legal status of this whole endeavour. What would be the official consequences for this woman and for her kids, if this whole matter got out of hand? Into the media and the judicial system.

"Sorry for scaring you like this. With your background, we had no real choice." Magda returned the necklace to Viola's hands.

Viola peeked inside it, and her suspicion was confirmed: the insides were missing the microphone. She cast a glance up at Magda, demanding an explanation.

"Whatever you might think about us, it was done for his safety," Magda pointed to Ingrid's kid.

"Feed the bullshit to them." Viola pointed at the kid and Ingrid.

"Calm down, Miss Voss."

"No. At what costs are they alive? Have you given any thought whatsoever as to the consequences?" she shot back at the doctor.

"At this moment, not a single country in the world has made CRISPR gene editing legal. Well, except China, who have admitted to performing the first tests. Despite this, this boy's embryo DNA was subjected to a CRISPR modification, directly modifying the nuclear DNA."

"Drop the tech facts. What interests me are people. What do you say to this boy when he grows up? I mean, how do you sell this bullshit to this Ingrid? Because she and her boy will have to live with this for the rest of their lives."

"People? Is that what you want to talk about?" Magda pointed towards one of Ingrid's boys.

"Rune would have been born autistic, and over the course of two years would have degraded to an irreversible point. At the age of three, his lungs would have collapsed. He would die a suffocating death," Magda voiced her opinion, then nodded towards the other kid.

And just as Viola fell silent, Magda caught a peek at her watch. As if on cue, a stream of kids burst into the playground, and proceeded to surround Viola and Magda with boundless laughter.

Right behind them, several women followed. The women had all their attention on the children, obviously watchful mothers, worried about the safety of their young ones.

Magda proceeded to point at the boys and girls who had just appeared.

"That's Arild. And he wouldn't have made it past the fifteenth week of his mother's pregnancy. By then his embryo would have to have been removed and discarded because it would be deemed life-threatening to his mother. And that's Line. Through our gene therapy treatment, she avoided a severe immune deficiency that strikes new-borns and leaves them with almost no defence against viruses, bacteria, or fungal infections. The "bubble boy disease." This time, when Magda finished, it was devoid of any showmanship.

Viola felt at a loss at these facts and what lay behind them. How could she dispute the very essence of her life's struggle?

"You really think that if I had listened to people like you, any of these kids would be alive today?" Magda said.

* * *

Ingrid and Viola stood in the middle of the circle, surrounded by the rest of the spirited and vibrant kids. It took only a short introduction from Ingrid, before the women launched into all sorts of jokes with Viola.

"You think these are normal?" Katrine said in reference to the children, with a playful smirk crossing her face. "Well, these turned out... okayish. But you should see the rest of them."

"The rest?" questioned Viola, and although she sensed some kind of pun arriving, she certainly didn't want to spoil the fun for the rest of them. And she was richly rewarded with all around snickering for feigning her ignorance.

"Yeah. The ones with twelve fingers and two heads." Katrine fired off the punchline and launched every one of them into a howling laughter. And when Viola joined in on the giggling, it was not because it was funny, but rather because she connected. An immediate warmth and trustful atmosphere radiated from them.

There was nothing feigned or artificial here, as they cracked terrible jokes, and spoke endlessly about the everyday stuff. The kind that, for most, led to boredom, but for them was an epiphany, simply because it was about their kids.

Despite all this emotional sharing, something less tangible kept bothering Viola. A strange undercurrent, maybe her sixth sense calling out to her. The problem was that she couldn't pinpoint where this was coming from. But her attention was constantly being drawn towards some glass door at the end of the kindergarten. Was someone watching her?

But then Viola's attention was drawn back to the women and their stories.

She learned about the delicate twenty-five-year-old Rene, who had come to the clinic from one of the northern most parts of Norway, the snow-covered, tiny town of *Kirkenes*. With a population barely reaching eight thousand, this woman had gone through hell, as the ultra-conservative orthodox population ostracised her when she decided to take her chance at IVF procedures.

Then there was Katrine from Bergen. The woman certainly raised more questions than Viola was prepared to answer. Usually, it didn't take Viola more than a few glances to profile anyone she met. But everything about Katrine screamed contradiction. The woman was, after all, in her sixties. Viola didn't want to pry into her story, she looked like a woman who cherished her privacy.

But still, Viola observed as Katrine shared an intimate bond with the toddler she had draped around her chest. And the way they eyed each other was too intense and dependent on each other for Katrine to be a casual nanny. So, she had to be family. Probably a grandmother.

But why did this grandmother come all the way from Bergen? And most of all, where was the mother of that child? During the two-hour talk, no one mentioned a word about her. So, when Viola finally voiced her question, everyone shot her weird glances, followed by an edgy silence, then finally interrupted by everyone exploding in laughter.

Viola couldn't grasp what the others found so hilarious, so she decided to just let the matter be.

But then, her train of thought was interrupted again, this time by a subtle flash coming from a remote corner of the playground. The unease she had felt from the very beginning was confirmed. Was that a flash from a photo camera? Or was it her mind playing tricks on her due to that blasted Remifentanil?

She felt the dubiety creeping along her spine again. It whispered to her that there was no Marianne here, only these happy women fulfilling their dream. Whispered to her she had been wrong about all of this, she had lied to her partner based on some insane notion, then she had betrayed the trust of everyone at work.

And, finally, she had deceived herself.

Chapter 21

Late Evening

Her fingers refused to obey her. They were bent out of shape. She hit them. Not just once, but repeatedly. Still, they crumpled away and prevented her from packing her bag and getting as far away from the clinic as possible.

Before she got to her room, she had stood huddled away in a corner of the kindergarten. She had watched the kids playing. But she knew better than to approach them. She had kept them at a safe distance.

She had wanted to flee, repeatedly, but the sight of them was the memory of a dope addict's first hit. Whispering to her, pervading her with thoughts the way only a drug could do. She had imagined their days. Careless, easy, filled with play and genuine laughter. It had made her body quiver out of control. And she had realised that there was no rehab for what she needed.

When she had gazed into the eyes of those kids, a voice in her had appeared. The same voice that had drowned her in longing. And when she felt that wash over her, suddenly the women's desperation wasn't something frightening. Nor even remote. Far from it.

It had the same unpredictable impulse that had driven her to have Markus, despite all the maddening odds. She knew exactly how these women felt. And when she watched their eyes connect with their little marvels, she realised they didn't think in terms of a possible future, one filled with pain, disappointment, or even death.

These women grasped at all the happiness they could get, in the here and now. This present was more than enough for them.

All of a sudden, she realised she couldn't stand being in the vicinity of these small creatures and their perfect lives. Not with this unabated need smothering away in her soul. It was enough that she had bombed her career and obliterated Ronny's trust.

She had to get out of there.

She had run to her room and begun to pack. Now, she eyed her fingers again. They were still cold, stiff, and useless.

* * *

That is when Magda rushed into the room and locked gazes with Viola, who immediately hid her hands beneath the bedcovers.

"I know what you are trying to do." Viola choked on her own words. She couldn't stand this anymore. Everything was splintering inside her. "These women. Their sweet little stories, these lucky kids," she hissed.

"What do you mean?" Magda asked.

But Viola only scoffed, shook her head, and got back to the packing. Useless old woman's hands or not, she was packing her bag and getting out of here.

"I showed you everything so I could convince you. You are right. But you are not seeing one simple thing. Do you have any idea what kind of hope this place can be for other women? For women like you." Viola jolted up.

A revelation flashed back and forth between the women. She sensed her eyes, her fingers, her own thoughts, everything about her, was cracking inside her.

And however much Viola tried to conceal it, Magda saw right through her.

This was exactly what Viola desired.

"How many years have you attempted to have a child? And you never gave up hope, did you?"

Viola felt shredded by this question.

"No... I... need to leave. Now." Just as she said these words, she began to flee; her feet carried her away in panic, to a place where she wouldn't suffocate on her own truth. But not before Magda moved in her way, grabbed her by the shoulder.

"See that paper hanging on the wall?" Magda pointed her finger towards a poster taped to one of the walls.

Viola couldn't understand what it had to do with anything. It was the most mundane poster of a mother nurturing her little one. But Magda gently pushed Viola towards it, and continued her argument.

"You see this paper? That's the single most beautiful thing in the world," Magda said.

Viola peered closer and noticed that handwritten along the lower corner were months in chronological order from left to right. Upwards in nice rows shone small heart-stickers. She couldn't quite count the amount of hearts, but on many months, the stickers went out of the paper sheet and onto the wall. And then it struck her, that one red heart meant a child born in this place.

"Isn't this fantastic?" Magda's face beamed at her as she referred to the hearts. "Don't you understand that they are what we are here for?"

She had arrived here convinced that she had to get to the bottom of one simple question: How could these women even think of giving up their lives into the hands of some freak experiment? Because, ultimately, that's what it was. An unproven technology that was barely in its infancy. And no other words than lunacy came to her mind when she considered it.

And then her mind was thrown back into the past, her last twenty years. A place where she had all but assaulted her body with countless hormones and other dubious medications during her IVF attempts. Despite this, she had persevered and had Markus. And right now she knew she was one of those women.

Was that lunacy?

When she glimpsed at these children for the very first time, it was as if someone had turned on an invisible switch inside her. Suddenly, she realised Magda was right. These small miracles would never have come to be, if not for this clinic's intervention in the natural course of things.

As her eyes focused on all the hearts on the poster, she had trouble counting them, there were so many. A part of her thought this was a breath-taking sight, but another part of her was just terrified. Of herself. Because she realised she had no idea what she would do next.

Night

Viola's bag was still unzipped with some clothes hanging out. At this point, it was the least of her concerns. The only thing that occupied her mind was how to make it out of the clinic.

She needed an exact tempo for her escape, fast enough so no one would catch on that she was leaving, but slow enough not to seem utterly desperate.

While nearing the reception, she felt everybody's eyes stabbing at her back. Curious and perplexed glances. There was never much traffic in and out of this place, but at this hour, in the middle of the night, it was unprecedented.

Viola was prepared for everything, even being forced to stay against her will. But she knew that if anyone got in her way, she would scream and claw her way out.

And this very thought, an uncanny determination, must have been written all over her face as she passed the reception, because no one even dared ask her what she intended to do outside. In the middle of nowhere, in a blasting snow blizzard at minus twenty-five degrees. Covered by her jacket but still wearing her patient's gown.

Viola turned her head one last time, and looked at the staff. There was no commotion or alarm – she was in the clear. But when she whipped her head back, she crashed into a wheelchair which barricaded part of the entrance.

Her heart jumped, and her body curled up. It was the albino boy, scrutinising her with intense reddish eyes. This time he looked frailer than ever, sweat trickling down his forehead at the mere effort of sitting upright in his wheelchair. Before she could utter a word, he gripped her hand, held onto it and squeezed it way too hard. She gasped in silence. Then tried to shake him off, but his nails just bit themselves deeper into the skin of her palms.

He pushed the chair towards her, and slid his quivering body up to her ear.

"She is here," he whispered.

Her wild eyes scrambled for the quickest way out of here, as she shook off his hand and finally darted out of the entrance. As she made her exit, her mind was dazed and muddled beyond reason.

And before she knew it, she was knee-deep in snow, barely able to barge forward. She attempted to cover herself, but it was useless. The snowfall just kept whipping at her body, and punished her face.

But then she froze as she felt something in her hand.

Inside her palm was a translucent metal container the size of a thumb. It couldn't have made it there while she packed, and certainly not while on her way out. So, that left only one possibility.

The albino boy.

He must have put it into her palm.

She inspected it closer and realised she had seen something like it before, as they were used to store patients' DNA profiles. Its outer appearance was just as anonymous as the rest of the clinic. No name, or any information, other than it was marked with the InviNordica's logo, their DNA helix.

But as she peered closer, she noticed two cotton swabs.

* * *

As Viola fought her way towards where Pål and Ronny had parked, an overwhelming dizziness gripped her. Her sight blurred out of focus, making further progress impossible. Her feet began to fail her, and her body cramped with the tension. At first she thought it was the minus twenty Celsius which wreaked havoc on her body. But that was not it.

As she finally reached Pål's parking place, she realised neither of them were there. Pål's car was, though.

She spun around, several times. And at every turn, she felt a growing confusion clawing its way into her mind, twisting her thoughts into an indecipherable tangle.

She had always had a clear goal, a concrete sense of a destination, one that kept her afloat. But now, as she stood here, in the middle of the snow-covered street, she had absolutely no idea where to go. And even if she had some kind of goal which would fill her life with new meaning, would she want to go down that road? Or was she simply deluding herself?

She didn't know where she belonged anymore. She didn't belong among the women who could become mothers. She didn't belong with the ones who could become pregnant. And she certainly didn't belong to those who could adopt either. So what was left for her? A childless emptiness? Was that the only thing for her in this world?

PART THREE: Demons

Vlog, 59th entry 23.4.2012

Her head slid into view of the webcam as she greeted her
public with a childlike smirk filled with nothing but
optimism. Two years had flown by since her first post
initiated this path. And at this instant, she felt on fire. And
why not? She had all the reason to be euphoric. She struck
a sensitive chord with her viewers, causing her public to
explode in numbers.

"Hello Dolly to you girls! Today is a special day. It's
two years since we started, and something extraordinary
has happened in my life. I've got you. All fifteen thousand,
two hundred and fifty-two of you, to be exact. That's
phenomenal, and that's Hello Dolly to you all!" she
shrieked into the webcam as her natural high climbed to
yet another mountain peak.

"Take Trine from Drammen. Thank you for writing to
me and sharing your personal story. You, darling, that's the
reason I am here. A year ago, Trine stood before a
gruelling choice between two places for her next IVF.
She'd used up her two attempts and had one last free

attempt available to her. But when the hospital explicitly stated she had only a seventeen percent chance of success, she changed her course and instead chose a private clinic that promised her a sixty percent success rate. But going private meant she also had to dig deep into her own purse. And as you all know, this one can crush anyone's piggy bank. I've been there too, Trine. I feel you."

"Everyone around her advised against the private clinic. But the only thing she had before herself was the magical number of sixty percent. A doctor at the hospital shook his head and told her the sixty percent is good, maybe even magical, because it's good to be optimistic, but not based on false expectations. She told him to shove his talk about false expectations somewhere. Then she left the hospital. Yes, the cost differences were dramatic, but it would all be worth it. The sixty percent held the key to the magical kingdom of fertility. If she was sure of anything, she was damned sure of that." She peaked into another dramatic curve of Trine's story. And she felt her body tingle as she built up the climax of her tale. Damned fine storytelling, that's what it was. And she knew that.

"But as Trine got to the hospital and went through the treatment, it ended in an abysmal failure. Drugged by all the hormones, emotionally shell-shocked, and barely able to fight for her rights, she confronted the clinic's authorities with their PR policies. And their response? They back-pedalled to all hell, saying that sixty percent statistic was only viable for a woman with a normal body weight. And since Trine was quite overweight, she supposedly produced way too many eggs. Then they pushed the following simple fact down her throat. It was her own fault, being overweight, that is. She was the one to blame, that she didn't read the fine print on their contract and statistics. She responded that it was no wonder she gained weight, when they pumped her full of Lupron, flare, and anti-flare protocols and whatnot. With a hormone hangover like nothing she had ever experienced before, she left, heartbroken and depressed. And as she concludes in her mail, this was her last IVF," she whispered in a subdued tone, delivering the punch line with the reverence it deserved.

"Phew, Trine! Some story! I am eternally grateful that you had the courage to open up like this, and share your personal experience with everybody. This means so much to everybody. But please don't lose hope. And, darling, please remember, you can't change the way your body is built, you can't change the damned crap shoot that the IVF cycle is, and you can't change the grief infertility put you through, but you can change the way you react to all of this in the future. You can tell yourself each and every day, what a miracle you are. With or without a child. You hear me! And I am with you all the way, darling. I am with the rest of you gals too! Remember, if you wanna talk, I am available to you all 24/7. Hello Dolly to you all!" She terminated the web stream and grabbed onto her laptop.

She checked her site stats and watched as the comments rushed in, her 'likes' soared, and her viewership blew sky-high. Her eyes burned with a compulsion she couldn't push away. No. She welcomed it with an open heart. She couldn't hide the fact, she loved every second of it. This was what she lived and breathed for.

But most of all, this was one step closer to the realisation of her goals.

Only two years away.

Chapter 22

Viola couldn't shut her eyes. Her tears had frozen a long time ago into some unrecognisable structure that stifled her eyes. Not that it actually mattered, after all, the only thing in her mind now was to just keep on walking. The direction wasn't really that important, and certainly not the goal. She just needed to keep on moving until dawn arrived.

Still, she felt a remote thought spinning away in some dark corner of her mind, telling her she could pick up her cell phone, turn it on, check if Ronny had left anything for her. But right now, that thought seemed distant, almost alien, as if it wasn't hers anymore. Not the Viola she had known. Not the woman who had chipped away her life, bit by bit, until there was nothing left.

And for every step she took, she became more and more convinced she was closer to forgetting everything. The clinic, her old job, her mother. Ronny. Everything had to go, if she was to survive the re-awakened flood. And she knew that if she was to make it till dawn, she would have to dig much deeper. She had to forget where she lived, where she worked, whom she was, but most of all, she had to forget Markus.

But as the dawn began to break, she stopped. She noticed an old couple standing in the middle of the street. Their hands were filled with huge chunks of bread, and were casually feeding them to a reindeer in front of them.

The huge animal's gaze was placated, as if it were a puppy yearning to cuddle. Its eyes showed without a doubt that it was more than thankful to be fed at this hour. And for every piece of bread that was shared, it stepped even closer to them, which caused their old, wrinkled faces to glow with contentedness. And for every piece shared, the old couple squeezed their hands together.

Bewildered by its warmth, the ice around Viola's eyes began to dissolve. Melted by the tears that trickled down her cheeks again.

She felt her chuckle, coming from some strange place. A happier place inside her, one that wasn't dead yet.

She yanked out her phone, switched it on for the first time since exiting the clinic, and saw a succinct message from Ronny.

Grønland, Police HQ, come ASAP!

Morning
"What do you mean he is not here? Check again! Ronny Larsen." Viola's eyes scowled at the man's refusal to cooperate. She stood at the Grønlandsleiret Police-HQ with a long queue of people behind her. And everyone was pissed at her, including herself.

It had taken her most of the morning to get into the city. The blizzard had crippled Oslo. Street lights were out, cars were stranded on every street corner, and the usual mayhem ensued. With her nerves jangled badly, and having gotten no sleep the night before, she barely managed to stand upright.

She had fought her way to this place. She had waited patiently, like all the others, for more than an hour. And now, this officer, who had absolutely zero clue as to her predicament, told her to beat it. So, at this moment, she felt quite justified in indulging in her anger, and smashing his face against that hard-edged pinewood desk. At least in her fertile imagination.

The officer, aware of her desperation, yet oblivious to her inner monologue, eyed her with contempt.

"Thank you, Madame. Next!" he bawled out, then moved his eyes on to the next person in line.

Viola was stunned. What the hell was that? She wasn't done. She spun around. A myriad of faces whizzed by her, and her mind tried to do the impossible: locate Ronny in this huge hall. But when this bore no fruit, it struck her that she was out of time. So she grasped at the only thing that made sense at that moment.

She began to scream as loud as she could. Repeating two words endlessly, until either her throat failed her, or she was carried away to the looney bin.

"Ronny Larsen! Ronny Larsen!"

* * *

Rarely had anyone made such a spectacle at the station, and to the bemusement of several hundred spectators, she was carried away towards the holding cells.

But before they reached their destination, a man appeared in their way, and before she knew it, he dispatched everyone around her.

She swerved around and immediately locked gazes with the stony-faced, older police officer. She scanned him, and realised that if someone could help her, this was her man.

About fifty, with obsessive attention to his clean appearance, quite probably a detective, Viola was certain this man carried some weight around the station. She was about to launch into a lengthy explanation, but his nod was more than enough to interrupt her.

"Miss Voss." The cop didn't even bother to phrase it as a question. He simply stated the fact. As she nodded, he continued with an underlying sigh in his voice.

"A mess, huh? You need to come with me. Now!"

Midday

The only thing that separated her from Ronny and Pål in the interrogation room was a one-way mirror. She knew they couldn't see her; it wasn't physically possible. Despite this, she felt Ronny's and Pål's eyes stabbing at her. Accusing her of everything that she was guilty of.

She quickly learned that the officer who had prevented her trip to the holding cell was the Chief Inspector. She had met him only five minutes ago, but just being in the vicinity of him already made her stomach convulse.

The man possessed an ambivalence about him, a quality that made him difficult to place.

The only thing she was sure of now was that his eyes seemed to drill right through her. And instead of exposing who this man was, she felt as if no corner in her life was left unturned by him. She didn't get nervous around people, so why did her knees feel like jello? Was he judging her? And why, all of a sudden, did she have a problem with this?

Beside the Chief Inspector stood two other police officers who witnessed their exchange. Chief Inspector pointed towards Pål.

"That man claims he was helping you uncover illegal criminal activity inside the clinic InviNordica," he noted with a flat neutrality in his voice.

But Viola knew that was exactly his intention, behind her possible yes to this simple fact, lurked many more questions. Ones she was far from prepared to answer.

She nodded, which immediately was taken as the first step towards a full confession. But then she pointed towards Ronny.

"I know that man. He is my partner. He was about to pick me up after my stay at InviNordica. The other man, Pål Skarbom, I do recognise him. He was very helpful in my search for a missing person. But that was two years ago, if not longer. And I haven't seen him since." She summed up the whole situation and wrapped it into as little drama as she could.

The cops exchanged curious glances, and she sensed an immediate tension developing in the room. She knew that she had given a preposterous explanation.

"Let me get this right. What you are saying is that even though your partner was caught together with Mr. Skarbom in the same car. At the same time. Listening in on stolen hardware from our station, it was... ummm... a coincidence?"

Viola eyed everybody and considered the consequences. Her mind raced through all the possible options and outcomes. The most sensible thing would be to come clean, help them both, explain everything to the police. Maybe in this simple action, she would find some understanding, maybe even some leniency.

Then her mind swept to the women inside the clinic. They weren't being kept as prisoners, and despite Magda's unnerving nature, Viola had no evidence to suggest anyone was being exploited. On the contrary, dreams were being fulfilled and lives saved. And there was the little matter of the metal container that rested safely in her pocket. What would happen if she revealed these facts to the police, here and now?

However she turned this whole mess, whichever way she decided to go, somebody got hurt. So she decided on the course she had always used in these type of situations, her escape hatch that had always worked.

She postponed the inevitable.

"That's exactly what I am saying," she answered simply. This was immediately met with a collective groan from the policemen. The Chief Inspector sent her a pained gaze. Then he fished out a Dictaphone from his backpack and pressed its button.

"Help. Help..." The Dictaphone sounded, and Viola heard her own voice while she was being put under, during the egg retrieval.

"The recording from the equipment. Sounds familiar, doesn't it?" the Chief Inspector said. And beneath these words, she felt the cop's concern for what she was about to do now. But Viola only shrugged her shoulders.

"I don't know what you are suggesting, Officer. If it's familiar, then that's only to you," Viola finished, firmly placing her bet on all or nothing.

The older detective held his gaze for way too long, drenching her with a perverse calmness. Was that his way of intimidating his victims? If it was, then it worked. Viola felt her limbs swell up with fear, her jaw clasp until it locked tight. She felt her pulse explode, and her throat gasp for anything that would resemble air. She knew she had pushed it way too far. But what options did she have now? Admit to her lies?

Her attention drifted to Ronny behind the one-way glass. She realised his face was in a gut-wrenching grimace. He was at his limit. This wouldn't have happened, if she had some control over herself. His life wouldn't be as screwed up as it was now. And she realised now more than ever, this man wouldn't have had to suffer, if she had managed to say no to this. To her craving disguised as a noble need.

But before she could make things any worse, the Chief Inspector clasped onto her shoulder with little remorse. Then he thrust her towards a more secluded part of the office.

* * *

The Chief Inspector's breath pummelled her face. She felt herself fumble backwards, and hit her spine against the wall. Her comfort zone had been broken by his proximity.

She saw it in his frozen eyes, laser-focused on how to pry apart her skull.

She expected he would launch into the legal consequences of her lies at any moment. He would draw out a long line of accusations, which not only would create a public scandal, with her right in the middle of it, but would also get her sentenced for a good number of years.

But his face softened, then he backed off a bit, and his lips whispered instead.

"A year ago, Pål incarcerated a boy. Small-time drug felony. Testified in court... But after the sentence, the boy decided he would rather hang himself than face his father. Turned out his father was Ukrainian drug mob. Two days later, Pål found his son and wife dead. Both hanged." He shared Pål's story out of nowhere. And it was done with reverence for this man's life.

She expected accusations, professional attacks, and if all else failed, personal ones. The only thing she didn't expect was the truth.

Now she understood that this man actually cared for Pål. There was no doubt about it, his words were grief-stricken, his otherwise calm surface now shaken. He and Pål had a history together, maybe even a close one.

"And Pål?" she prodded gently for the rest of the story.

"Soon after, he was diagnosed with post-traumatic stress disorder. The guy is a mess. His mind can't remember half of what he has been through. And the other half is all jumbled. The experts tell the family lies, that it's a coping mechanism. They even tell them he will get through it. I just tell them the truth. It's hell. And he is still living it." The Chief Inspector uttered the words, but from the looks of his face, he had difficulties coping with this himself.

She had come along, gotten some strange ideas into Pål's head. Made him do things he couldn't possibly take responsibility for. And now the Chief Inspector, by telling this simple story, was pleading with her to straighten things out.

Her mind felt smothered under the implications. She gazed at Pål in the other room, and realised the Chief Inspector's story had altered Pål's face. Or maybe just the way she perceived him. The creases in the middle-aged man's face were tinged with the weariness of a man lacking hope. The sheer weight of his skin, carved all the life experiences into his face. And all told the same story: no amount of good intentions or compassionate deeds would turn this man's life around.

"That man. He is... my..." The Chief Inspector stalled as he immediately realised he had gone too far, revealed way too much of himself. He collected himself, backed off emotionally, and continued in a more distanced tone.

"He faces charges now. And you are in a unique position to help him." He finished his moral appeal to her.

Rarely had she been so shaken by someone's words. Not only by the story itself, but by the simple fact that she saw how deeply she had crossed her own values. The same qualities she fought so hard for in her stories, but failed so miserably at in her own life.

She could still turn this around. She knew that.

And she would do it. Right this moment.

She took in a big breath, while she repeated to herself that the first words would be the hardest. After that, everything would get easier.

"I've got nothing to add." She heard the words uttered somewhere in the room. But she had difficulty connecting them to a person. She looked around, but found no source. Surely, it couldn't be her. After all, she was about to tell them the truth. But as she glanced into the Chief Inspector's face, she began to have some doubts. And as the silence continued, the doubt grew into an absolute certainty.

The words had come from her lips.

The Chief Inspector's eyes filled with regret. He was done with her. And without any more ceremonies, he looked over Viola's shoulders and nodded to another cop.

"Release them. For now." He turned to walk out.

This was all she needed to hear. If she had to stay here one more minute, she would shriek at the top of her lungs. Not because of this man's story, but because she hated being around herself.

And as she began to race for the exit, she heard the Chief Inspector's words carve into her again. She swerved around, but only because she had to.

"You know what I learned later on? Pål's family was threatened by the mob before his testimony. He could have avoided all of this. But he stood up for what he believed in."

She realised she wouldn't make it out of this place without hearing what she feared the most.

"I've always admired your stories, Miss Voss. That's why I was somehow expecting the same integrity from you." His voice had turned into a whisper and held all the more power.

And this time there was nothing neutral about his assessment of her. Only a conclusive judgement on her character.

Chapter 23

Evening

She had longed to throw up. She had prayed for it while at the toilet, but nothing had come up. She had thought her body couldn't take any more of this battering.

But then the Chief Inspector had ordered Ronny and her to exit separately from Pål. And she had felt relieved. She knew she wouldn't be able to handle any more of the ex-cop's accusations. The guy had done everything possible to help her. And when he had needed her help, she had betrayed him.

And now, as they made their way out of Grønland's HQ, the feeling that she was about to hurl all her intestines onto the sidewalk still pervaded her body.

Still, she made sure she thrust Ronny as hard as she could towards the cab. She clenched onto his hand even tighter, sent him a forced smile, and did everything not to glance back.

They were just reaching the cab when Viola felt someone's presence glide in behind her. Before she could react, Pål blasted right at them, his adrenaline pumped up through the roof, his eyes delirious from zero sleep. He yanked at Viola's neck and grabbed onto her jacket. She shrugged him off, tore herself away from his grip, then rushed towards the cab door.

"Hey, Lady! Stop! Hey! What the fuck was that back there?" he spat out at them both. She glimpsed him from the corner of her eye, but didn't dare to turn around. Instead, she pushed Ronny into the cab, doing everything she could to avoid the confrontation.

But this wouldn't be enough, as the ex-cop threw himself into Viola's face.

"You have any idea what it is like to have a stranger coming to your apartment three times a week? Just because everybody thinks I am... a fucking danger to myself?" He cursed the words at her, and she knew he had every right to do that.

She glanced into Ronny's eyes and watched as confusion began to cloud his vision.

"Pål, please. I had no choice back there. I..." she started, but halfway through the words just petered out into nothingness. This was futile and she knew it. How could she explain to this man what was at stake in that clinic, in her life, without sounding like a raving egomaniac?

"Bullshit. Go back there. Tell them the truth. This thing with InviNordica, that was my ticket back to my work... to a normal life." Pål's words stung her, and the more she heard, the more she felt a need to escape.

But as her eyes went for the cab's door, Pål grabbed for her throat. The man's massive hands smothered her while Ronny just stood there and didn't even budge an inch.

"And do you know what my life feels like? Like I am on a fucking trial and Kafka is doing the judging," Pål rasped at Viola. And after all, she couldn't blame him. Had she been in his place, she would have done the same. A long time ago.

Finally, Ronny woke up from the stupor he seemed to have been in, and threw himself at Pål. He grabbed the cop, forcing Pål to let go of Viola's throat. Instead of halting his rage, though, it escalated, now channelled at Ronny. And where Pål's mind had still exercised some restraint due to Viola's sex, in Ronny's case all the consideration was dispensed with.

Pål twisted Ronny's arm, crunching it against his shoulder, headbutting him in the face. Ronny was pummelled down, his blood splattering all over the curb. Viola attempted to get up, but wasn't sure where she was. Her mind retched out of sync with reality, spewing up indecipherable images.

Still, she registered bits and pieces. She saw Pål, or was that his hands? Maybe even his feet. Kicking, battering. Was it at Ronny? At this point, she wasn't sure of anything. She saw a knee drive into Ronny's throat; Pål's face contorted in agony.

"You know what your relationship is?" The traffic noises blasted at her senses as people gathered around them. Despite all of this, Pål's words carved themselves into her brain as if someone separated them from the rest of reality and amplified them right into her eardrums.

"A damned lie. Mitochondrial disease? Ring a bell? And you know what that means? Baby cripple. That's the best she will fucking give you."

She had dreamed of meeting a guy like Ronny. And suddenly this wish had been fulfilled. There he was. Prepared to go through hell for her.

And just a couple of hours ago, she had made the impossible journey, had made the unfeasible jump. She was about to conquer her demons tonight, and tell him everything, tell him about her disease. All the truth that had poisoned her for the last twenty years. They would have hugged and she would have cried, and if he had a little bit of heart, maybe he would even have forgiven her. Eventually.

But now?

The cop staggered away from her into some blurry nothingness. Then her eyes strayed towards her man. She barely caught a glimpse of Ronny's blood-spattered face, and there was nobody at home. She whipped her head around at the countless people who were observing them, pleading for help. But nobody lifted a finger.

She had no idea how much time passed. It could have been seconds or minutes. Finally, she forced her body to get up. She was barely able to support Ronny's battered body, as she pushed him into the cab.

Chapter 24

When they got home, they had still not exchanged a single word. And she did everything she could to make sure that it stayed that way. As she ran upstairs, her mind spun endlessly on a simple sentence.

"A fifty-fifty chance. Willing to gamble, Madame?" The words reverberated in her mind, but she couldn't place their origin. Viola fled to the only place where she was certain the door would remain locked. The bathroom.

She let the tap run, just to uphold some kind of pretence. Then it struck her that for the first time since this havoc started, she was finally alone. And just at this realisation, her body crumpled to the floor, as her throat gave in to a silent wail.

Her life had always been a broken roller coaster. But nothing had caused more of an upheaval than the endless row of IVF cycles. Then, one day about five years ago, she met an acquaintance, while abroad. This particular doctor mentioned a new variation of the IVF treatment, three-parent IVF, only performed in Spain. She learned this IVF specially catered to certain rare genetic diseases, including

165

mitochondrial disease. This was the most serious step towards helping women like her.

Still, she held onto her resolve, and felt an immense inner strength when she turned down this opportunity. She would not go through another bout of hormonal hell and pulverised dreams. She knew what that road meant, what kind of inner emotional desert it left behind. Never again.

She returned home, but after only two days, she found herself in feverish pursuit of what that treatment really entailed. She met doctors, specialists and whatnot. Most of them wouldn't even discuss this with her. But the ones that did, painted a similar picture of this treatment. Considering her condition, this was not only illegal in Norway but most of all, a huge gamble for her and the child's health. Although she might make it, there was still a fifty-fifty chance the child wouldn't. "Are you willing to gamble, Madame?" one of the doctors summed up with a smirk on his face.

She let the thing go and returned to her job. The people in her stories were the only thing that filled the hole inside her.

But soon enough she realised she couldn't sleep anymore. This escalated into an eating disorder, and finally, a leave of absence. After two more weeks, she was on the plane to Barcelona, torn inside by wants, needs, rights, and wrongs. Hope she would finally fulfil her dream, and a clear realisation she had broken a sacred vow to herself.

Two weeks later, her embryo transfer was a resounding success. For the first time in her life. She couldn't believe it.

A dream came true, and a nightmare was about to begin.

She was jolted back to reality by a knock on the door.
It was Ronny.

Late evening

She had opened the door, and he had politely stepped in, without touching her. Then he had reclined on the floor, as far from her as possible. As they glanced into each other's eyes, she felt a wall separating them now.

"I need to know. Please," he whispered. Beneath his words was a desperate plea from a man whose whole world had just been wrenched away. Whenever their gazes connected, a jolt of pain passed through Viola. She knew she had lost him and this attempt at a normal conversation, this was just him seeking closure.

"He lied. Pål lied," Viola heard herself say. And it came as no surprise to her; these words, the lies, came with a chilling ease to her. After all, they weren't hers, she reasoned with herself. They originated from some other part of her. A big chunk of her that couldn't deal with the stuff she had gone through all these years. This fragment was willing to do whatever had to be done. Fleeing, lying, even hurting people, just so it would keep all the bad stuff away.

She gazed at his face, and immediately registered a deeply hidden annoyance. The truth struck her right in the gut. The veil she had draped over his eyes for the last two years was lifted now. Whatever she said or however she said it, it didn't matter.

"Tell me I am wrong, but for the past two years you've done everything to avoid the subject of kids. And with your career and all, I could understand so I never pushed it. But it was the mitochondrial disease, wasn't it?" He began to utter his accusation, but she instantly shook her head.

"No. Pål was out of control. Lying," she said in a final appeal.

"Lying? It's been two years, and I still don't know how Markus died. Was it the mitochondrial disease? That's what happened to him? For Christ's sake! Is that normal? Or just another lie?" The secrecy, the lack of openness, these were indeed the terms she had forced upon their relationship. She had hoped he had accepted them, but she realised she had been naive to think this wouldn't have repercussions down the road. This was kept sequestered inside him, spreading like an out-of-control weed. The kind that were impossible to get rid of. And now was the time to deal with them.

"Markus died in... an accident. It had nothing, absolutely nothing to do with this. Especially not Pål's lies." She barely forced the words out of her throat. Her path was paved with many lies, whitish, greyish, even some black ones. Some heavier for her conscience than others. But this one felt like one stone too much.

Ronny's gaze pierced right through her, saw the raging struggle inside her. Then he just stopped and shook his head. Pushed himself up, then trudged towards the door. His eyes revealed the truth behind his silence. There was nothing more to talk about.

When Viola realised this, she was struck by utter panic. Maybe this man hadn't come in here to finish off their relationship. Maybe he wasn't seeking closure. Maybe he had approached her so he could reach out to her. To give her one last chance to come clean.

Moments ago, she would have given anything to have him out of here. But now, as she understood his intention, she knew she had blown her chance.

"Ronny, I am sorry. Please. Sit. We can talk..." The lump in her throat smothered away her words. Still, she fumbled at anything that would make him stop.

Ronny's body halted as he was stung by the intention behind her voice. But as he turned to face her, she realised his face was skewed in an expression she had never seen in this man. Anger ate away at him, and only now could she see how betrayed he felt.

He had done so much for her, accepted so much, without a single accusation or complaint. But everyone has their limits. And she sensed Ronny was reaching his.

"Remember me saying kids weren't important? Well, they are. I didn't want to put pressure on you. I lied. I thought... no, I *hoped* you would come around. I hoped for a family," he hissed at her, his nerves ripping him apart.

"Wanna talk about lies? Someone's been through my mails. Bills. Daily. Is that normal?"

There were many days when she pondered how to approach him with her suspicions. Given the right situation, done gently enough, maybe this wouldn't feel like an all-out assault on him. A suspicion of his intrusion into her privacy. But right now, at this instant, this felt like nothing but a futile flounder. Something she had been certain she would never use.

But here she was, and there were the words.

"What the hell are you talking about? You can't be serious? Is that an accusation?" He was taken aback by the course their confrontation had taken.

If she had earned something with him, it was his respect. So, when he glanced at her now, she felt like he was looking at a complete stranger. He certainly never would have thought she was the type of person who would lash out at others, just because her inner child, which was like a leashed dog, got kicked in the ribs way too many times.

Ronny's head shook with pity. Then he turned and began to leave.

"It's not me. Or my fault. I... I lie. That works. Only way... to get by. Can't even.... Fucking... Can't tell the truth from the lie," she said as she tried to stop the flood.

She had always been terrified of this. Even the simplest private details felt like someone was hanging an anchor around her neck. But once she started, she pushed away the barrage of fear and pushed on.

"They all leave. Everyone... leaves," she whispered and felt the rusty anchor begin to melt off her neck.

He eyed her, and despite her truth, she wasn't reaching him. His anger clouded his eyes, a thick wall between them.

"Mitochondrial disease. Markus. It's all true." She laid out the words carefully, in the hope she would punch a hole through to him. Her last attempt.

But he only shook his head. Drilled his eyes into her.

"You know the job offer in Damascus? That was like the worst fucking career opportunity. Setting me back for many years to come. I was still willing to do that. For you. For a family. But now this?" He glared at her one last time, then all but ran out of the bathroom.

Chapter 25

As she began to wake up, her mind still refused to adjust to yesterday's exchange with Ronny. Viola's bloodshot eyes gradually gazed at the mess in her bedroom. Still in the same clothes, with the whisky bottle emptied on the floor, her head was battered. And then, it all came crashing down on her, in all its grimy vividness.

She had waited all night for Ronny to come back. But he never did. So, she went for the only whisky bottle left in the house. She told herself she had stopped drinking. She would never touch the bottle, not after Markus. But it was a more than fitting occasion yesterday. It was certainly much easier to start than to stop. The rest was an indistinct blur.

Now, as she fumbled out of her bed, she laid her eyes on Ronny, who sat on the bedside. Her heart sank as she glanced at his bruised face. She noticed there were two bags beside him. Both were packed. He must have let himself in and packed while she was sleeping. She tensed up again. Was he back for another round of yesterday?

"Leaving?" she asked. How long had he been sitting there?

"I've gone through your bills, your mails, your stuff. Several times. I want to stop. No. I know I need to stop. But the fact is... I can't."

She couldn't believe what she heard. She never focused on the what-ifs. Especially not this one, which she had trouble believing in the first place. Could her nearly perfect partner actually be a jealousy-stricken liar and intruder?

No. This wasn't possible.

As he admitted this, she didn't feel any emotions. There was no outrage or resentment left in her. Maybe she had used up her share on herself.

On the contrary, she felt grateful that he had shared this with her. She realised she felt closer to him. Their mutual flaws had levelled the playing field.

Instead of mulling further over this, she drew closer to him. Then just lay her head on his knees. As she saw into his eyes, there was more than a fair share of tears. Something he tried to wipe away in embarrassment. But she touched his hand. Then stroked them away with a gentleness that rarely felt that good.

Morning

He caressed her along her spine as they lay naked on the bed. When she began to doze off quietly, she wasn't assaulted by grief or the constant guilt. Present was only satisfaction. Something she hadn't felt for quite some time. An afterglow from the sex, a simple pleasure which caused her to disconnect from her mind, from these emotions. The only thing that was left was the sheer delight of simple presence, without her thoughts. The best vacation she could have from herself. If only for a moment.

But Ronny's soft, yet inquisitive words pierced through her dreamy veil.

"So what, now?" he asked. She tried to push it away with a smile, but noticed the insistent nature of his eyes. She elbowed herself up, and faced him.

"After this mess. Well... the only thing I can do is crawl back to my mother. Beg for anything resembling a job."

He smirked at her assessment, which at this moment felt genuine.

The deadline Anne had given to Viola as an ultimatum had passed two days ago. Viola knew she had blown it, and after behaviour like this, she had no idea how Anne would react.

But she felt it would be different this time. This time, she would indeed come crawling back on her knees. If she was sure of anything, it was that she wanted to regain her life.

As she mulled this over, she noticed a renewed glow in Ronny's face. Maybe she read way too much into it, or maybe there was some renewed respect towards her in his eyes.

"And the clinic? Did you find Marianne? Or any answers?" he asked.

"Only more questions," she whispered. Ronny nodded as he understood not to push it any further.

Yes. She felt it would be different this time.

Chapter 26

Late morning

As her eyes woke up from the slumber, her body yawned from pleasure. She glanced around herself and noticed he was in the shower. She felt good about herself, a state quite rare in her everyday life. But it wasn't every day that she conquered her demons. Managed to open up to such an extent. To anyone. And Ronny was still here. Prepared to give her another try. She felt a warm glow spread through her body as she felt a sense of simple gratitude that she had him. A partner with a heart big enough to overcome his emotions and forgive her.

She stretched out and proceeded to repeat her new mantra to herself. She felt fine. She was great. She was done with that crazy blip on the radar. Most of all, she was done with Marianne. This was the day she would get her life back on track. Just as she had so many years ago, she would now stop chasing after mirages, and regain her much-needed footing. Only this way would her inner harmony be restored. And these were just a few kinks in her life, new learning experiences, nothing she couldn't take care of.

As she turned on the bed, beaming with newfound contentment, she caught a faint glimmer on the floor. She stretched out her hand to inspect what it could be. And there it was.

The metal vial from the clinic.

It lay beside her bag, which it must have fallen out of. It was just as she remembered it, with the InviNordica's DNA helix stamped on the side.

As she reached for it, her heart stung in her chest, and her mind gave off a blaring warning. Wasn't this day supposed to be a new beginning for her? Her hand froze.

Was the boy telling her the truth? Or had he been forced to give her the vial by someone at the clinic? Why was a sick teenager at a fertility clinic? After all, he seemed like he was a patient.

And what about Ingrid? The whole thing just didn't make sense. The recording she had seen at Stine's might have been dark and fuzzy, but certainly not blurry enough for her to doubt the woman's identity. She was sure of herself. She had seen Marianne. She had studied every crease in her face for the last three years.

And Ingrid was not Marianne.

So, that left only one possibility. The clinic had attempted to push lies onto her. And maybe Marianne was still inside there, completely unaware that Viola had been so close to her. Even if her suspicions turned out be true, what about the women there? Her initial suspicions of a medical institution taking advantage of women's rare diseases simply didn't fit into the whole picture. At least not what she had seen. Their happiness, their intimate contact with the children, all of this was genuine, something that would be impossible to stage. This much she was certain of. So how did these pieces fit together?

Her mind spun in all directions, but was suddenly torn away by a cough behind her. She fumbled the vial under the bedcover and faced Ronny with a grin.

Had he seen the DNA vial, or was she just being her neurotic self?

"You okay?" he asked.

She bared her teeth in a self-assured smile.

"I am great, hon. Just great."

After all, this was the day she would get her life back on track.

Noon

Her hands gripped tightly onto the steel wires. No. They didn't grip the fence. The wires had barbed themselves into her skin, and her hands wouldn't let go. On the other side, a school playground filled with kids roaring with laughter. She stood there transfixed, eyeing their slightest movements. Their subtle, quirky emotions, their tiny, sweet dramas which meant the world for them.

Earlier this morning things had been simpler. Her goal had been in sight. But for every step she had taken towards the *Aftenposten's* offices, towards her new, better life, the doubts had begun to seep into her body, squirm like rotten worms under her skin. And before she had known it, she had found herself standing behind this fence.

This playground was very much like the one she had gone to with Markus. Despite being only three, he would fearlessly shoot onto the biggest swings, then scream for her to push him higher, faster, quicker. His joy drove her nuts with happiness, pushing her mind into the absolute here and now. She had never experienced such utter simplicity and bliss. Yet this didn't last. When he coughed one too many times, then made a few complaints about being tired, she decided he was too weak to go outside. The doctors told her he was ok but they never visited the playgrounds again. After all, why take unnecessary chances with his potential condition?

She had no idea how much time had passed behind this fence. But she would have stood there for much longer, if not for a woman who jolted her back to reality. Her face was contorted and spewing anger, as she lashed her body into the fence on the other side.

"Hey! Lady! Whatcha doing there? Dontcha think I don't see you!" the woman spat out at her. If not for the fence, this woman might have pummelled her with her bare fists.

And she knew better than to stay around here to find out if there was a gap in this barrier. She twisted herself, backed away, then dashed across the street. But the woman kept at her, thrashing her fists into the wires like a baboon out to wreak havoc.

"I see you, Lady. Standing there an hour, what the fuck are you? Stalking my kids! You a pervert, Lady?" Viola was already on the other side of the street, but still heard the incessant shrieks from the woman.

She hurtled forward for a couple of blocks until she felt safe enough to catch her breath. Yet, as much as she gasped for it, she couldn't catch it again. Her eyes were drowning with tears. She was choking. She beat her chest, once, twice. One more time.

It wasn't the run, nor the woman's fault. It was the black hole in her chest. It smothered her. Wrapped itself around her throat like some limbless reptile with saw tooth jaws. And despite that she finally managed to regain her breath, she knew there was no point in returning to work. Pretending she was fine. Maybe she would manage to deceive everybody around her, but her time was up, and she couldn't dupe herself anymore. She realised this black crevice would never go away. Because only one person in the world knew how to melt it into bliss.

Markus.

* * *

The snow plunged down on Viola's windshield as she tried to make out the details of the building in the distance. Her eyes squinted as the granite sign on the building slowly coalesced into focus. It read simply "Aurora Biobank". She recognised it as her goal, and whatever her plan had been earlier today, it had all changed now.

Her eyes drew to her clenched fist. In it was the metal container she had received from the albino boy. She eyed the name on the vial. She knew it proved nothing. But even if it turned out to be Marianne's, what proof would that be? At best, that Marianne had been a patient, but did that mean she was still there?

She had no idea what it held, or if it would give her any substantial answers, but she made a couple of phone calls and quickly realised she could test its contents for the Mitochondrial disease. And do it off the records, which was key at this point. This was something she could work with, this was something she couldn't pass on.

So why did she feel so dizzy?

Along the way to *Aftenposten*, she had passed the kindergarten, and her reality seemed to have warped into some parallel dimension. She had been pushed kicking and screaming down the rabbit hole. Only this hole didn't lead to any adventures in a far-off fantasy land. It only led to pain.

What was she hoping to gain? Did she want to find out if it was Marianne's DNA? Or did she intend to save a woman, someone who might not even be alive? Maybe it was to save the women at the clinic? If they needed saving, that is. Or was it just to fill that empty hole in her chest?

She could still return. Get back to the office. Have a chat with her mother. Maybe even get a job. It was still not too late.

She stopped herself.

Screw it.

Late afternoon

Viola glanced at the technician's girlish fingers. They were quivering. And pretty soon, she noticed that he kept sending twitchy glances over his shoulder, constantly checking to make sure no one was coming.

She had hoped to get into this place without calling any attention to herself, but when she looked into this man's petrified eyes, she realised that if anyone asked, it might prove more difficult to get out of here.

She had used the better part of the morning to bombard old-time acquaintances whom she presumed owed her a favour. Unfortunately, most of them didn't see it quite the same way and simply told her to get lost.

Finally, though, she had managed to pull in a heavy-handed favour from an old journalist pal. In no time, Viola had access to the Aurora Biobank's lab. But through the backdoor.

Normally they performed only DNA fatherhood scans, since this was only a privately-owned service facility. But she quickly learned that this rear door gave her access to the technician who was able to perform deeper genetic tests, including rare diseases. This was the perfect opportunity. An off-the-radar facility, with an off-the-records guy.

Only nobody mentioned to Viola she would have to deal with this little man, with his nerves about to pop. And since the corridor was filled with people, mostly staff, Viola knew that any one of them could drop into the lab and start asking importunate questions.

"Mitochondrial disease analysis in half an hour? This isn't Seven Eleven, Lady," he scoffed at her.

"And how do I know you are not just one of those journalists wanting a scoop on our day-to-day operations?" His left eye twitched at the very thought as he unpacked the cotton swabs from the vial. A sigh passed through Viola, she wasn't about to share the truth about her occupation.

As his monitors flashed into view, a myriad of analysis data flowed in. The techie's face twisted into an unsettling smirk.

"You sure this is real, Lady? The results, they are all over the place."

"What?" Viola leaned over his shoulder and eyed the screens. Whatever diagnostic software was being used, the program threw off a myriad of random errors. All of them were contradictory. Her eyes scanned over them, forcing her mind to spin at possible conclusions.

"Yeah. You are right. Unless... unless... Is it possible these swabs belong to two separate individuals?" She thought it was a long shot, too obvious a solution, but at this point, anything was worth a try.

He cringed at the stupidity of the idea, but punched away at the keyboard. Pretty soon a 3-D scan of the analysis source flashed up on the screen. His face flinched as they both realised the cotton swabs were indeed from two different people.

He cringed as he shot her an uneasy glance. She waved this away as a lucky guess, and pointed him back towards the screen. As he realigned the two samples, she realised they were nearly identical.

"Mother and daughter." Adrenaline shot through her body. This was it. Inches away from her answers.

And as the techie nodded in confirmation, his body suddenly froze. His eyes squinted at the monitor. Froze for a longer moment. Then spun towards her with exasperation filling his face.

"Hey, Lady, where did you get this from, huh? This must be some fucking joke to you? Isn't it?" For every word that he spat out, his tone grew more confrontational.

"Hey. What do you mean? Please! Tell me what you see there," she begged and leaned over to see the LEDs, but he blanked them out, then pushed her towards the entrance.

"Get out of here! Right now. Get the hell out of here. Before I call security!"

And before they knew it, his shrieks caught some unwanted attention. Concerned glances were directed at them from the passers-by. A man halted and stared.

Viola realised she had about ten seconds before the whole thing blew up in her face. She whirled on her heel, and raced for the door.

* * *

The blizzard blasted into her face as she desperately attempted to locate the keys to her car. Where did she hide those things? She was absolutely certain they were in her jacket, in one of the pockets. She dug even deeper into them, turned them inside out, but still nothing.

Her mind tried to make sense of what the hell had happened back at the lab. She had been promised this guy was trustworthy. At least enough to get her errand done. She had counted on this. Despite this, she had gone in there and lost the most substantial proof she'd had in years.

And now? She had not only lost the DNA profile but also her car keys. For Christ's sakes!

She glanced at her numb fingers. Way too cramped to be of any use now, the cold had eaten itself into her bones. She punched her car several times, then let hopelessness take over her body as she slid down against the car door.

She had gone down into hell, and this was rock bottom. She had finally hit it, and would now freeze to death beside her car, in what might be the most nonsensical death of this century.

Then she felt a chuckle come up from some undefined place inside herself. This plain conclusion cheered her up. At least now things couldn't get any worse.

Then she felt her phone purr out a vibration. She slid it out of her pocket with her skewed thumbs.

It was a text from her mother.

You on the plane, girl? Viola began to smile to herself.

You've been nothing but disappointment in my life, blurted out the next SMS. Viola felt her chuckle turn into a giggle. She was wrong. She could be sure of one thing, if things could get worse, they probably would.

Sorry? Anne asked Viola in the third SMS. But with Anne, the apologies lasted only until the next message. One that would arrive about ten seconds later.

I've booked another plane for you. Be there. Or I will fire you! Viola shook her head, but her chuckle only increased. She couldn't help herself anymore. These messages were a hoot.

Strike that. I cancelled the booking. No second chances. This threat made her bawl out in laughter. And it hurt. In a good way.

You there? another SMS burst in. Viola cackled at this.

Sweetie? I love you. And as the last message arrived, Viola's laugh launched into a howl.

As she leaned backwards, she bumped into the car's door. And as she did that, it opened.

With ice-covered eyes, she barely saw through the haze. But as she pushed at the door further, she realised it had been open all along. She had simply forgotten to lock it. And as the keys came into sight, she realised they were still in the ignition. Just as she had left them.

Chapter 27

Earlier, Viola had been more than prepared to return to *Aftenposten* and convince her mother that her life had changed. For the better. She had recuperated from a temporary disability, which was nothing to worry about.

She had even prepared a whole tale.

But that was then. And now, everything had changed.

At this moment, the last thing she wanted was to stumble into Anne. She sneaked into the *Aftenposten's* offices with one goal only. Get in, talk to their IT expert, get her answers, then get out. And do this before Anne realised Viola was here.

That was the plan anyway.

In practice, things had gone wrong from the moment she set foot there. For one, her feet left a long trace of smudgy footprints on the office carpet. This would be perfectly normal with the winter blazing outside. But she had not foreseen the brand new off-white carpet which Anne had installed.

As she entered the open space area, she felt everybody's smirks stabbing at her back. Her idea of an inconspicuous entrance had flip-flopped into a feeding frenzy.

But she wasn't about to stop and indulge in any unnecessary conversations. She blasted her way past everybody's glances and into the IT section of the offices.

* * *

Viola could barely see over Jorunn's obtrusive shoulder. The woman's fingers whizzed in hyper-focused bursts across the keyboard.

Viola and Jorunn were both in the Hole, the place where all of the administration, backup, and security work of the *Aftenposten's* servers happened. Viola figured Jorunn was a woman in her twenties, although it was quite difficult to pinpoint, with the girl resembling a champion sumo wrestler.

The Hole got its nickname from Jorunn's offbeat interior design habits, which transformed the office space into a medieval-looking dungeon crevice, with her as a self-proclaimed "Dungeon Master". All the lights were out, except the incandescent LEDs lined up on the desks.

And to add to the charm, the Hole was thickly layered with chips and sushi leftovers, all of them more than a week old. Viola sighed as she saw the waste dump. Even Anne couldn't make Jorunn see reason. Not after Jorunn prohibited any activities that resembled cleaning. All this due to the servers' sensitive nature.

But Viola couldn't care less about the mess. She was certain she had seen Marianne in the video stream on her blog. But when she landed at the clinic, the blogger was gone, replaced by another woman named Ingrid with an identical recording. At this point, even Viola began to doubt herself, and the only way to confirm her suspicions was to check the WordPress logs of Marianne's site. And this was where Jorunn's White Hat hacker skills came in.

"Sorry, can't help you. Short of breaking into the ISP provider hosting Marianne's WordPress site, there is nothing I can do. And I am sure you wouldn't want me to do that anyway. Right?" Jorunn swerved her huge body to the side.

184

"Right! Uh-huh. Right. But... why wouldn't I want you to do that?" Viola knew exactly where this was headed, but it didn't hurt to play stupid. This was her territory. If they took the next step, it would mean breaking the law. And the Norwegian law didn't take this lightly, with a minimum sentence of five years. Not to mention the legal repercussions for the newspaper.

Viola had lost count of how many times she had asked for Jorunn's services. Always in the name of a good cause. One more pressing than the other. But no matter how dramatic the situation, or how tragic the fates of the people involved, the girl always turned Viola down. And not because she couldn't do it, but out of principle.

"Come on, Viola. You know why. I just can't." The woman repeated the same old story. It was clear to Viola that Jorunn didn't want to turn her down. They had always been on a good foot. Sometimes even approaching personal. And considering Viola's aloofness, this was quite a miracle.

"How are you holding up?" Jorunn changed gears and prodded Viola softly. But when Viola's eyes faltered away, the hacker mulled this over and continued more brashly.

"Tell me. This thing. The blogger. You quitting your job. Is this connected to you somehow? Personally?"

Viola knew Jorunn was sensitive, and her silence would hold all the answers the young woman needed. So, the safest bet was to let the question peter out into nothingness.

And as the silence drew out, Jorunn glanced at Viola.

"You know. Your mum. She is not so bad after all. Maybe she will even have you back. Sure you don't want to talk to her? Come back to us?" Jorunn never stumbled with her choice of words, but she did now.

Viola was touched as she felt an emotional attachment below these words. But the only thing she could do was shake her head. And when Jorunn noticed this, she sighed again.

"Give me two hours. I will get you what you need." The woman voiced her decision, then squeezed Viola's hand tighter and glowed toward her.

* * *

"I used a chain of a dozen or so different bugs in the WordPress binaries, which gave me partial editor privileges. From there, the road to critical vulnerability wasn't long, and with remote root access, I was able to download the blog's SQL database and its most recent backups." Jorunn was feverish from excitement. She then pointed to two text files.

As Viola eyed them, she felt perplexed. Whatever was so obvious to the Dungeon Master, was completely incomprehensible to her. And Jorunn must have noticed Viola's reaction, because she smirked in amusement, then clicked on two texts.

"These SQL databases list the media files that are uploaded to the WordPress site. If you compare these two, you will notice a video file has been deleted and re-uploaded within a very short period of time. Two days, to be exact."

"I appreciate this, Jorunn. But I can't base my story on a database hack. It's too vague. Other than that, I now know for sure that someone replaced the media, this gets me nowhere." Viola's stomach felt heavy as her mind churned away at the possibilities. This was not enough. One video file tampered with, that could be purely coincidental.

"Nowhere? Inconclusive? Well, grab some sushi, girl, put up your feet, and watch this!" The young woman pounded away at her keyboard, and it was immediately followed by two video streams that started simultaneously, side by side.

Viola felt a surge of electricity punch through her body. Four years, countless dead ends, and even more sleepless nights. Only now did she have this. The single most irrefutable piece of evidence since she started digging into this case.

Her eyes widened at the two videos. Each one, by itself, might not mean much. But both, side by side, they could only mean someone had taken great care to cover their tracks.

One stream showed Marianne and her kid, and the second one, Ingrid, choreographed, dressed, and lit to look almost identical.

Evening
Viola's legs felt incapable of supporting her as she reeled out from the Hole. Her mind was a jumbled mess as all the questions stabbed at her with their sharp edges.

Why would the clinic go to so much trouble to record a similar version of Marianne's video? The obvious answer would be to cover their tracks. But what lay behind this? Had Marianne become too big a liability for them? And if so, what did they do to her after they found out about the recording? Was she even still alive?

Every one of these questions demanded a rational explanation. Something her head wasn't capable of delivering right now.

She had to get the hell out of here, before Anne caught on to her. The last thing she needed now was a confrontation with Anne's should-haves, impropers, and unacceptables.

But as she twisted her body, about to flee, her eyes locked onto a familiar set of wrinkled brows. Right in front of her.

Her mother.

* * *

Viola repeated her story several times. And for each telling, her mother's face grew more wary of the details. They both knew it was a house of cards, about to crush Viola.

As Anne listened, somewhere in the distance, Viola heard a pen as it made a grating noise against Anne's desk. Its every single beat hammered Viola's pulse into a gallop, as Anne's eyes pierced right through her.

"That's it? Is that supposed to impress me?" Anne tested the words in her mouth, not really sure what she thought about her daughter's proposition.

"Frankly, ever since Markus, I am sceptical about you." Anne jabbed at her daughter.

"Markus? How the hell does he have anything to do with this?" Viola fired back.

"Everything. How long since you've been to visit his grave?" Anne wouldn't let this go. Viola knew she had no one to blame but herself. And the mere mention of her son bristled every single hair on her body. She had to redirect her mother's attention before this ended in some kind of brawl.

"Please... I am willing to do anything, Mummy."

Anne sent a glowing smile toward her, then threw an envelope on the table.

"Something for you. Dropped on my desk earlier today." Anne pointed towards the plain envelope, which had no addressee nor sender.

"Maybe not a Middle East correspondent job. That one went to Jon," Anne said, making sure to stress the name.

Viola's body froze. She was about to lash out, but then restrained herself. The guy was barely twenty-five, with little experience. But he more than made up for that in looks and charisma. Something that didn't go unnoticed with Anne. But she had difficulty believing her mother would cross that line. No way.

Maybe there was something else behind this. Maybe Anne simply wanted to hack away at Viola's dignity. If she couldn't have the job, Anne could at least give it to the least suited person in the paper. Viola realised this smelt of paranoia, but she often enjoyed indulging in her neurosis.

But then she collected herself and did the only thing that made sense.

"Are you kidding me? Of course!" When everything else failed, an act of humility would be the best tactic.

Viola glowed as she unwrapped the envelope, which revealed a set of pictures. But before she knew it, her throat compressed in a wrenching, silent cry. She felt her knees were about to collapse as she struggled with the effort to keep standing.

The picture set depicted the interior kindergarten at InviNordica. It also revealed the identity of each and every woman at that place. But the worst part was that Viola immediately recognised the situation. This was the exact time of her presence. Viola fumbled through the pictures, expecting the worst.

Finally, she laid her eyes on the last image, and just as she expected it, there she was. Only, she had her back turned towards the camera. A mixed blessing that filled her with contradictory feelings. Every woman's identity was compromised, but hers wasn't. And while she kept up her poker face, she felt the ground give in. How the hell did Anne learn about this whole thing?

"A tip from an anonymous source. This place. A clinic. InviNordica. And there is some substantial evidence pointing towards illegal gene therapies." Anne summed up the whole thing without any hidden meanings.

"Who is your source?" Viola blurted out.

Anne responded by grabbing the picture with Viola in it. She played with it between her fingers, then locked gazes with Viola.

"Anonymous. And will stay that way. But only if you manage to do your job." Was Anne talking about the source, or her own daughter?

Anne knew about everything.

"So, what do you want me to do?" Viola swiped the envelope back.

"Can you manage, *nothing*?" She pursed her lips innocently.

"What do you mean, *nothing*?" Viola said calmly, but everything in her croaked at the suggestion. Had she heard her mother right? She tried to wrap her head around this. Something that went against everything she believed in. The manifesto, the family tradition, all of it evaporated in a micro second.

"No more questions. What I need to know now is, is my best watchdog up for the job? Or do I have to worry she will run off somewhere and mess further with everything?" Anne stabbed at Viola, making her intention perfectly clear.

An unnaturally long pause followed. Finally, Viola just nodded to Anne and decided there was nothing to add.

"Believe me, it's for your own good." Anne sent her a compassionate glance.

Viola sneered, twisted around, and began to flee the room. But she didn't make it to the door before Anne halted her with a cough.

"You never answered me about Markus." Viola bit down on her lip as she heard the words behind her back. She couldn't afford any more escalation. So, she tucked away her ego, contained her burning anger, her unresolved needs and motherly traumas, then turned towards Anne.

"I haven't been to his grave," she whispered.

"Since when?" Anne pursued the matter to its bitter conclusion.

"Since the funeral."

She fled the office.

* * *

Viola lashed out at the dashboard in her car.

Why did Anne bite down so easily on this truth? After all, her daughter had failed her so miserably with the Middle East correspondent job. She had betrayed her own mother. And everything she stood for. So why were there zero repercussions?

190

Her mother played tough, but one thing had changed. Beneath those refined games was an old woman's attempt to save her daughter from herself. A desperate cry to save her family. But this wasn't rooted in some family sentimentality. Viola had no doubts about what lay behind this.

Anne wasn't doing this for her daughter. It wasn't done out of concern. But out of fear for her own name.

Viola took in several deep breaths, and her head began to clear.

After she had come out of the clinic, her mind had been tainted with serious doubt. But now everything crystallised. She felt herself reaffirmed on her course of action. She needed to do the opposite of what her mother had told her.

She needed to find Marianne.

Chapter 28

Late evening

She had waited all day outside his lab. She was hoping he would exit alone, and for once, something had gone right. The scrawny man made his exit with no company, leaving the way open for Viola to go after the lab technician from Aurora Biobank.

Before he managed to reach his ride, she slid herself between him and the door. With an innocuous smile across her face, she made an attempt at formulating her first plea for help.

"Hey, Lady! I told you to leave me alone," he hissed at her as he stepped back.

"Please. This test. I need to know the results. There are lives at stake here." The guy seemed unhinged, and her jumping him in the back alley didn't help.

"What? You bring those phoney samples to me, and now what? You people from the Health and Welfare department are some piece of work, huh? Leave me alone, once and for all, okay?" He spat the words out at her and pushed his way towards his car.

"Hold on. Please. Please." She flashed her journalist credentials in his face. And as he glanced at it, he recognised her true identity.

"Uh-huh. Okay, I get it. You are not from the department?" He shook his head in dismay. "And you are not here to check up on me or our business? Or do a story on us?" He still had trouble grasping the simple truth behind her identity. She nodded impatiently.

"Listen, Lady, why do you think I reacted the way I did? Especially when you bring me a sample that couldn't possibly be human. Someone else..."

"Hey, hey, stop! Did you just say 'not human'?" she said.

"Similar. Think 99.9 percent similar. But that's how far it got. Would quicker go for an ape than a human. Both females." He summed up the facts, which suited his world view completely.

"Wait, wait. Is it feasible this was human after all?" She pushed an alternative version of truth at him. But his initial expression told the whole story.

"Lady, do you realise what 0.1 percent means in this case? Monkey for sure. Unless they had the best from MIT at their disposable and millions worth of high-tech gear for some kind of gene editing. Not for another ten years, and certainly not in Norway." He smirked.

"Like Clustered Regularly Interspaced Short Palindromic Repeats – editing and splicing? In other words, CRISPR?" she interjected, instantly stopping his ironic chuckle. "Did you do a pass for the mito-disease?" She disregarded his baffled face, and pursued the matter further.

"Yeah, I did. Mother had mitochondrial disease, as you suspected." He pursed his lips.

"And what about her child?" Her eyes strained with great force at him. And it struck her how much she needed to know this. How much she longed for this answer to be something other than what she expected.

193

"No traces whatsoever."

He shook his head.

As Viola heard the final confirmation, she felt a surge pass through her body. She suspected there might be some doubts as to the results. She was prepared for a no. God, she was used to them. They had covered her life like an impregnable carpet.

So the next best thing would be an approximation. A ballpark figure. A fifty-fifty chance would be fantastic.

But this? An unequivocal one hundred percent. This only left her body trembling. The impossible had indeed been made possible.

* * *

Viola squeezed herself into the car. She fumbled the keys into the ignition. The car was freezing, so why was she burning up? This was no ordinary fever yet, at this moment, she didn't care. She had all the confirmation she would ever need from the techie.

Maybe, just maybe, she had warped everything inside out. Maybe she had mistaken the past twenty years for being real.

And what was happening now was the very first real thing in her life. Yes. That's how it was.

* * *

She was about to start the car when a set of headlights blinded her. She squinted her eyes and soon enough glimpsed a dark figure approaching her. She clutched at the steering wheel, realising the car in front of her had blocked her exit.

Before she could do anything else, a stocky palm knocked on her side shield. She was about to start screaming when a familiar face pressed itself up against the glass – the Chief Inspector from the police station.

Her mind gorged on all the paranoid configurations imaginable. What was this man doing here at this late hour? How did he know she was here? He must have followed her. And if he had, he must have seen her with the lab technician.

"We need to talk," he practically growled at her, and before she could protest, he heaved his body inside the car and threw a tablet onto her lap. Her body bristled at this behaviour, but his nod wouldn't take no for an answer.

She gripped the tablet, and several images were revealed to her. Viola recognised them as the English couple she had seen while she was in the waiting room at the clinic.

"London based. Wealthy. And about to raise hell. Legal dispute over a breach of contract. But InviNordica is making sure this gets squashed before it hits trial." The Chief Inspector didn't mince any words, and judging from his composure, he was about to bulldoze over Viola's lack of cooperation.

"Contract? What contract?" she queried, wanting to get at the core of the truth. He smirked back and pointed at the next page of the pdf document.

This answered her question. An official agreement that laid out the legal terms of the IVF treatment. At first sight, it had all the standard legal stuff, disclosing nothing out of the ordinary.

Her legal knowledge was as barebones as it could get, but there it was, in plain sight, measured with the clinical precision of an AutoCAD architectural drawing: the exact expected measurements of a child's body. "And no less than one hundred fifteen cm at age three and four months." These measurements proceeded to trace the baby's physical evolution up to the age of fifteen years. A myriad of different body measurements were given their own expectancies. All done with little room for error.

"What the hell is this?" The words somehow stumbled out of her mouth, but there was no afterthought. Her mind began to feel muddy. Uncertain. What did this mean? Was this even real? And if so, then where did she stand in all of this?

The Chief Inspector grinned at her, apparently amused at her confusion.

"These people aren't suing InviNordica for failed IVF attempts. But because they had a dream. If you can call it that. With swimming quickly becoming one of the major elite sports in the UK, they set out to for their girl to become a top-level swimmer. But things didn't quite go according to their plan." He recited the facts, yet beneath the words was unabated scorn. This man had made his judgement a long time ago. And it was without compromise. His finger raced to the next page and pointed towards even more data, to some foetus measurements expectancies.

"Get this. Their two-year-old daughter's body is not performing up to the contract's spec." He guffawed at his own words, "So they are suing InviNordica's ass to kingdom come." He delivered his punchline, and gave off another hoarse chuckle. Viola locked gazes with him and threw the tablet into his lap.

"This is some sick joke, right?" she hissed at him, with no more patience for this. This was enough to extinguish his laugh. He shook his head in denial.

"Miss Voss, this is very real." He flung the words at her.

Viola realised he wasn't a man to waste anyone's time with some petty evidence. The document he produced was real. All the more reason for her to get him out of her car. As soon as possible.

But as she nodded him out, he drilled his eyes into her, making sure he got her undivided attention.

"If our suspicions turn out to be true, the women involved in this thing are risking a minimum sentence of five to six years. And you are looking at three to four years for obstructing justice. But if I have any say, and believe me, I will, then I will see to it personally you get way more. Just so you remember what it is like to use sick people for your own agendas. Are we on the same page, Miss Voss?"

196

All of a sudden, Viola felt caged, blocked at every corner. However she turned this whole thing around, the implications would leave her life in upheaval forever. She needed to breathe, needed some focus, but this car, this man, everything was crushing in on her.

"I will make you a deal. I will get you off on probation, two to three months. You walk away all clean."

"In exchange for...?" she croaked out at him.

"For telling me what is going on inside there." He stated this as plainly as possible, without a grain of emotional baggage. And as she eyed him, she knew this man would carry out his threat without even the slightest flinch.

"Officer, I was at the clinic for one day only. They treated me professionally, and I have nothing to add. Now, if you please?" she whispered, then pushed his door open.

Without any protest, he climbed out of the car. Relief passed through her as he slammed the door behind him. But then he leaned his head against the window.

"Pity about your mitochondrial disease and Markus, huh? If I were you, I would probably do the same thing. Only this time, Mummy won't be around to save your ass. And the only rehab you will be doing will be behind bars." He grinned at her, then nodded her off.

She stamped on the gas and revved away.

If there was one thing she was certain of, it was that if their paths ever crossed again, it would be her downfall.

Night

Her foot was still glued to the gas pedal when she realised she was running on empty. She had driven blindly, hoping this endless, lightless forest road would lead her to some answers.

She hadn't expected to be ambushed by the Chief Inspector. The threats were simple and direct this time, but she didn't expect any less. She had earned them, after abandoning Pål like she had.

But this didn't shake her. What turned her world upside down were the simple, yet undeniable facts about InviNordica.

Surely this document had to refer to something other than a living and breathing human. A being of flesh and blood, with chromosomes threaded through each of its cells. With a soul radiating from the deepest recesses of its being. A marvel of life. Someone who would put all their unconditional trust in her mother from day one.

Yet, having seen that contract, she realised this child was little more than a piece of re-engineering, a proof of concept, set up to some ideal specification by people who expected more.

A lot more.

She felt queasy just thinking about it. Her mind was spinning into the dark corner tainted by the memories of her son. There was a clear border that separated her and those parents. She was certain of that. After all, these people had clearly made their baby into some twisted construct. They had done this out of some desire that she couldn't quite grasp. A superficial want.

Then she held herself back. Because she realised it was easy enough to judge their choices.

But when she thought about it, wasn't it every parent's unvoiced wish? Didn't we all yearn for our kids to be more resilient, smarter, stronger, more attractive, more able to handle the tough hurdles of the current world? And didn't we invest all our savings, and our time, to give them the best chance possible, the best shot at a future? Sending them to the most prestigious schools, giving them the best tutors, feeding them the most nutritious food, and showering them with the latest educational toys. All done in the name of giving our loved ones a head start in this rat race. And did anyone judge this course of action?

So why shouldn't these people be allowed to do what she had just seen laid out in that contract? Were they any different to the rest of us?

She had no problems with this part. She could maybe even see a part of herself in their actions. But then the other sort of questions appeared. The ones that weren't so easily answered.

Would their baby's success make them more fulfilled? And who was this done for, ultimately? After all, how could they know if their needs and dreams would also be their kid's? With such high expectations, how would these people feel if their kid turned out to be something less? Would they love it as much as if it had been perfect? Would they be able to love a cripple? And would they understand what unconditional love really is? That it wasn't built upon wants, needs, or expectations, but on giving themselves to their little ones, loving them and accepting them as an autonomous entity.

Where was she in all of this?

There was the mitochondrial disease. While she didn't quite understand these people's actions, her Markus had come to be out of pain and necessity. Surely that had to count for something. If not for this necessity, Ingrid's boy would never see into his mother's eyes. She could question these parents' motivations for building the perfect specimen, but could she question Ingrid for saving her child from a certain death?

Still, the doubt hammered away at her. Bit by bit, her conscience crumbled. Was she actually any better than them?

Suddenly, she stopped the car as the snowed-in forest road ended abruptly. She eyed the surrounding area.

And realised she was at a dead end.

Chapter 29

Thursday, 18th February 2016
Dawn
Viola stepped out of her car and ploughed through the knee-deep snow towards her apartment. She hadn't made it to the door before she was greeted by Stine's worn face. The old woman was shaking from the unbearable cold, yet she stood there as sturdy as a rock at Viola's door.

"You wanna come in?" The last thing she wanted was Stine occupying her apartment for the rest of the morning. But as she glanced at her, she felt sorry for her. Fortunately, Stine shook her head to Viola's offer but barricaded the entrance with her body.

As the old woman removed her wool hat, it struck Viola what terrible shape she was in. Feverish eyes, bloodshot from lack of sleep, sunken cheeks – she was falling apart. And it somehow struck Viola as ironic, each of them with their lives torn to pieces, each with their own drama playing out at a high note. Viola knew this wouldn't hold for much longer. Stine's heart wouldn't hold, nor would hers.

"You found her, didn't you, Miss?" Stine shrilled the words at Viola with a delirious insistence, while her trembling hands unpacked a container of Snus, probably the only way for the old woman to soothe her nerves.

"Stine, please. I have zero proof she is in there." Viola sighed, hoping the softness of her tone would somehow take off the sharpest edge of Stine's turmoil.

But upon hearing Viola's resistance, Stine grabbed a huge chunk of Snus and started to cram it into her upper lip. Satisfied with a moist hit of tobacco, her body relaxed enough to collect her thoughts and continue.

"Miss! Why should I, a stupid farmer widow, have to explain the simple things to Miss? Huh? She is in there. One hundred percent sure." She chewed through her Snus, then spat some in front of her.

"So now we have that settled. Yes?" Stine pursed her lips into a hard circle.

"And Miss is gonna go in there. And Miss is gonna get my Marianne back home. Right? Or I'll have to go to the police. To get their help, of course. Maybe even today." Stine added the words, but to Viola they seemed far from an afterthought. Had she miscalculated this woman's intentions? Were they a part of some kind of scheme? Viola's body strained at the mere thought.

"I told you I have no proof she is in there. But for the sake of argument, let's say she is. Do you think the police will roll out the red carpet for her when they find out what's happened inside there? She will be just as much an accomplice as everyone else." Viola pushed her argument, but immediately saw she wasn't getting through.

"So maybe Miss should hurry, then? Huh? With me going to the police? Surely?" Stine smirked at her line of logic, which smelt nothing short of extortion. And one thing was sure, Viola wouldn't be blackmailed, no matter how broken and desperate Marianne's mother was.

"And your conscience? Isn't that your daughter?" Viola questioned Stine, but the moment she uttered the words, she realised a simple fact. This woman lived by different ground rules. If she had a conscience, it was applied only when it was convenient.

And as if to confirm Viola's thoughts, Stine chuckled hoarsely.

"Me, Miss? Me? I've killed animals with me bare hands since I was five. Small pleasure in every day. And I care for my whole family, even if some of them are alcoholics and wife-beaters. And after what that girl has gotten me through? All those years, all the worries and those sleepless nights." Stine hissed at Viola, while baring her Snus-infested teeth. "No. No. No. Two years of this shit. Enough! She is in there! Mark my words! She comes home or I go to the cops. Then she and the rest of those mito-d sluts will end up on the front page of Miss's newspaper." The old woman spat the words with vehemence.

Yet it wasn't the old woman's deep-seated contempt that jolted Viola's mind awake. It was the mention of the other women that fired off all the red lights.

Had she heard Stine correctly? How could the old woman know about the other women? After all, Viola had never mentioned them to anyone. Most of all not to Stine.

Viola locked gazes with Stine and searched her eyes for any clues.

Still, Viola wasn't about to let this go that easily.

"Mito-d? What sluts?"

"Miss. I'll go to police on Monday. That's four days to find my daughter and get her out." Stine's eyes glared at Viola, letting her know their talk was finished.

Then she spat out the rest of her Snus on Viola's shoes and left.

Chapter 30

She was back at her home, up in her bedroom. The only positive thing right now was that Ronny hadn't yet come home from the night shift. She considered herself lucky, as there would be no confrontation. Their relationship wouldn't bear that. She knew it would be easiest if she vanished. Just like Marianne. Maybe this would raise a lot of questions but, ultimately, it would also save a lot of heartache.

But then, she felt someone staring at her back. It was him. He stood behind her. Observed her. How long had that been?

"What's going on?" Ronny voiced his question, searching her face for any clue to the reason behind her frenzied packing. Yet, this time, his words were tainted with fear.

"Gotta go away for a job. Be back in a few days."

"You going back there? To that clinic?"

"Where the hell did that come from?" She was in an uproar, but was stung by the hypocrisy behind her reaction. How could she be angry at him when he had shown how far he was willing to go for her?

"From the same place, where I watched you sacrifice that policeman's reputation. I know you. You wouldn't do that if there wasn't someone valuable. Back there. This is not one of your stories. It's your body. And what about your condition?" His tone was filled with pleading, begging her to stop this. But she wouldn't stop. No. She *couldn't*. Her choice had been made, and the only thing left for her was to flee.

She eyed her bag, all packed and ready, grabbed it and began to leave. As he saw that, she felt his disappointment hanging heavily in the air. She knew what he was thinking: wasn't he worth more than this? Hadn't he given her more than she was giving him now?

She knew he was at an emotional cliff edge. It was only two days ago that he had almost left her. How much more beating could they take?

"You've fought half of your life for a relationship. Lied about your condition so we would be a couple. And now... after all this shit. Look! I am still here..." She saw it in his face; he couldn't grasp why she behaved this way.

"And now you are going to throw it all away?"

Her stomach clenched into a knot as she heard his words.

"Because after this... I can't anymore. I just can't." She had known it was coming, but he had finally said it.

Somehow she had hoped she would make it out the door before he managed to summon enough strength to voice his feelings. But there it was. The plain truth.

When she broke the silence, she did it with a nod. She was fully aware of what he had said. And accepted it.

This only aggravated him more.

"Who the hell are you doing this for, really? Is it to help that woman? Or just..." His voice grew even more desperate.

"Go ahead. Just say it!" She pleaded with him to finish what he was going to say. She saw it in his twisted lips.

There was no going back now. He took a deep breath, then let it all out.

"Just to fulfil your own fucking needs, right?"

Ronny never got his answer, nor any confirmation. She knew that if she stayed here long enough, she would have to be honest with herself.

And at this point, it was just asking way too much of her. It was easier to run out. Sacrifice what they had.

Chapter 31

Morning

Pål had nightmares. Many of them. He dreamt he wet himself in bed like a sickening brat. But when he woke up, he realised it wasn't a dream. The bed was soaked.

Then he heard the doorbell, and immediately cursed at whoever had dared to wake him up in the middle of the night. But as he drew the curtains away, sunshine punched itself through the drapes. His blinded eyes rushed towards the clock. It was ten twenty-five. In the morning.

And the doorbell still wouldn't stop ringing.

He dragged himself towards the door, as he tried to make sense of his bathrobe. To tie it up, make himself decent. Right or left, this or that. It didn't matter anyway. Why did he care, really? He wouldn't open that door anyway. He never did. Because there was never any reason to.

Despite this, he slid next to the doorframe and remained there. He put his ear to the cold steel and listened.

"Pål, I know I made a mess..." He heard a faint whisper on the other side. It was that goddamned

206

journalist. Wasn't it enough that she ruined his life once? Or was his recollection of the past jumbled up again?

"Pål, I need your help. How is that for pathetic, huh? I need your help with those women."

The begging tone in her voice gave her away, he realised she was desperate. Probably way too scared to go back there by herself.

Lately, nobody wanted his help. At least not since... not since... *Him* and *Her* disappeared from his life.

He preferred to call them that. Him and Her. It was easier. More detached. It kept the worst monsters away. The ones that broke some people. But not him.

He slid even closer to the doorframe and listened. Yes. She was still there.

"All these years... I pretended to be okay. You know how that is?" she whispered to him.

She should speak for herself. Maybe she had problems, but he was just fine.

Except that no one else thought so. Certainly not his shrink, who barged into his apartment twice a week. He treated Pål like a retarded child who couldn't even manage a quickie to the toilet, much less taking care of the mundane things, like paying the bills, or even buying groceries.

Maybe Pål forgot some things. From time to time. But it was nothing serious.

"And I just know... some part of you cares." He heard her whisper a plea thickly layered with despair.

And these words reverberated in his mind.

But did he really care? Maybe a long time ago. Before the essential stuff got ripped away from his life. However much that damned shrink had tried to confuse him, he had a clear recollection of why he lost his son and wife.

Well, sort of.

And on the other side of the door was a woman who had bombarded what was rest of his life to shreds. So why should he care about what she had to say now?

"Yes, you do. Otherwise you wouldn't listen to me now." He heard her choke on her words. Was she crying? He breathed in and listened.

"I don't... care." Pål croaked out the only words he could manage in response.

Immediately, he heard a rustle on the other side, and felt it as she slid closer to the door. He silenced his breath and felt her next to him. Viola's words, his thoughts, they didn't really matter. Nothing she said would sway his decision. He would never open that door.

And then, tears began to streak down his face.

What the hell was wrong with him?

It was because of the door between them. This steel frame, a barrier, made this intimacy possible. Something that would have never happened if he saw her eye to eye.

This proximity, between him and her, it was the closest he ever got to a simple hug. And he felt something he hadn't felt since he lost his family.

A little bit of human.

A sigh passed through his body as he pushed away the lump in his throat. His whole body quivered, he knew he would regret this but he reached for the bolt and began to unlock the door.

Late morning

Viola sat beside Pål in his car, and took in the subtle features of his profile. His skin was stretched across his face as if his corpse had received an all-too-eager makeover at a funeral parlour.

As she eyed Pål, her gut feeling told her this man would never find his way. His family, their deaths, his condition, the irrationality of it all, made Viola think he would never recover. And none of this was his fault.

Yet he had let her into his apartment, listened to her plea, and finally said yes. Despite what she had done, how she had treated him, he was still willing to help her. Only this time it was different.

208

This time both of them were risking so much more. She had received a clear ultimatum from her mother, and right now, she was headed towards the clinic, about to go against everything she had promised Anne. This choice was irreversible, personally and professionally.

She knew she had built up a hall of false mirrors. A kaleidoscopic insanity which couldn't hold for much longer. Standing right in the middle of this, she had lost track of which image of herself was the original one, her true self.

Yet when she eyed Pål right now, she realised here was a man who had lost it all. Then lost himself. Despite this, he was still with her. Willing to help her. And all of a sudden, her problems felt quite insignificant.

Maybe he didn't have anything to lose anymore, maybe he felt some kinship in their mutual hell. Or just maybe, he realised that the only thing that made sense at this point, was to be of help to others.

She eyed Pål, squeezed his hand.

"Thank you," she whispered.

PART FOUR: Crash

Vlog, 120th entry 3.2.2014

"After three attempts, the dice were rolled. *Riksen,* Oslo's university hospital, told me to get lost. They didn't have anything more to contribute to my pregnancy. When I asked them for a recommendation to another clinic, another IVF, they told me to take it easy. Think about it. Reconsider my options... Come again! What options? No fucking way. So I've found illegal ways through the Net and through social media. Because the Norwegian Health System won't lift a goddamned finger to help me. And what do you know! Immediately, I got branded as one of those hysterical fertility tourists. Willing to pay up hard cash. No better than a prostitute. But I am not a whore looking to sell my body. Don't you see this is about something entirely different? I won't take it easy." Sara wrenched her voice into the web camera while Marianne sat beside her.

The blogger realised that Sara couldn't contain her tears any longer. They began to roll freely down her cheeks, streaming her mascara all over her face. Marianne's eyes lit up as if with fire, the way of an anchor-woman when she felt she had one hell of a story.

She wiped the smirk off her lips, and slipped into the field of view of the webcam. Then she nodded with full emotional engagement.

"Listen to her, gals! Sara here is one of my most ardent followers. She came here all the way from *Bodø* – that's 2000km to you folks. And she did it just to talk to me and share her story. And by God, what a story it is!" Marianne pepped up the audience with her blistering enthusiasm.

Meanwhile, she noticed Sara had become unglued. She halted, then threw herself over the girl. Hugged her to herself. And while she stroked the weeping girl's forehead, she proclaimed to her public:

"If anybody tells you that you need to take it easy, they are goddamned liars. Sara here is barely thirty. But from thirty-five, the quality of her eggs will dramatically drop off, and her time will be running out. What then? Will she still listen to those liars? That she should be fucking taking it easy?" She finished and grabbed Sara's head, then forced the woman to look her right in the eyes.

"Sara! You are on the threshold of a cliff with your fertility. Don't let anyone tell you what to do; you have options!" Marianne knew she had to make this girl see the truth. And she was getting through to her as Sara nodded sheepishly back to her.

But then Sara stopped and whispered to the blogger.

"Marianne? I met a man recently. Warm, compassionate. Do you think I should talk to him about this?" Sara stumbled with the words but finally voiced her question. Then she glanced at Marianne, her eyes filled with respect, looking to the oracle for life advice.

But as Marianne heard this, she glanced Sara over, then shook her head in disapproval.

"I don't have any man to share my grief with. You know why? Because I am sure I won't find one who understands me. And you know why? Because I am ashamed, just like you are, girl! Because everyone around us thinks you've failed as a woman. You are a second-class citizen, baby. A convict of your fate. Do yourself a favour. Forget about him, dear."

"But, but he is so considerate. Maybe I should talk to him? Maybe he would understand?"

"Sara! Sara! Baby! Get a grip on yourself. Just listen to yourself. Hear that? Just think about it. The one thing you were meant to do, that only we can do, you've failed at. And miserably at that. Remember who you are, Sara! And if you should forget, then just listen to your period. How do you feel when it comes around?" The blogger held Sara close to her. Whispered to her. Marianne knew this girl needed her more than ever. Sara was lost, and it was her duty to make her see this fact.

"It's a joke?" Sara asked, but was unsure if her answer was the correct one. Then she focused her tear-filled eyes on Marianne's face. And the blogger clapped at her like an obedient dog.

"That's right, girl. It's one cosmic joke. And the last laugh is on you. What's the point? That's how you should feel. The period is a fucking taunt! And so is this man. Because when he learns the truth, that's how he will think about you. Right?"

Sara nodded back a resounding yes with her puppy eyes.

While she still caressed Sara with her fingers, Marianne switched off the webcam and grabbed the mouse to see her site statistics. This was one stupefying show, and she expected nothing less than a flood of comments and bravos.

She caught her breath. And congratulated herself. She was good.

No. No. No.

She was freaking amazing!

But as her eyes scanned the results, she felt knives carve into her throat. She couldn't believe what was happening. Her show was dropping like a boulder in the water. People were switching her off like she was some kind of leper. It was a damned exodus.

Chapter 32

Magda sent Viola another weary glance. Behind the older woman was an entourage of a dozen doctors. And all of them watched Magda restlessly.

When Viola had arrived at the clinic, she had fought a small battle with the staff at the reception desk. But no amount of pleas would convince an otherwise serviceable team.

Viola realised how quickly things change. After all, just a couple of days ago, everyone here was prepared to do everything to satisfy her slightest whim. Yet now, it was obvious nobody cared about her recent stay, and even less about her genetic condition.

So, when the nurse at the desk had finally issued an implicit warning that Viola's badgering would cause a friendly visit from the local police, Viola had blasted right past the desk and through the clinic.

She knew this was short-sighted, or maybe just plain stupid. And indeed it had caused an immediate uproar, but it had gotten Viola all the way up to Magda's office, to her doorstep. Where Viola had stumbled upon the female CEO with her band of followers.

And now, as Viola's eyes went back to Magda, she realised she had about ten seconds to convince Magda about the authenticity of her motivation.

The presence of the doctors didn't help. Viola wasn't sure how much they actually knew about the CRISPR splicing activities in their own clinic. But if she presumed right, probably only a few select people closest to Magda had any idea how far things had gone. Viola had a hard time imagining any more would be involved, certainly not in Norway, and definitely not on a larger scale. She gathered most of the doctors had a strong moral spine and would never even consider these kinds of human clinical trials.

So this made the matter even more difficult, since she couldn't reveal her conditions or what lay behind her last visit. And the last thing she wanted to do at this moment was use Magda's secretive trials as leverage against her. Viola knew Magda wouldn't be blackmailed, and even if Viola were to do it, it would only be a bluff on her part.

"Sorry, I can't allow you inside again." Magda pursed her lips as she thrust the plain fact at Viola. Something Viola recognised as an irreversible decision made long before she set foot in this place.

"Doctor. Should we continue our rounds?" One of the doctors locked gazes with Magda, suggesting this was not the time or place to comfort patients with way too much baggage on their hands.

Viola winced at the doctor's impatience. She had come way too far to blow it now. She wouldn't be stopped by Magda's brush-off, and certainly not by this entourage of overpaid middle-aged schmucks.

"Just about finished here," Magda bit back at the doctor, reminding everybody who was still in charge. Anne and Magda shared a lot in common, and this uncompromising demeanour was further proof of that. If anything, it made Viola feel right at home.

"Miss Voss, you asked why I won't let you in, right? Well, let me recheck my facts..." Magda's words were drenched in sarcasm, as she drilled her eyes into Viola. "After lying to my staff, after that microphone stunt, you suddenly realised how badly you need to become a mother again, huh?" Magda rasped at Viola.

"Goodbye, Miss Voss."

"What do you know about my fucking need?" Viola spat the words hoarsely at Magda's back. This got everybody's attention. The CEO stopped in her tracks, swerved around, and searched Viola's face.

"Doctor, this is nonsense. Send this lunatic off." One of the doctors summed the whole situation up quite succinctly, but Magda held him off with a steely glance. Then she nodded at Viola to make her case.

"You know what? I was twenty-three years old when I hung a sign over my bed. It said: *And this too shall pass.* It was a comfort that however bad things got, someday they would get better. And since then, everything I did, every choice I made, was in an effort to survive. I never shopped at malls during the days, as there would be too many kids there."

Viola felt her chest constrict again. An invisible force stemming from these words, causing her to gag on the lack of air. But she had to go on. No matter what.

"I shunned relationships just because I knew where they were all headed. That row of questions, which I wasn't prepared to answer. What about babies? How do you feel about them? No pressure, but you are forty and time isn't on your side, huh? Maybe we should up our frequency, you know? Go about it a little bit more scientifically? Maybe you are not relaxed enough? You should really take it easy, huh? Those kinds of questions." She couldn't breathe.

"I deleted my Facebook account so I would not have to look at those gut-wrenching new baby pictures all of my... ex-friends were sharing. And every time I applied for

216

a new job, I was terrified that the people there would attempt to get to know me. The real fucking me. A person." She felt anger wash over her whole body. Yet this time, the anger felt like a relief. It fuelled her mind, and pushed her farther and deeper into the pain.

She summoned up the little strength that she had left, gasped for a deep breath, then spat out the rest.

"I survived by running away for twenty years. And you know what? I still have the very same sign I hung up all those years ago. But by now it's some fucking joke. A naive reminder that certain things just never pass." By the time she was finished, she was trembling uncontrollably.

"So, do you still want to debate my need?" she finally spat out.

It was as if she had dropped a bomb in the middle of them. The doctors' faces were drained from this public confession as their numb eyes shied away from her direct gaze.

Magda fished out her phone and speed-dialled.

"Get Miss Viola Voss a room."

Late afternoon

Viola's toes cramped as she stood on the freezing tiles of the changing room floor. She tried to wiggle them to get some warmth while she changed into a patient's gown.

Still, the change had gone according to plan. No one had bothered to check her bag. Inside the bag were her cell phones. Two of them. One was packed in casually and was meant to be found and confiscated. But there was the other one. And it was crammed into a side compartment, private enough to survive even the more thorough search. It was the key to her plan, the only way she could contact Pål after she got settled in.

And as she glanced up, she realised she had a nurse and some kind of clerk before her. Both of them bored their eyes into Viola as she changed. Not exactly her idea of privacy. But they didn't seem too preoccupied with Viola's distress.

The clerk nodded the nurse off, suggesting some privacy. And as the nurse disappeared, he flung a bunch of papers in front of Viola, then presented himself as the clinic's legal advisor.

He told her he was there to make sure Viola understood the legal side of these contracts. First and foremost, what it entailed for both sides, as the man stressed several times.

Viola knew what that meant. This errand boy dressed up as a lawyer was here to make sure she signed all of them without so much as a squeak of protest. And as the man laid out all the NDAs, contracts, obligations, and payment plans, he went over all the terms of Viola's stay.

"That NDA, that's standard-type issue. But since you will be progressing to the west wing of our program, it has some non-standard paragraphs. Please, consider them as perks," he whispered and opened up the payment plan as proof.

Her eyes scanned over the treatment costs, medication costs, lodging costs, clinic's services, and so on. And as she realised the prices had been slashed by close to ninety percent, uneasiness crept up on her.

How many women did they get through this door who had mitochondrial disease? A disease found in one of fifteen thousand women. Take a wildly optimistic guesstimate, five a year. And how many of those were desperate enough to proceed with the treatment? Make that one, maybe two.

How many cells filled with fresh mito-d did they get out of them? Surely more than enough to recompense the costs of the treatment. Embryonic stem cell research was a big deal, and her kind of cells were a hot currency. And even if the patient didn't give her permission, it wasn't exactly a guarded secret that some clinics divided the single cell after Pre-implantation Diagnosis. A second cell was created, the perfect specimen for further stem-cell research. Outrageous private IVF prices, topped up with behind-the-scenes cell-research, that was one way to ensure the company's steady growth.

She knew her condition was special. And she was sure she would receive preferential service. But as she glanced at the numbers, her stomach wrung inside out. They didn't just need her, they were desperate to have her.

She pointed towards the payment plan, and sent him a questioning glance.

"The clinic's policy. You are on special terms, Miss Voss." He grinned at her. And she proceeded to sign the thing. Once she was finished, the lawyer grabbed her bag and emptied it out onto the table.

Nice, neat.

And without even a hint of Viola's approval.

One of the phones fell out.

"Hey, that's private stuff." Viola whipped up her head and sent the man a sharp glance. But he grabbed gently onto Viola's shoulder and hushed her protest.

"Miss Voss, if you care to take a closer look at the NDA, the document you just signed, you will see we are forced to do this. Precautionary rules. For your safety. And everyone else's," he assured her, and sent her another one of those placating grins.

Then he felt over her bag again, and this time his face lit up, as he located and fished out the second phone from its concealed compartment. With glee on his face, he tucked it away into one of the clinic's baggies. And with it, Viola's plan.

"Like you see, Miss Voss, you are on special terms."

Chapter 33

Evening

She had a very limited timespan to find any clues to Marianne's whereabouts. And the only way that would happen, would be if she found Ingrid.

But she had no illusions about whether Magda had made sure the staff would be paying careful attention to her whereabouts. And sure enough, there was rarely a moment where Viola felt completely alone. Whether it was a nurse watching her during a diagnosis, or some other staff member, she couldn't get away from the prying eyes.

So, she came up with a half-measure. She informed the head nurse about her spinal disc hernia that demanded frequent movement, especially walking. After some hefty discussions, and way too many protests from the staff, she was finally allowed to take longer walks around the clinic's premises.

This gave her the required pass to search for Ingrid. She trotted as fast as she could without calling unnecessary attention to herself. But she quickly found out that this would prove more difficult than initially thought. There was an unusually low count of patients in this place, and most of the rooms were simply locked. In a matter of two hours, she was not only stumped but empty-handed.

When she finally found some patients, she made her inquiry about Ingrid. But no one seemed to be willing to help. And the last thing she wanted to do was ask the staff. Way too many ripples and unwanted attention.

At the end of the day, her body felt punished. Not from the walking, but from the unease lashing at her mind. She kept reminding herself she was tough as hell. But the reality was, she was anything but.

In situations like this, she couldn't stand herself, or her weaknesses. They seeped through like a leaking roof and flooded her all over: worries she had ruined her life in the last week, doubts she was doing it for the right reasons, and self-flagellation over what she had done to Ronny. And even her mother.

The longer she stayed at this place, the worse this would get, she knew that. With her plan in shambles, Ingrid nowhere in sight, and Pål waiting for a call that might never come, she realised she had no idea what to do next.

Night

Late at night, Viola slumped down in the darkness of the TV room. Not because she needed to be here, or because she wanted to watch whatever was on the tube, but because in the murkiness, only occasionally lit up by the TV, she could quietly vent her frustration.

She had nowhere to turn, and tomorrow wouldn't be better. She would be faced with even tougher choices, as Magda expected her to proceed with the treatment.

Her attention was immediately drawn to the tube. On it was one of those sci-fi movies from the early nineties. A title with Ethan Hawke that Viola had failed to see. She rarely had time for movies or books, and certainly not some kind of wild dystopian speculations about a possible future. She watched Hawke's graceful features, yet she couldn't bring herself to remember what the movie's title was or what it was about.

Her mind wandered back to her situation. What the hell was she doing here? She had to accept it, Ingrid was gone. She would never see that woman again. And with her, all the answers Viola was hoping for.

And the more she thought about this, the more she realised there was only one way out of this. It was time to stop. Tomorrow, she would pack. Then leave this place for good.

All of a sudden her thoughts were interjected with a barely audible racket, originating from a chair way back in the room. Viola twisted around and noticed a familiar contour. She got up, and as she trotted towards a woman hiding away in a secluded corner, she heard a stream of barely audible words.

"Damn, damn, damn..."

And as Viola came even closer, she realised the words were interspersed with an occasional whimper, delicate enough so as not to be heard by anyone else watching the telly. Soon enough, Viola recognised the face.

It was Ingrid.

* * *

The last time they met, Viola couldn't tear her eyes away from Ingrid's radiance. The girl possessed an out-of-this world glow, something only a fulfilled body and soul could hope for.

Yet now, as Viola first glimpsed Ingrid, it was as if she eyed someone else. A torn face smeared with crass layers of mascara. Viola wondered if the woman was able to see anything beyond them.

But most of all, the woman's glow was replaced with a helpless dullness. She avoided direct eye contact with Viola while her posture told the whole story, it looked as though someone had given Ingrid way too many benzodiazepines. Either to calm down her nerves, or maybe just to shut her up.

The young woman's weakened hand scribbled slower than a two-year-old learning to draw. While she attempted to put down something unintelligible on the piece of paper, she gnawed at herself in a subdued whisper. As Viola approached her closer she finally heard what the young woman was saying.

"Am I a bad person?" she flogged herself. It was clear that for every time she repeated this sentence, it slowly evolved from being a question, transformed into an answer, then finally ended up in a full-blown judgement on herself.

Some place deep inside Viola, maybe the place where her heart used to be, was moved by this sight. Viola knew that once she would have done everything to soothe Ingrid's pain. Under normal circumstances, that is. But these were not normal circumstances. Viola needed her answers, no matter the consequences or moral hangover this might spew up later.

"Please, what's going on, hon?" Viola probed gently at first, but the woman failed to respond. Instead she continued to mumble to herself.

"Am I bad?" she said and tried to lock gazes with Viola, but her eyes refused to obey her. Her words were then immediately followed by a sob. This time a little bit louder. Enough to draw the staff's attention.

Viola noticed one of the nurses made eye contact with them, worried some incident might be afoot. Viola rested her hand on Ingrid's shoulder, then caressed her subtly. The woman relaxed enough to become quiet.

"They promised me it would be perfect. You see that, don't you? But now, it isn't. It's anything but. And I wanted so badly for my future kid to have a better life. You see. Don't you? Huh?"

"What? Your future child? Don't you have a child? Who was that kid back there when we first met? Wasn't he yours?"

"Whaaaat? No. No... Did I say that? Nooo... Silly me... I didn't say that. Did you hear that? I've got my son, Tobias." Ingrid struggled to make sense of what she had just said and, all of a sudden, she began to chuckle at her herself. Viola couldn't be sure anymore what the woman actually meant. Not only were her eyes fogged up on some drugs, but she was losing her mind as well.

If Viola was to get anything from her, she had to hurry, before the woman's awareness retreated. Or worse, the staff grabbed her and took her away. And maybe the way to go about it was to give the girl a little reality check. Maybe even scare her.

"Ingrid, I know people like that. If there is anything they made you do, forced you to lie, anything at all, you need to tell me now." Viola whispered in a hushed, yet urgent tone.

Yet as she put the pressure on Ingrid, the woman's eyes remained just as fuzzy. Viola was losing patience and gripped her arm, pressed Ingrid into her chair and slid close to her. Then fumed into Ingrid's ear.

"Listen, girl. What you are going to hear now, your future might depend on. I am not going to repeat myself. Tomorrow or the day after, at the latest, this place is going to be swarming with cops. Now take a look around. Do you see anyone else reaching out a helping hand? No. I am the only one you've got. You have to tell me who was that boy you were with. Because he certainly wasn't yours." If Viola didn't have a hold on the young woman's arm, she would have attempted a run for it, in spite of her condition. Ingrid's eyes fluttered with panic, sobering up, reassessing her situation.

"The clinic. They promised to do the fix. Splice a couple of genes in my future child. Only a couple. But now they say there might be side effects..." She gulped up everything at once.

"They can't help you with the mitochondrial disease treatment? Is that it?" Viola pursed her lips at Ingrid.

"Mitochondrial disease? No... No. No. No. Not that. Another gene. They said they could do it but his immune system might get damaged." Ingrid's voice began to take on a feverish pitch. Until it reached the nearby staff. Viola tempered Ingrid while she eyed the nurse.

"What gene?" She pressed Ingrid with even more urgency for the rest of the truth.

"What? Ah... his homosexuality gene. I am a Christian after all. But I still want to have him. You see? Does that make me bad?" She explained herself then searched Viola's eyes for approval.

Viola's mind went numb as she heard her. Was it some kind of joke? She checked Ingrid's eyes once again and it began to dawn on Viola that it was anything but.

As her eyes wandered, they fell back on the TV again. She began to recognise the movie again, something about some kind of dystopian society subdivided into groups. What were they? Valids and in-valids, some genetic haves and have-nots. Yet, the movie's name still escaped her.

Viola's mind snapped back to reality. She realised she still hadn't got what she had come here for.

"So, who was that kid when I first met you? Why did you lie to me? Did they force you?"

But before she could do anything, Ingrid curled up into her own shell and began to sob for real. And this time, it took only a couple of seconds before the nurse was upon them. Before Viola could intervene, the staff member dragged Ingrid away to her room. And when Viola wanted to accompany them, she got a scolding glance from the woman.

Viola was left alone in the shadows of the television's queasy lights. As her eyes took in the movie again, she could see that it was nearing its finale, as the main character, despite his genetic limits, managed to attain his goal. Despite the hurdles, he packed his body onto the spaceship. Made his way to the stars, and with it, he fulfilled his ultimate dream.

225

Viola watched the ending and felt bitter. She was struck by how blatantly false it felt. And she realised she had never felt farther away from her own goals than at this moment. She still had no idea if Marianne was here, nor where to look for her if she was.

But when she was about to get up, something fell out of her lap. She leaned over and picked up a crumpled piece of paper. On it were scribbled a few words.

Marianne is in the west wing.

Chapter 34

She felt bed railings as they cut into her thighs. Her thoughts should have focused on Ingrid's message. Yet the only thing that pounded at her mind was how deeply these rusty railings carved into her body. This felt familiar for some reason, as they made her body ache all over. Maybe because it was just like the dream she held onto for so many years.

She had always had a clear picture of herself, a woman who pushed on. Someone who got things done and accomplished her goals, no matter what came her way.

Yet now, when she approached her destination, her body folded into some unfamiliar sickness. Her mind spun uncontrollably in all sorts of directions. She knew exactly what she should be doing now. So why was she sitting here, wasting precious time?

What Ingrid had shared with her was undeniable. However much Viola tried, she couldn't explain away the facts that had been shoved right in her face. These women's greatest weakness was being ruthlessly exploited. She saw it in Ingrid's eyes, and immediately recognised this could have been her.

If Viola had learnt anything in her life, it was about dreams that could bring down the whole house. These kinds of dreams were the easiest to take advantage of. And the people at this clinic seemed to have made it their business to do so.

If she called the police right now, it would be the right thing to do. The most sensible way out of this. It would put a swift end to everything. Both for these women, and certainly for her dreams.

And maybe then, her hopes, her dreams, the ones which had poisoned her a long time ago, they would finally be released. Giving her room to breathe. Giving her a chance to start her life over again. Something she didn't doubt would be good for her. After all, didn't someone tell her they were the root of her suffering?

Yes. It would be a new start.

Then it began to dawn on her that through all these years, despite that Markus brought into her life ceaseless worries, bottomless angst, and grief, he also brought with him the most blissful moments she had ever experienced in her life. The ones which carved themselves into her soul, and showed her what it meant to be alive. Did one recompense the other? Was the price she and Markus paid for her dream worth it?

Then her eyes fell on the scrap of paper from Ingrid. And all of a sudden it was clear. There would be no call. No police.

She wouldn't let go of the dream. She couldn't.

Friday, 19th February 2016
Morning

Viola was looking at the sealed door to the west wing. The night had taken a brutal toll on her. With less than an hour of sleep, she was barely able to keep her legs straight.

The moment she approached the door, she realised this was a fortress, electronically hooked up to biometric fingerprint scanners, with the small bonus of CCTV cameras recording each entry. She wasn't getting in here, that was obvious.

And she had found no way to get in touch with Pål. Had he given up on her? It wouldn't surprise her. Their agreement had been for a daily update yet two days had passed with zero contact between them. The poor guy probably felt she had abandoned him yet again. And even if Pål decided to call in any law enforcement, it would most certainly be way too late. She was on her own.

But she also had a plan. It was as simple as it was desperate.

Her train of thought was interrupted as she caught a glimpse of a staff member who approached the door. He swept his thumb through the fingerprint scanner and made his way into the west wing corridor.

She knew she would be recorded, leaving traces of her entrance. But she also knew this gave her a time window, way too short, but maybe still long enough to make her way through the west wing.

If Marianne was there, she would find her.

But as she swerved her body, about to make a run for the door before it closed, she heard a familiar voice behind her back.

"Miss Voss!" It was Magda, and the only question was if the woman had spotted her mad plan of rushing into the west wing.

"I was... umm... About to do tests. In there?" Viola reached for the closest thing to an explanation, but couldn't help herself that it turned into a question.

She knew she was making an ass of herself. More than that, she was about to jeopardise everything she had fought for, if she didn't come up with something more credible. Her thoughts were immediately reflected in Magda's response.

"Right. Probably not in there. Anyway, I was looking for you. I am sorry, but you have to leave us. Now." Magda announced her decision without any further reasons, her eyes already pointing Viola towards the exit.

"What's going on?" Viola couldn't grasp what lay behind Magda's decision. Surely, it couldn't be that she was standing here. But then it struck her, there must be something more.

"Read the NDA? Maybe you should have thought about it before you dragged your mother in here," she lashed out.

"But I didn't! Viola protested. The last thing she would do would be to invite Anne there. Anne had made an ultimatum preventing her from approaching this place ever again. Had her mother had second thoughts after Viola's visit?

"Yes, you did. Or is that a freak accident that she is in the reception right now?"

"Do you think I want a story with this? If so, then why am I still here? The easiest thing would be to pick up the phone and talk the cops into paying a visit here. Has that happened? And the last week, I've broken the law way too many times to count. I've sacrificed two of my most important relationships. Just to be here. Please. Give me twenty minutes to talk to my wobbly mum. I can calm down her nerves. I can also reassure her there is nothing to fear. That's all I ask of you." She knew her plea was filled with desperation, but at this point, she didn't care. Anything to put out this fire.

Chapter 35

When she made her way into the reception, she realised there was no Anne there. Distraught, she looked around until her eyes landed on a woman's back.

When the woman turned, her mouth spat out another piece of Snus. Then she welcomed Viola by baring her rotten teeth. Stine.

"What the hell are you doing here?" Viola whispered, all the while peeking over her shoulder at the agog nurses who, from the look of things, had more than enough time to eavesdrop on their conversation. Viola pushed Stine aside and towards the entrance, preventing any unwanted overhearing.

"Come again! What the hell I do? What is Miss doing? Huh? A mess. That's what Miss is doing." Viola quickly grasped that the old woman was fuming with uncontrolled anger.

"Do you have any idea what you coming here might cost me? How will I find your precious daughter if I get thrown out of this place? Listen! This whole thing, it shouldn't be my problem anymore." Viola glared at Stine. It was about time to set the old bat straight.

"Not Miss's problem?" Stine whispered hoarsely, and proceeded to dig into her purse. Something that turned out to be way more difficult than initially expected. Viola watched as the woman's frustration escalated, yet this time not because of Viola but at the mess inside her purse.

"An officer. Chief Inspector from Grønland. He paid me a visit yesterday. Asking questions about Miss Viola. Nice little fellow, ain't he? Huh?" Viola heard Stine utter the words, but she had trouble focusing on their content as she watched Stine bare that sick grin again.

"So...?" Viola's words trailed off in the most anticipatory manner. She knew this didn't bode well. Her intuition, which for the most part didn't fail her, gave off blaring warnings of what was about to come. And soon enough, Stine pushed an innocent-looking envelope into Viola's chest.

And when she opened it, there they were, the rest of the pictures Viola had received from Anne. When she first laid eyes on them, they were mostly of the women here, playing with their kids.

Amongst them, there had been the picture that could implicate Viola in the whole affair. But it was way too vague and could be called into question by any legal proceedings. Anne may have used those pictures, but simply as a deterrent, to prevent Viola from digging any further.

Yet, right now, Viola eyed what she presumed to be the complete set. The pictures that her sixth sense had screamed existed, but which she had never seen.

Until now.

And there it was. Leaving no doubt as to her identity. Full frontals of Viola, smiling, listening. Perfect material for glitzy centrefold close-ups, if one so wished. Only this time, the only centrefold Viola would be making, would be as the main story of her own paper, her reputation and persona shredded beyond any repair.

"So, if I give this to him. Does it make it Miss's problem?" Stine lashed out at Viola with the obvious, and only now was Stine showing her true self, something even Viola didn't expect of her.

But what worried Viola more were the clear implications of what had happened behind the scenes. It began to dawn on her that these pictures weren't some crazy fluke, an accident that just happened by itself. Far from it. They had to have been part of a plan, much earlier on. But by whom and for what ends? This was something she couldn't grasp.

"Stine, if she is anywhere, it would be the west wing. But it's way off limits to me. The only way to get in there is if I do the treatment myself." Viola voiced the only clues she had to go on, hoping it would placate Stine, but the only thing it managed to do was collect an indifferent shrug from her.

"So?" Stine slid closer to Viola. And as Viola felt the old woman's ragged breath on her chin, she thought she would vomit. Not because of the smell of her rotting teeth, but mostly because she knew what Stine would demand from her.

"I can't," Viola whispered.

Despite that she gave out no concrete information, just the mere mention of the treatment, gave voice to a most tangible horror. Viola wasn't about to risk the remaining shreds of her sanity. She wasn't about to throw herself into the emotional snake pit called her past. And Stine would have to deal with that. Without any explanations.

But what followed was only silence filled with Stine's indifference. Viola realised the old woman wasn't prepared to empathise with her inner drama.

"Personal reasons. Dammit," Viola added, and made sure she left no doubt. But the old woman's face blanked out.

"Miss, I care diddly shit for personal reasons."

233

Viola's mind raced, and her stomach churned into some impossible knots. She realised now there might be no other way out, other than to share her truth.

No.

Bringing back those memories would grind her to dust. And even if she summoned some strength to talk about them, would Stine even care? Viola's eyes locked with Stine's, then she shook her head no. Stine eyed her, sighed, and pushed the envelope into Viola's hands.

"Keep them. I got my own. Bye." She screeched her rubber boots as she made her way towards the exit.

This abrupt end shook Viola. She had presumed she held the best hand. It was she who had the mitochondrial disease. The very thing that gave her a free pass to this place. And it was she who had managed to talk Magda into something that resembled trust.

But that was before Viola found out about Stine's pictures and her intentions. The woman had no second thoughts about going further with her blackmail.

Still, what terrified Viola most at this moment were the consequences of the whole matter. She knew what some parts of the media did to people like the ones in the clinic.

She had always tried to remain unbiased in each of her stories. She knew that credibility was the most important thing a journalist could possess. But she had seen way too many of her fellows blurt their own political and ethical attitudes right out into the open. And then they had tried to convince the public their stories remained impartial. And she was certain that the same men would sit high up on their moral stools, and pretend neutrality while they lashed out at the clinic and these women's actions.

No. She had to stop Stine, no matter the cost.

"What? Wait. Listen!" she begged Stine.

Viola's voice was loaded with a strong undercurrent of desperation, and it had an impact, as it stopped Stine and focused her attention back at Viola.

"Listen, I was never supposed to have Markus. But I didn't listen to the doctors. They warned me. Even if the child made it through the pregnancy, the odds were heavily stacked against him. Yet... I still didn't listen." Viola dug for a deeper breath.

"And when he was... born... he was healthy. Can you imagine that? And then, he was in that bathtub one day... and he... he... just slipped. But it was nothing. Just a small, stupid bruise from hitting the side of the tub. Surely it was my fault. But he was okay. He was okay," she babbled. "But then he just fell asleep. And... and... never woke up again. The doctors told me it was because of a genetic defect. He was sick after all. Mitochondrial disease. And the fall, it made the defect come back." Viola was about to implode, the past crushing at her every pore.

The strain was just way too much, and her body began to shudder. Her hands gripped at the railing, seeking some support, yet she realised too late that there was no railing there. She barely recovered.

Her senses began to shut down. One by one, they abandoned her. Her hearing submerged below some thick, fluid substance, her sight blurred out of focus. But she pushed on with the confession with the faint hope that she would convince the old woman.

"Not a day goes by when I don't wake up with a burning desire to still have a child. But then I remember Markus. Every day I wake up and dream that some doctor will tell me I can have a child again, and it will not be some 50/50 crap shoot but a guarantee of success. And every day I tell myself I must be mad to even entertain these thoughts. This is never going to happen. Then I came to this place and I finally met this doctor. She made this promise to me. And right now I understand, I can't. Do you understand what you are asking of me? I can't. I can't do this. Not for you or anyone. Never again. I see that now." Viola spewed out the last words. And as her whole reality slipped away from her, she held onto the only comfort she had left. She wasn't doing it for herself. This was for their children.

Stine stepped back.

"Miss does the treatment. Only way to make up her sins."

Late morning

Her pale fingers jerked at the patient's gown, digging into her thigh again. Her mind kept sliding in and out of the grimy reality, in and out of focus, Stine's words still echoed away in her head, wringing her into a decision she wasn't ready for.

Then her mind was yanked back to the present, as she felt Magda standing over her.

"All sorted out?" Magda eyed Viola, and judging from her expression, immediately sensed something was way off.

"I had doubts..." Viola said.

"If you could get rid of her?"

"No. If it was worth it. Any of it..." she said, but caught herself in the sheer stupidity of this act. Did she still have any illusions Magda could change any of it?

"And now?" Magda's concern was clear. Viola understood she was doing very little to placate Magda's growing concern. But here she was with her gut torn to shreds. Here she was, pressed up against the wall. The gene therapies were readily available to her, the dream of her life, a healthy child, was within her reach.

And if that wasn't enough she was still convinced she was doing this for more noble reasons, other than her own need. The women who needed to be saved. They were her sisters. And if anybody understood their struggle, it should be her.

Only she had gone through as much as they had. Only she understood what it was to arrange her life according to one desire only. And only she knew what it was like to finally get pregnant but still battle with self-doubts. How it felt to wake up every morning and disbelieve everything

236

about this miracle of life. Unease and constant checking. Checking for the heartbeat, checking for the gestational sack. Only she knew how the pregnancy was tainted with fear instead of celebration. And why shouldn't it be? After so many of the disappointments that infertility brought with it. Why shouldn't she do everything to protect herself from a potential heartbreak?

She glanced up at Magda, bit down her teeth, then put on her best smile.

"I am ready for the cycle."

Chapter 36

Saturday, 20th February 2016
Afternoon
They said the operating room with its cushioned table was state of the art. So why was her body twisted into some freakish position? The table cut into her thighs and distorted her spine.

The whispers from the nurses enveloped her. The less she heard them, the more her fears surfaced, spinning her mind into some murky interpretations. Were they commenting on the folds around her stomach? Maybe something was wrong with her diagnosis? Or simply just making fun of her? Anything to make it through yet another boring day.

Her eyes glanced up at the LED screen just over her. In an instant, it lit up and exposed a glass catheter that slid into view, revealing what she presumed to be the embryos. They were neatly lined up in rows on the glass surface.

One of the doctors loomed over her with his burdensome smile. She could feel his breath. Was she imagining things or was his breath tainted with alcohol? Barely noticeable, covered by a heavy aftershave, but still there.

Although she had little technical knowledge of the inner workings of this profession, she recognised him as an embryologist. His stubby finger led her attention towards the LED screen again, suggesting some vital information was coming.

"Miss, please direct your eyes to the screen. I need you to select the embryo numbered #X045 and #X053, which are the best suited specimens. Can you confirm the choice?"

How could she choose between what was in front of her? Each embryo stemmed from her body. A part of her. Each one the possibility of a life.

It didn't take long before her prolonged silence collected the staff's curious glances. Maybe some of them were capable of concern, but right now, she only sensed impatience.

"Miss Voss. Are you okay?" A voice prompted her.

What will happen to the rest of them? Yet, she didn't have the strength to voice this question. For them, it was pure formality. If she had got as far as this table, she shouldn't be asking in the first place.

The staff would inform her in their most casual tone that considering her age, she was a suitable candidate for the insertion of two embryos into her body. Simply because of the smaller chance to conceive her own eggs. Of the fifteen possible lives on the screen, two, at most, would make it into her body. The rest would simply be frozen or dispensed with. How silly of her to even care. After all, wasn't she getting what she came for?

From the look on the medics' faces, everybody realised she was having second thoughts. Soon enough she also heard sighs. After all, for them, it was the most peculiar thing to go through. Especially at this stage.

"Dispensed with?" she heard herself say out of nowhere, even though no one had said anything that might cue her strange question.

And this confused the medics even further.

239

"Miss Voss. Do we proceed?" the embryologist pressed at her with his question. Viola grasped for any kind of resolution within herself. She knew that if she aborted this moment, there would be no going back. No second chances.

It was all about freeze, flush, repeat.

All these doubts were only her sentimentality talking. She asked these people questions that she already knew the answers to. The IVF industry had a mission to help women in need. It communicated to women all over the world that their fairy tale ending was just an embryo transfer away. And they did this despite discarding thousands of embryos each year. The clinics would protest this, and reassure everybody that the embryos were frozen for later use, at least those that were deemed worthy. But could anyone be absolutely sure which ones were deserving of life and which ones weren't?

Nobody cared to mention this, much less object to it.

So maybe it was silly of her to dwell on these minor details. Way too many of the hormonal drugs, clouding her line of reasoning. This clinic had good reason to flush a couple of lives down the toilet.

"I confirm." Viola clenched her teeth and voiced her final decision.

Freeze, flush, repeat.

Late afternoon

As she was wheeled towards the west wing, she expected to feel something.

Yet, right now, everything escaped her. Despite no drugs being used during the procedure, she felt her mind was eroded, barren of thoughts. Her emotions were blunted. Whatever happened back there, one thing was sure, something broke. Inside her.

Despite the numbness that seemed intent on consuming her, she stared at her necklace, and remembered something crucial.

240

She had done all of this for a reason.

Soon she would find Marianne and get her home. Not only that, but she would get the women out of this place. Lead them to someplace better. She had no doubt it would all be worth it.

And as her consciousness began to slip away, her lips repeated the words. Again and again.

It would all be worth it.

Chapter 37

Late evening

There was some part of her that was still aware, even though she was sleeping deeply. This part didn't cling onto the suffering. Maybe because it wasn't her. In this place, this other self couldn't quite comprehend why Viola struggled so much; what all the drama was about. Yet there was no judgement in her observation. Instead, an all-encompassing warmth radiated from her towards Viola. And she called out to Viola, to burst open that gaping hole in her chest. Open her heart and fill her with the only thing that would heal – an endless ocean of silence. Something that had always accompanied her, in her heart, but which she had buried so deep, and tried so hard to forget.

When she finally woke up, the vague memory of *Her,* the one that was filled with the permeating silence, became a distant speck in her consciousness.

Only to be replaced by a cellular camera lens aimed straight at her. And behind the camera was a woman Viola thought she would never see again.

Marianne.

* * *

Viola rubbed her weary eyes again, her mind still adjusting to who sat in front of her.

She had never met Marianne, never seen her in real life.

But here was a young woman, with unusually self-assured body language, a demanding gaze, one maybe even bordering on conceit. She was nothing like what Viola remembered. Or imagined.

Or maybe Viola just assumed way too much? Maybe she had created the perfect artifice.

Viola was about to speak when some movement from behind Marianne's bed caught her attention. Was there someone else behind Marianne? Viola wanted to get up from her bed but was interrupted by the Blogger's hands which shoved her cell phone camera right in front of Viola's eyes.

"Get that thing out of my face," Viola said.

"Don't you see? I am here to get you out." She repeated herself, and hoped the words would in some way realign Marianne's behaviour.

"Me? Out? You kidding me?" Marianne chuckled back at Viola. And her face strained with impatience. Marianne shut off her phone and leaned across the bed.

"Do you still not get it? I need you to do the story," Marianne said.

"A story? There is no story here," Viola protested and hoped she made her point succinct enough so they wouldn't waste more time on this.

"Not *a* story. *The* story. About me and my future children." Her eyes bored into Viola.

"What are you talking about? What children?"

Marianne scoffed at Viola, swivelled around on the bed, reached down and dumped a small child onto her bed.

Right this moment, everything clicked into place. Before her was the boy that she had endlessly scrutinised in the video snippet on Marianne's blog.

243

Tobias.

Before she could adjust to this fact, Marianne jerked him awake despite his moans of protest.

"Isn't he lovely?" Marianne twisted the boy's head like a race-horse to present his best profile. The boy groaned at the abuse but Marianne immediately proceeded to hush him down. When he refused, she disregarded him and faced Viola again. "And my soon-to-be wonder. It's official now! My latest IVF cycle is successful and Helen will become a reality!" The blogger pointed to her currently flat stomach, then flashed Viola with her grin again.

"I don't get it. Why would you do this? Risk these children's lives? And what about the recording on your blog? And the photos taken in the kindergarten? Is that blackmail?" Viola demanded.

"Blackmail? Silly! That's motivation. Just in case you didn't see it my way. And from the looks of it, you have some problems adjusting to my perspective, huh?" The blogger's stare shifted, jerked around the room, agitated that Viola didn't share her enthusiasm.

"You can't be serious?"

"Honey, I am damned serious. I've gone through too much pain not to get ahead in life. There are girls here who've already had their CRISPR kids. But if you ask me, they are too stupid to see the obvious, the opportunity this represents. So it is only my god given right to be the first one to go public with this. Huh! Right? That's not a story? That's history, baby! Me and my little ones."

Viola's mind ground to silence upon hearing the words. Somehow she had hoped they would leave room for ambivalence, another interpretation. Something that would give her hope. Anything. Any reason would be a good reason.

But no matter how she turned Marianne's words in her head, there was no doubt about Marianne's motivation.

And when Viola laid her eyes on the blogger again, it was all too obvious.

Marianne's eyes demanded Viola go along with her. And when they were met with zero response, the young woman's face twisted in anger.

"Don't you see? You are exactly who I needed. From the very beginning." Marianne spat out the words, losing her remaining patience with Viola.

"From the beginning? You staged this whole thing? Didn't you? The comment, the video? Those pictures? A set up?" Viola uttered the words half-hoping she was wrong.

Marianne only shrugged her shoulders, her innocent gaze neither denying nor accepting the accusation.

"Uh-huh... Maybe not too bright, but from the best paper, right?" Viola heard Marianne mutter.

What had she done for this girl? It wasn't just some sacrifice. She crucified her job, her relationships, everything that she believed in. For *what*? For this girl?

"Do you have any idea what they will have to go through in their life if you turn this into a story?" Viola struggled to grab onto something, to look for some shred of humanity in Marianne's actions. Maybe a shot in the dark, but at this point, one last appeal had to be made.

But Marianne brushed Viola off, grabbed her Tobias and squeezed him towards herself. Then aimed the cam at her own stomach and him.

"I know damned well what they will go through." She smirked as she made a gesture with her cam. And soon enough, she started recording yet another chapter in her story.

"They will be my small, shining starlets."

Chapter 38

Night

She couldn't recollect how she got here. Wherever here was. But as she jerked her head around, she realised she was in a toilet, in one of the cubicles. Her bones ached all over; stiff and bruised. She couldn't recollect how long she had been here.

Had she been searching for someone?

She would have been just as happy with staying there, if not for a distant sound. Her eyes jarred towards the thumping resonance. And only now did she understand, it was someone knocking on the door to her cubicle.

She barely managed to get up to her feet, and as she unhinged the door from its lock, she was greeted by Rene.

Despite all the fuzziness clouding her head, Viola remembered the woman, an outcast from the northern part of Norway. This recollection brought an inner glow to Viola.

Rene's face turned bleak, as the woman's eyes ran up and down Viola's body. Viola didn't quite understand what the fuss was about; after all, she felt a little shaky, but otherwise was just fine.

But when Rene realised Viola didn't comprehend what was going on, the woman moved away from the mirror behind her.

A glimpse is all it took. In the reflection stood a woman whom Viola didn't recognise. Surely this wasn't her. This wretched-looking thing in the mirror had smeared and dried mascara across her face. It was a bleak phantom, ready to hunt the halls of some mad Luna Park. She rubbed at her eyes, but the apparition still stood and eyed her with a quizzical expression.

Then Viola's eyes ran to her fingers, and she realised she had blood caked under her nails. As if she had tried to dig at the floor tiles, and shredded her nails and skin to pieces.

Maybe this sight was sufficient, maybe it grounded her just enough, since suddenly, everything flashed back into her mind, reigniting her neurones, putting all the missing pieces back into place.

She remembered how she had scuttled in here after Marianne's revelation. She recollected now that she had torn her fingers up against the tiled floor until her nails bled. And as she emptied out her aggression, she had lost track of time, she forgot where she had been, or what had happened.

If her mind had stayed long enough in that place called the past, she was bound to melt down, beyond any recovery.

And she almost had.

* * *

Rene jumped closer to Viola, and with all the nurturing of a distraught mother, supported Viola's mangled body.

"Oh my god, hon. Come. Come now. Only your body acting crazy after those damned IVF hormones," Rene whispered and slid Viola down onto the floor.

As if by a sudden realisation of where Viola was, her body lost all strength, and gave into Rene's hands, then

247

folded onto the woman's knees. This got even more sympathy from Rene, who began to caress Viola gently.

Despite that this was the last thing Viola wanted at this moment, her senses immediately gave into this tenderness. She couldn't recollect what it was like to be touched, at least not in this way. Even if Ronny soothed her, this was something else. It wasn't the intimacy of a lover, or a man's hand, but a mother's delicate strokes barely touching her child's forehead. This sensation spread through her whole body. And all of sudden, Viola's body quivered with a radiant energy. A surge of warmth rushed into her heart.

Peace.

As she felt Rene's nurturing fingers, she couldn't help remembering her Markus. How many times he had lain in her lap, and although he was way too uninhibited, had just way too much vibrancy in his body, she still savoured those few short moments when he was tired enough to be caressed. When he just snuggled into her hands, and made the sweetest purring sounds, something that lulled her heart into a wholeness.

But as Viola's eyes moved back to Rene's face, her mind was drawn back to the here and now. She glanced into her eyes, and realised that maybe not everything was lost. Maybe this woman might be able to help her. If Viola couldn't do anything about Marianne and get her home, maybe Rene could convince her.

This woman would surely see that Marianne's reckless actions were about to rip apart everything she and the others had fought for. And Viola felt as if she finally found a way out of this seemingly impossible situation. With the help of Rene.

This was her last chance; yet this time, she sensed she would succeed. She would make things right, because she understood why she fought so hard.

It wasn't only for those women's children. If she could rectify one thing in this screwed up world, it would be that Markus didn't die in vain. It would be for the moments when he had placed his sweet face in her lap.

Late night

"Rene! I need your help. Please." Viola's intuition rang with a reinvigorated zeal. She raised herself up on her arms and locked gazes with the woman.

"Marianne intends to go public about this place. About everything."

"So? Is that a problem?" Rene shrugged her shoulders and returned Viola's gaze.

"Don't you see what you are risking? Your child, the other children, police – they will take the children from you!" Viola's mind scrambled in search of the reason why she wasn't reaching Rene.

But then Rene moved into Viola's face.

"Just because my Trond had an M1 and M3 CRISPR neurodevelopment modification done to him, you wouldn't understand any of it. No one in my hometown did. Not my family, nor my friends, and least of all my husband. My *ex*-husband, that is."

"What do you mean M1, M3?" Viola pressed Rene to explain herself.

"That's a group of about thousand genes, responsible for our intelligence quotient. Don't you see, I don't want my kids to go through the things I had to. Do you know what it is like to work ten hours a day at the cash register, just because I never got past high school? Do you know what it is like to become everyone's laughingstock, just because you can't make it past the most basic math tests? For some, university is a dream. For me it was high school, but I didn't even make that. That's why I am here. I am not going to let that happen to my little Trond. You see that? He is never going to be called a slow coach, a poor learner, or just plain retard. No one is going to take away his future from him. Most of all not you."

"I... I don't..."

Viola was now the last person to take a moral stance on anything. Was the young woman making the right decision? Was she giving her child a better start by taking this wild chance? Or was she simply hurting him? Maybe Viola was just narrow-minded. Maybe the lack of the insight that intelligence gave could be deemed a handicap, just as mitochondrial disease. And maybe Rene's Trond, of all people, deserved a better life than what Rene had been given.

Viola's mind reeled in the face of these questions. And however shocking Rene's actions were to Viola, the young woman's perspective wasn't. This reached Viola's sensibility. Weren't Viola's choices grounded in the same reasons, which drove her to do things, reasons many people would have trouble accepting? This didn't magically set things right, nor did it excuse Rene's actions, but it made Viola question what was right and wrong in this matter. And if that happened, she always paid careful attention.

But however much she empathised with Rene's life story, it got Viola nowhere closer to a solution.

"Please. This is exactly what I am trying to tell you. If you don't help me, everything you've fought for will be in vain. Including your son's future. Do you want to lose custody of him?"

"Take your fear and spread it somewhere else. I would be crazy to want to go back. With those kids kicking the shit out of my son and my family trying to lock me up in an asylum." Then the woman jumped up and raced out of the toilet.

Chapter 39

She felt people swarming around her, maybe the staff, circling her, observing her like some cornered animal. They had been watching her for some time, but after she hissed them off, they all kept a safe distance. Probably until Magda arrived.

She had been wrong about a few things. She had to admit that to herself now. She was wrong about Stine. She was wrong about Marianne. She was also wrong about this place. She thought it to be important, and the very idea that these women were fulfilling their dreams seemed to be something to fight for. Actually, when she thought about it now, she had been wrong about everything.

Only this time it was different. This time it was too late.

For some time she thought she heard church bells somewhere in the distance. It was Sunday, and just the proper time for the believers to gather around the church's warm fire, lit up by their faith and hopes. She thought this to be a poor joke, to be reminded of such people and their faith. If any of them lost everything and still came out

251

smiling, still convinced it was God's generous hand, that it was all for the better, she would call them a bunch of liars.

Her incessant stream of thoughts ended as she saw Magda approaching.

"I will take it from here," Magda whispered to her staff despite their warnings. Everyone thought the clinic's security would be a better fit for this situation.

"You okay?"

"So, you plan to...?" Magda prodded Viola one more time for a reaction. Searched Viola's eyes, for some contact.

Then she felt herself utter some barely audible words.

"It's all... This place. The women... you. It's all lies." Viola forced the words out of herself. Yet they didn't feel liberating. No relief was to be had.

Still, if there was something she could do, it would be to confront Magda with her own deceit. Was that why she was here?

"Before you pass the final verdict... Please, I think you need to see something."

* * *

Viola followed Magda with hesitation.

Magda's eyes passed another fingerprint scan, which unsealed the doors to a more secluded space in the facility. The tight security, coupled with surveillance sensors, suggested they were entering a section that held importance for the older woman.

And with every unsealed door, another layer of her mask would fall away. Until they reached their destination and Viola glanced into her eyes. Magda's transformation was striking, her granite features replaced by weariness.

As they made their way inside a simple patient room, Viola realised she stood in a teenage boy's room. There was a huge TV screen accompanied by a games console and all the latest games to play. Cupboards with private clothes and a general mess only a boy his age could accomplish. If Viola didn't know better, she would have thought she had entered someone's private house, not a clinic.

Amongst all of this everyday normality, the room was populated by one simple bed, and a host of medical scanners, vital signs monitors, and respiratory analysers. Between these instruments, Viola also noticed a nurse present behind the bed.

Yet what struck Viola the most, was the lone stainless steel bedpan that rested against the bed. It wasn't the urinal itself that was so extraordinary, out of place. It was the stains of blood that blended in the urine, swirled by themselves and told a whole story – one Viola wasn't sure she wanted to be a part of.

Before Viola saw who lay in the bed, she somehow sensed it. Her sixth sense whispered to her that it would be the boy. The same one she had met twice in this place. The frail-looking thing who had revealed one of the most well-kept secrets of this place.

"This is Tony," Magda barely whispered to Viola. And Viola noticed the woman's tone was filled with reverence.

As Magda sat on the bedside, Viola could see the woman's face underwent yet another transformation. Her eyes brimmed with fear. Was she concerned for her dying patient? Or was there something else Viola failed to see? Something more at stake.

"Contrary to everyone's speculations about some kind of genetic experiment, Tony is living proof of what happens if you don't do anything about mito-d. In Tony's case, the abnormality of his nuclear mitochondria caused his Leigh disease." Viola realised she couldn't stand this anymore, no matter how sick this kid was, nor how flooded she was with pity, she had to get out of here. But before she could budge, Magda's pleas whipped away at her again.

"Please. He is sliding into irreversible mental decline. His central nervous system is slowly giving way. Causing vomiting, dysphagia, seizures. He's been extraordinarily brave all these years, but now, he doesn't even have a year." Magda drew her fingers across the boy's whitish skin, soothing his temples. Despite the apparent truth, Viola refused to believe any of it. It had to be fake, a road-side show, no matter how convincing the act. And the damned old woman just wouldn't stop, she kept chipping away at Viola's remnants of humanity.

"He is the only reminder that if I leave things as they are, people just... die."

"You know what? I think you are serving me crap. Maybe it's poetic crap, but nonetheless it smells and tastes like crap. And it certainly doesn't make it alright that you milked those desperate women's needs for your own research." Viola spat out the accusation at Magda.

"No Miss Voss. Yes, they are pioneers and I would be lying to you if I said there were no risks involved. But everything we've done with them was up front, clearly communicated to them, with their full acceptance, even if it meant staying here for two years under our supervision. That includes using the data collected from their cases for our own R&D lab." Magda defended herself but Viola noticed the older woman was clearly losing her composure.

"Come on! You can serve the bed time stories to those kids. But you can't make me believe these women stayed here willingly for this long." Viola said.

"That's exactly what I would have you believe. Given a choice between leaving and making themselves available for our observations, for their babies' safety, every one of them accepted our offer." Magda whipped back at Viola.

"For fucks sake woman! Maybe you want a Noble prize for your exceptional effort in the field?"

Magda's composure almost broke under Viola's provocation. She was about to reply with everything she had, but something held her back. Whatever it was, she took a breath, then another one, eyed Viola then proceeded to whisper back.

"When I created this place, my stance was simple. I drew the line between cosmetic therapies and curing genetic diseases. I wanted to help women like you. But to my surprise, the commercial demand for preventing the hereditary diseases was practically zero. People didn't want healthy kids. They wanted better versions of themselves. So, to stay financially afloat and develop the necessary know-how, I broke my own rules."

Viola looked into Magda's eyes and for the first time something stirred inside her. She began to grasp how far Magda had gone with this place. This realisation twisted and churned inside her. She swept her eyes towards the bed, lingered on the boy's barely heaving chest. Her eyes quivered with hesitation as the story was laid out in front of her.

"And if I had to, I would do it again. For my son, Tony," Magda whispered, letting out a barely audible sigh, and with it the secret that tainted everything she had done in her life. Gone was the defensiveness or the pretence of the CEO of this clinic. Left standing was a lone woman who had a dream, and somewhere along the road, she had lost sight of her ideals. And ultimately herself.

* * *

Magda shut the door behind her, sealing off Tony's room. Silence permeated the air between them as they made their way down the hall.

As Viola recollected Magda's confession, she realised that her heart resisted being moved by emotion. It repelled anything that could generate empathy in her. Or at least pity for Magda and her Tony. Had Viola's fight to keep away her own pain made her insensitive? Even to someone who shared a similar fate?

After all, Magda's tragedy was Viola's past. All twenty years of it. But when Viola thought about this, this woman had gone much further. She had not only rearranged her personal life according to the laws of a crippling disease, but she had built this place in the hope of helping him and others like him.

Not only that, but when confronted with a dead end, the end of funding for the research necessary to help Tony, Magda proceeded to do all the wrong things, for what she thought were the right reasons.

For the first time since Magda had shared her secret, Magda's eyes searched for contact with Viola. At first Viola was far from willing to return her gaze. But when their eyes finally met, something stirred in Viola. She shivered all over her body, finally moved by the circumstances that turned this woman's life into a living hell.

She saw an older woman who had burned down her whole life, and just like Viola, sacrificed everything for her kid. And what did life pay her back with? A dying son. And at that moment, Viola felt moved by the truth in Magda's eyes.

"What happens to him if this place shuts down?"

"He could still walk a month ago. Then there was the chair and now he can barely get up from bed. Without the care we are able to give him here, his life span would be reduced to a few weeks. Best case scenario." Magda shared this fact with her, and this time Viola didn't question its validity. She didn't need to because she had already made up her mind what she would do next.

"If it were up to me, this story would never make it to print. Still, my silence won't be enough here. Give me a day? Okay? I might have an idea how to fix things," Viola said, and with her steadfast gaze, left no room for doubt that she was one hundred percent behind Magda.

The older woman eyed Viola and wanted to know more, but instead just nodded, her face filled with gratitude.

Chapter 40

Morning

Viola peered into Marianne's room, and observed the woman punching away on her mobile phone. The blogger had obviously been more effective with the smuggling in of her phone. Marianne's frantic typing was interspersed by constant checks to see if anyone was paying attention to her.

Viola was sure of one thing: This would be far from easy. However mission-oriented Marianne wanted to appear, Viola had learnt the hard way what lay behind that fatuous country smile.

When Marianne finally finished her task, she hid the phone under her bedsheets.

As Viola entered the room, Marianne's composure stiffened. But the blogger quickly covered it with a reassuring grin.

"Dear, I've done some thinking. And you are right. This opportunity is unique. I will help you go public with this."

"You will? That's just amazing, hon! I am so happy... but are you sure?" And it was quite obvious, despite the mistrust, that Marianne still played her role perfectly.

Viola knew Marianne would not be swayed by her sudden friendliness. If anything, it would only make matters worse, and make her more suspicious.

Viola's mind raced for a solution. When Marianne had revealed her plan yesterday, she had uncovered a couple of crucial facts about herself. The most obvious one was that she not only distrusted Viola but also everyone else. How could she not, considering her life was built on the assumption that everything was a poker game? The only way to get ahead was by being the best hustler in the room.

Yet, Marianne also revealed another fact about herself. She had constructed her whole life around one single thing. However warped it was, Marianne would stop at nothing to get into the limelight.

* * *

"I couldn't be more sure. You know, I thought about you and everything. I've been through hell. All my life. So I am a bit weary of people finding out about my condition. No. Not weary, terrified. So, I can imagine what you will be going through. And..." Viola allowed her voice to quiver with emotions. "And right now, I feel it's as if I've let you down. And that feels as if I also let myself down. Do you see how much you mean to me? And the best I can give you is my support, because I think what you have done for others... that's priceless. And I realise now that you and your children deserve to be at the centre of attention. Because you deserve to do more good." Viola whispered the words with appreciation, and hugged Marianne to herself tightly.

Slowly, she felt her words making a dent in Marianne's armour. No. Actually, they did far more than that. They left a huge gaping hole that turned Marianne into a misty-eyed teenager dreaming of stardom.

"Yeees! I knew you would come around. And just in time. I received my plan from my lawyer yesterday." Marianne jumped up from her bed and fished out her mobile phone. Her reservation was gone now, replaced by a child-like belief that Viola was on her side.

"Plan?"

And as Marianne's grin stretched her lips, Viola had the sensation that her problems were about to become a whole lot larger.

"What do you think, silly? My business plan, of course." Marianne shrugged her shoulders with the innocuousness of a schoolgirl, then proceeded to download the pdfs to her mobile.

Noon

Maybe she had schemed to use her mother, Stine, in order to get to Viola. To make her do exactly what she ultimately had done. This fact couldn't be pushed away.

Yet, despite her shortcomings, Marianne had gone through the same IVF hell that Viola had. The ups and lows of the ovarian stimulation, the hopes awakened then ground to smithereens after the endless shots of progesterone and oestrogen. And the two weeks of waiting for the final judgement.

Over and over again.

And if this experience had taught Viola anything at all, it was how unique life was. What a true gift it was, this tiny breathing organism, a true marvel of what life had to offer. It had made her realise what it means to be grateful for the thing in life which most women take for granted.

With this mind-set, Viola simply failed to see how a business plan related to such an intimate matter as Marianne's childlessness. Even for someone like Marianne, it would be quite a stretch.

No.

Viola repeated to herself, she had to have faith in people. And even more so in Marianne.

* * *

"Hello Dolly, you darlings!" Marianne hugged Viola close to herself and bared her bleached teeth for the selfie.

259

In a matter of two hours, Viola found herself dragged through countless photo sessions. What was supposed to be humble memorabilia for the blogger's future children, turned out to be selfies pumped up on PR-steroids.

However hard Marianne tried to justify this to Viola, none of these shots seemed like cosy photos intended for the preservation of a family's memories. But Marianne only chuckled this away, and pushed Viola on to the next task on her tight schedule.

The blogger posed with a grin on her face. She posed with a solemn face. She posed exasperated. Marianne even managed to shower water all over herself to get what she called that sweaty momma look.

And right now, as Marianne bared her stomach to her best ability, she told Viola to wait for her cue before she snapped the photo.

Then she burst into tears. But when too few of them flowed, she began to grow impatient. She squeezed at her face as if this would alleviate the situation. But when it didn't, she hit herself. Once, then twice. Her face twisted in pain. Then she waved to Viola, the cue for her to grab the pic.

"Hello Dolly to you gals!" she whispered into the cell phone as tears trickled down her face.

Early afternoon

When they found themselves back at her room, Marianne aired a lot of questions. Each one more peculiar than the last. And every one of them twisted Viola's insides even further into some freakish knot.

Marianne questioned Viola about optimal schedules of the post-InviNordica time schedule. It seemed she had separated them into phases. Although Marianne didn't share explicitly what was on her mind, it became apparent she had planned some kind of launch. But for what, and to what end?

Then she pushed Viola for information about media reviews and the press. Clearly, this was why she needed Viola, the expert in her field, and now an accomplice. And as Viola let the young woman talk, making sure the girl got more than enough praise, Marianne's mouth loosened and her boasting increased.

Soon enough, Viola was holding Marianne's mobile in her palms. Viola realised that it had a document with a clear timetable for her business stored on it. This included a complete marketing launch, media appearances, intended media outlets, a whole social media strategy with precisely chosen channels and partners. Also included were draft contracts for book, movie and TV rights.

The specifications were endless, and as Viola's trembling hands tapped on Marianne's phone, her mind tried to take all of this in. Double-check, then triple-check if this was for real. But however hard she tried, she found nothing to tell her otherwise. Marianne had left nothing to chance.

And as Viola glanced at Marianne, finishing the financial summary in her business plan, Viola noticed a tiny footprint, a copyright text that specified the plan's conception date. Dating it back more than six years. About the time Marianne started up her blog.

"This must be a mistake. This thing. It's six years old?" Viola stuttered out the words, but even before she voiced them, the comprehension began to flood her mind.

Viola had pushed this away for far too long, tried to soften Marianne's character, attempted to explain away her shortcomings. But in the face of these facts, her heart ground to a halt.

This young blogger had carefully planned this for over half a decade. And now Viola wasn't sure anymore what came first: the blog with its noble intentions, or this plot. Maybe Marianne had this plan already in mind when she initiated her blogging activity. And her whole mission to be of support to the infertile community was a lie from the very first moment.

"Oh. A mistake. Yes." She smirked at Viola, and her cheeks bloomed yet again with an aura full of gratitude at Viola's help. But this glance only made Viola's body shudder.

Yet one fact didn't add up to Viola in all of this. Why had Marianne stayed in the clinic for so long? Why didn't she just leave InviNordica when Tobias was born? That must have been the easiest and the most tempting solution. To cash in on her plan and fame as soon as Tobias came along. Instead, Marianne stayed around for another two years. Nothing about this woman's plan seemed to be a coincidence and certainly not two years.

"Ok. I see. So, Helen was a mistake as well? That's why you waited around for two years. Just because of a mistake?" Viola prodded Marianne but didn't have high expectations for any deeper truth from the young woman.

"Viola! How could you say something like that? I am surprised by your lack of heart. Helen was never a mistake. I had her planned from the very beginning. Long before Tobias. There had to be two of them. Spaced apart at least two years from each other. It couldn't be any other way. Don't you get it? Silly!" Marianne cringed at the lack of understanding.

Viola tried to wrap her mind around what the blogger was trying to tell her. Then it struck her, maybe there was hope for Marianne after all.

"You stayed here to make sure Tobias was ok? You did this for him? Didn't you?" Viola voiced her idea, and hoped this would be the case. Surely this could in some way redeem Marianne's character.

"Yes! Yes! You couldn't be more right. This was the only way my plan would work, don't you see that? I had to be sure he was ok. Just imagine what an idiot I would make of myself in the media if he turned out bad. But now that I am sure he is ok, I can proceed with Helen, you know."

"Everything for the media, right?"

"No. No. Of course not. This was done for Helen's safety."

"Right." Viola went along with the blogger but her words were already tainted with sarcasm. The damage had irreversibly been done. Viola had pierced right through to the core of this woman. And at this realisation, Viola began to choke. She felt crushed by everything. As much as she had been taught to keep an open mind, she could not grasp this.

Marianne's conscience had more than six years to reflect on what she was doing, scream out how she was bludgeoning herself, and what she would be doing to her children. Wasn't that enough time for some kind of wake-up call of the soul?

Yet, nothing happened.

Viola had seen it on so many occasions. People always had noble reasons to do horrible things. But this? To despise and abuse human life? One life brought into this world two years ago, and now another? All this just to make sure a plan was fool proof? This fact was simply irreconcilable within Viola.

Her body reeled, swaying out of balance at the implications. If these children lived, Viola couldn't fathom what kind of life they would have. A mother obsessed with glitzy stardom. A mum who had turned her kid into an efficient tool.

What would happen when the fame faded, or even worse, when the mother realised the children failed to serve their purpose? And would the future teenagers see the absurdity of how they came to be, or comprehend that they existed only so their mother could attain her goals?

Would they understand they were cursed from the beginning? Would they feel they were only a means to an end?

Marianne snuggled into Viola's shoulder, and her face beamed with teenage excitement. By now, the blogger's gaze was enamoured with Viola. Ready to destroy her life, and the life of her coming child.

"I gotta give it to you. Just knock-out amazing. Everything." Viola's eagerness was forced, which Marianne failed to notice.

"Just one more thing." Viola halted Marianne and took out the girl's phone from her own pocket, then shoved it into her face.

"There is more than enough on this to put you in jail. Three times over. Or you can just pack and come back with me to your mother. And keep your mouth shut." Viola's tone hardened and made it clear these weren't just empty threats.

"That thing? That won't hold up in court for even five minutes. Or didn't you see how vaguely it was worded? It could just as well be the PR launch of horse manure."

"I wasn't talking about the business plan," Viola said and pressed a button that brought up the Dictaphone app that had been running in the background during the last four hours. Viola stopped the recording, then pressed play again. Marianne's voice, clear and distinct, came through the cell phone's speakers.

"And they will be my small shining starlets..." Marianne's giggles trailed off and were stopped by Viola's finger, which terminated the file and brought up a share button.

Marianne's grin faded immediately as she heard this. But Viola had one more card to play. Her ace.

"If I push this, the file will be uploaded to our FTP server at *Aftenposten*. More than enough proof for tomorrow's headlines. So, do you think I can convince you to go back home?" Viola asked with all the politeness she could muster.

This time her argument was met with silence. This was Viola's best shot. Her only shot. So why did she feel so shaky inside?

Maybe because right this moment, she wasn't sure what would happen if Marianne said no. This was a huge gamble, not only with this girl's life, but everyone else at this place.

Chapter 41

Evening

Half an hour later, Magda and Viola watched as Marianne crammed her belongings into her makeup bag. The decade of planning that had gone down the drain was evident in the blogger's face. So, she kept her mouth shut, and filled the bag with the few possessions she had left.

Viola had more than a few reasons to be happy. For the first time in two weeks, she had a good reason for hope.

And now, number one priority was to get the women and their children out of here. Then erase all the files on them. Viola knew she had to sever all the connections between the children and this place.

Yet at that moment, a blaring noise reached her ears.

Everyone raced to the window, the source of the sound, and Viola realised the noise originated from police sirens outside the clinic.

Her mind reeled in panic as she saw InviNordica was surrounded by a flurry of police cars, and a whole squad was preparing to enter.

* * *

The adrenaline exploded through her veins and scattered her mind into chaos. She lashed her head around, attempting to regain her much-needed balance. She needed to think. She needed a solution.

Things had happened faster than the speed of light. One moment the police were about to enter, and the next, she heard shouting, cries, and panic from all over the place.

The police had come in sheer force, two dozen men, specced out to the teeth. Maybe an ordinary sight in Paris or New York but hardly in Norway.

Viola couldn't shake off the feeling she was in the middle of an international incident, involving fundamentalist extremists. But here she was, and the only danger she could think of was the crying of the innocent children caused by the police. Nobody was prepared to help anyone, much less the women and the children.

"Why the hell would you call them?" Viola hissed at Marianne, unloading all the blame on the girl, while her hand clutched onto Marianne's arm. No matter how much Marianne assured her she would keep her mouth shut, Viola wouldn't let go of her. If she desired to shine, Viola was more than prepared to fulfil her desire, handcuffed and dragged away by the police.

"Don't you get it? With that recording, I would be crazy to call them." The blogger threw out the same answer one last time. Up until now Viola's mind refused to accept this. Yet this time, the words finally reached her.

She halted her body, swallowed a big breath, then re-focused. Maybe the girl wasn't lying, maybe she was even right. Her calling the police just didn't make any sense.

Then it struck Viola, something that should have been obvious from the get-go. Marianne was an egomaniac, but she was not stupid. She had vested her fortune, her body, and most of all, her offspring in gene-editing superstardom. No. Marianne wouldn't do anything reckless to jeopardise her raving vision of the future.

But if there was one character who was just as prepared to pull the trigger on this place, and rattled enough in their brains to throw away everyone's safety, Viola didn't have to look farther than Marianne's family.

"Damn your mother. Couldn't she wait one more day?" Viola spat out at the woman, and immediately, as she voiced her conclusion, she knew that Stine's lack of patience would cost everyone here dearly.

"Hey. Don't blame me. She is the one who's been threatening me to wrap up this whole charade. All these amateurish ideas with the recordings and whatnot, that was just to appease the old hag. To speed up the process. If she didn't ride my back every day, I would have done this with some genuine flair." Marianne defended herself and by the time she had finished, Viola noticed that the blogger already regretted what she had just said.

With the police about to blow the whole place wide open, and detain everybody on the premises, she had about ten minutes to do the impossible: get the women out of here, before the police seized them. But that wouldn't be enough. She had to erase all the digital records that connected all the patients to this place. And for this, she needed Magda.

Without even realising it, her hand let go of the wriggling blogger. Viola's eyes scanned along the hall, then homed in on a pair of hunched shoulders. It was Magda and she was about to disappear up the stairs and lock herself inside the clinic's private section.

Evening

Viola ran after Magda and cut her off before the first biometric checkpoint. Two seconds later, the entrance would have been sealed off, and with it, Viola's chances at a rescue plan.

She grabbed the woman but was met with a wrenching hostility as Magda's eyes bulged with fear.

268

"Haven't you done enough already? Leave me alone!" Magda spat out at Viola, then tried to shake her off. No matter the circumstances, Viola knew she couldn't do that. Viola realised this raw emotion wasn't so much about Magda. Rather it was about her dying son, hidden behind those doors. A helpless child who, in a few moments, would lose his mother. And Viola felt a pang of guilt. Here she was, stood in her way, preventing the last intimacy Magda was bound to have with her son.

She slid up to Magda's face, tightened her arm, deadlocked her eyes, then whispered with maddening urgency.

"Please, I need to know where the files on the women are. The treatments, the diagnoses, everything digital. All of it!" Viola tried to reach Magda, while she kept scanning the corridor, aware that at any moment the cops would be filling this place.

While the words hit Magda, and with them Viola's intention, the older woman was coming undone, unable to think straight, much less act.

"Since the trouble started, I've erased it all. The sensitive data, that is. Except on my laptop. Uh-huh. My office. First floor. No backups." She digested the most crucial fact, and then grabbed Viola's hand and shoved an ID-access card in her palm. As Viola eyed the card, she nodded with gratitude.

Magda twisted around, punched in the code, ran her finger through the bio-scanner. And as the doors slid apart, she looked at Viola one more time. She pressed her lips together.

"You know, you can still get away. It's not too late. For you, that is."

"Please... go to your son," Viola said. As she disappeared behind the door, Viola eyed the ID-access card. Indeed, she could still run, she had all the means. This card would get her out. Maybe for once she should think of herself. Her own future.

269

Chapter 42

She had done the impossible. She had managed to avoid the clinic's staff, she had gotten past the army of cops and even made it past their rabid dogs. But she had no idea that her biggest obstacle would be the women themselves.

Her body quivered with impatience as she faced a thuggish bunch: Rene, Katrine, Ingrid, and behind them, three more women, accompanied by bleary-eyed, toothless cries from their babies. Despite the barrage of confusion and fear on display, the women's gazes were filled with a seldom-seen defiance.

One thing was certain, none of them had trusted Viola when she set foot in the clinic. And with the police storming the premises, scaring their children witless, this didn't improve. On the contrary, it provoked wild speculation and suspicion. All of this was aimed at Viola, making her responsible for the current tragedy.

No matter how much she pleaded, none of them were prepared to hear her out.

Rene's face was stretched into a sneer. After she had refused to help Viola at the toilet, her attitude hadn't changed. She seemed ready to support any of Katrine's decisions, no matter how ridiculous.

Katrine was the leader and brains behind this group. With gritted teeth and a warrior-like stance, she was ready to pulverise any arguments Viola might have. Whichever way the decision swayed, Viola knew it would be either through some kind of truce with this woman, or over her dead body.

But the worst was Ingrid, her posture beaten to a pulp, her eyes muddy and about to sign off for good. It was written all over her face, for this woman there was no tomorrow.

"In two minutes, the police will come through this door. And they won't be asking questions."

Her mind was racing in multiple directions at once, the approaching footsteps from the police, the barking dogs, all the possible escape routes, and the six women who were about to jump at her.

"So? This is crazy. What are we? Criminals?" Katrine hissed at Viola, and she knew instantly that this was a dead end. Unless she back-pedalled on her tactics, the cops would be carrying these women out, kicking and screaming. And if she didn't do anything to soften up the leader of this pack, Katrine would sabotage everything.

"In their eyes, you will be."

"Forget it! We are not going anywhere." Katrine shouted at Viola, and this collected its fair share of support.

"Please? Damn... Okay. I ask you to consider only one thing: You've risked so much coming here. Having your babies. It took a helluva lot of guts. I admire you for that. I really do. But the moment these people come in through these doors, you will have to give up everything you have fought so hard for, including your kids." Viola realised what she was saying, the implications for each of them were earth-shattering. But there was no way around it.

A murmur spread through the women. And suddenly Viola realised she was winning them over. One by one,

271

they nodded their agreement. Each one giving Viola the necessary support. And not a second too late.

Still, one of them remained.

Viola's eyes landed on Katrine.

"Listen to *her*? Back home we hear this shit every day. It's all lies. Don't you think you will only be making it worse by trying to run from the police? That's like admitting to something you didn't do. Our case is clean. Calm down, everybody. We are staying."

"Stop," an unfamiliar voice pierced through the murmurs. Everyone whipped up their heads, and a dozen eyes fell on the one person who hadn't spoken a single word till now.

Ingrid.

The delicate girl was practically convulsing, barely able to handle the temper rippling beneath her skin. Yet she summoned enough spirit in her to make herself heard.

"You are all goddamned fools. Listen to Viola. How do you want to spend the next seven years raising up your children? Do you want to spend them in peace somewhere in the country? Or do you want to spend them in litigation hell, in courts while your kids are under child care services or being adopted? Do you want to face conviction? Lose everything? Including the most important thing, your kids?" And while she flailed at them, she drilled her eyes into each one of them, making sure she was heard.

Then she stepped towards Viola and stood behind her, showing her unwavering support.

Viola saw that Katrine wanted to fight back, oppose Ingrid, and ridicule them, but the words failed her. This time Viola felt a tinge of hope. Before anyone uttered a word, she felt half the battle was won.

And as one after the other stepped forward towards Viola, she realised they were about to put their lives in her hands.

Chapter 43

Her tears exposed something within her that still testified to her humanity. She wiped them away as quickly as possible.

Tony was oblivious to what was going on, at least that took away some of her pain. Lately, he was in no man's land, too advanced in his condition to be lucid, yet still too strong to slip away for good. And she didn't really know which one would be for the best.

As she heard the police bang on some distant door, about to blast into the room, she knew their time was up. And she realised, with an inevitable looming incarceration and endless legal battles and repercussions, her life was about to get a whole lot more complicated.

There remained one question, though. Would she go through this alone, or would she drag him further down with her? It all came down to one simple question: who was she doing it for?

Magda watched his twitchy fingers, and choked on her barbed breath, her throat as dry as the desert.

She had to stay. She doubted that she felt love for him. Guilt would be more appropriate. It hung around her neck, like a steel anchor that would eventually drown her.

The guilt had been the most consuming. Her companion for the last fourteen years. What was she thinking? Did she really think she could give birth to a healthy child? In her condition?

However much she sacrificed herself, however many hours she put in, nothing would erase the guilt. Reminding her that the only reason this boy existed was because she had fulfilled her own want. A thing which, she now reflected, wasn't real, just a mirage.

* * *

Viola swiped the ID-card, and expected to be greeted by the opening of the balcony door. Yet the digital lock only burped back with discontent and refused to let her pass.

Viola cursed inside herself. This hadn't gone to plan, but lately, nothing had.

She had scheduled to contact Pål, right after she entered the clinic. But when the staff confiscated her cell phone, Pål was left dangling outside without any reassurance she was fine or if they would proceed with their plan.

She wished he would still be outside, but maybe she just hoped for a miracle. This was asking a lot of him. Maybe too much. After all, the last time they saw each other was on Thursday, three days ago.

She had to face the facts, the most probable scenario was that Pål had left a long time ago, and even if she was successful in getting everybody out, there would be no one outside to help her.

Her quivering fingers swiped the card yet again, but the response was exactly the same. She slid her nose up to the digital read out, and eyed an error message that blinked in her face.

"System override. Silent alarm initiated."

She whipped her head around, and tried to maintain as neutral an expression as she possibly could. She swept her eyes over the trembling faces, all of them lost, everyone looking to her for leadership, expecting her to provide an escape route. And not in half an hour, but the next two minutes.

What was she supposed to tell them, that she had been blowing hot air when she said she could help them? It was all for show. They might just as well return to their rooms, and wait like sheep for the cops to take them away. Made into some freak side show, then fed to the media, which would gorge on them, then vomit them up when they had served their purpose.

She eyed the kids, half of them already in tears and the rest silent enough to sink into a trauma.

As she realised this, something primal kicked inside. Wrenched at her. Told her she hadn't come all this way to be stopped by a damned door in her way.

Viola searched the room and saw a chair. She grabbed it, then smashed it with full force against the window. She expected a mountain of glass to come hurling towards her, but nothing happened. Not even a dent in the window.

She realised she needed something with more weight. Way more weight. But as she glanced around the room, there was nothing substantial enough. Either too small or too large, way too unwieldy to get anything done.

At the same time, she heard several shouts just outside the hall. The cops were rounding up all the patients. She had sixty seconds before they noticed the door to this room was locked.

There was no way around it, she knew she would have to do something desperate. When it flashed into her mind, she had no illusions about it; her idea of desperate was not only stupid, it was also dangerous. The sort of stuff done only in the movies. And this wasn't the movies.

Viola nodded the women to the back of the room, stepped back herself, caught a gulp of breath, kicked back, then sprinted towards the balcony, and threw herself at the glass door.

At the moment of impact, she felt as if she crashed into a pool of water, although this surface wasn't liquid. It had huge, sharp fangs, and many of them cut into her body. As she came blasting through the glass, she felt torn apart, her body convulsing into shock, even before she landed on the other side. And as if the countless glass pieces didn't hurt enough, the balcony's unwavering granite floor only confirmed this might be the last thing she would do.

Seconds later, her eyelids exploded open, and she felt as if several men had given her a brutal beating and were still kicking and bashing at her skull. Still, there was no time for minor details.

She eyed herself, and realised several small glass shards were pierced into her body. And as she pressed her body to the side, she wanted to bawl from agony. But she clenched her teeth, then hissed at herself to stay awake. To stay conscious. Alert. She couldn't let them down. Not now.

Then suddenly, through the haze of pain, she saw a man down below. Someone racing towards her.

It was Pål.

* * *

Magda knew she had come to terms with her own lies, voice her hypocrisy. And the impossible choice became her only option. It made the act she was about to carry out possible.

He was still unconscious and would probably remain so until she had finished. She stroked the few hairs he still had left, his hair loss caused by the chemos she had forced on him in an attempt to halt the inevitable, but had instead ravaged his body.

She would be sixty in two years' time, if she lived that long. All her life had been one incessant flurry of movement forward, an energy that couldn't be contained, channelled into this place. It had taken her thirty years to come this far, to reach this point. Yet, it would only take

276

the next two minutes to tear down everything. Including his life.

All it took was a few silly buttons on the life support machine, the only thing that separated him from here and somewhere else. A place she wished existed, if only for his sake.

She pressed down on them, turning off the two ventilators that pushed oxygenated and humidified air into his lungs. As they powered down, their rhythmic pumping faded away into silence. And with the newfound quiet, she could feel some part of her disappearing into a dark crevice.

She knew she wasn't finished, though. She proceeded to pull out his thoracotomy tube, which protruded from his chest, the only thing that made sure his lung was constantly drained after it had collapsed a few months ago. As she did this, it felt as if she had pierced her own stomach with a dull knife, grated it and twisted it inside.

Despite this choking pain, she focused her mind on the only comfort she could have at this moment. She was sure he couldn't feel a thing, that he slid gently over the threshold without sharing her pain.

So, she kept on.

One cable at a time, one button press after the other, she separated him from this world. While stroking his hair, making sure that if he was still present in some way, the only thing he would feel would be her love.

* * *

Pål still didn't know why he had waited this long. On several occasions, during the last three days, he had fired up the car and driven away. Each time, he had made it past a block. Maybe even two. Then he stopped.

Shortly afterwards, he came hurtling back like a dog on an elastic leash, whipped back into obedience by his master.

And as he stood there again, time flew by, his temporary parking spot turned into a camping site. And his stay became an unintended vacation in hell.

He didn't know what to think. Was she ignoring him and just needed to hitch a ride to the clinic? Was all that talk just some empty words, thrown at an emotionally starved old geezer who was willing to do anything for something resembling a whiff of compassion? Or maybe he had it all wrong. Maybe she had done this for him out of pity. Maybe he was simply insignificant. And along the way, she had simply forgotten about him. After all, she was saving the world.

At this point, after a mind avalanche like this, his breath felt like a steel scraper against his throat, grating his nervous system to shreds.

He knew exactly where these kinds of situation led. The doctors warned him about it. He had to restrain himself. He knew he was harmless towards others. Not that he wanted to harm anyone.

Still, it didn't mean he couldn't hurt himself. And that felt good. It was at least some illusion of freedom. And any way would do, as long as the physical pain numbed out the real pain. The one that really hurt. The moments with his family that he still remembered.

So, he punched at anything in the vicinity, anything hard enough to matter. During the arduous wait for Viola, it was mostly the steering wheel or the dashboard. Sometimes he broke a few bones, yet this time, it was only bruises.

After a bout like that, he had blasted away from the vicinity of the clinic, but again had screeched the car to a halt, further down the street. Then he had returned again, and parked just outside.

The obedient dog.

But then he had seen the women climbing out.

And now, as he helped each one down the gutter, his doubts left him, his anger dissipated. Replaced by an energy he didn't know he had in himself anymore. The same one that made him into one of the hardest-working cops in his career.

One after the other, the women made their way down the wall. Slippers, patient gowns, children and babies draped across their chests, everyone shivering from the cold. None of them prepared for what waited outside.

As he ran his eyes along the crowd, he failed to locate Viola amongst them.

"And Viola? She here?" He threw out the question and the women immediately sensed his concern, then one by one they shook their heads in dismay.

"She disappeared right after you started helping us down," someone cried out from behind.

"Can't wait. Gotta go. Now!" Pål screamed and pushed everybody towards his car.

* * *

The Chief Inspector felt a sigh pass through him as he eyed the axes ripping the door apart. Everything, including breaking open this simple door, had taken an inordinate amount of time.

This whole investigation had been one long streak of wild cards. But the last one, his squad entering this clinic on a Sunday, without a green light from his boss, this was the point of no return.

He heard the maligning voices at the station, the ones behind his back. He was just about done for, almost buried for good. He had the wits to face this fact, he knew it to be true, yet he gambled everything on nothing more than a hunch.

And unless he came out of this with something akin to total success, this stunt would bury him and his career. The simple fact was that he couldn't return empty-handed, not after today.

But then everything had gone wrong. His men had entered the premises half an hour ago, and the only thing they had managed was to blunder their way through the almost empty clinic. They had set off all the alarms that could be triggered and seized the suspects he had no use for. Amateurs would fare better.

They had arrested a couple of oblivious young women, whom he would have to release in a couple of hours anyway. And he was sure that after they had come down from their feigned trauma, they would set their lawyers on them.

Then his men had shut down the surveillance system, but the only thing this generated was even more mayhem, as several crucial sections got sealed off. Including the room they were trying to get into now.

Yet he had a good nose for these things, and it told him that behind this door were the answers he was searching for. And as he watched his men blast open the door with their axes, an opening revealed itself.

Moments later, his boots crushed at the glass shards strewn across the marble floor. His eyes scanned the room and instantly caught the broken glass door. He swerved his body in between the protruding glass and rushed out onto the balcony.

As he whirled around himself, a simple fact reached his mind. Whoever had crushed this door, was long gone. And with them, probably his last chance at solving this case.

* * *

Viola was battered and left a trail of blood behind her. She shuddered in agony at the few glass shards still in her body. Yet, she was still standing upright, on her feet. After the impact through the glass, she had lost way too much blood, her mind fumbling with even the simplest of tasks. But as long as she could shuffle her legs back and forth, she knew she would be all right.

So it was nothing short of a miracle that she had made her way towards Magda's office without being detected. Her time was about to run out, she knew that.

But as she faced the door now, she was almost home. Yet, one tiny hurdle remained. The alarms had jammed all the doors, and this door, made of oak, wouldn't be so forgiving towards her body. This left only one option, Magda's card. She swiped it once, twice, but this yielded the same result as upstairs. Everything was sealed.

She pivoted her body around, searched for anything resembling a solution, but quickly realised this was a dead end.

Then, as if on cue, she heard all the alarm systems come back online. Whatever had brought this on, it couldn't have been timed better. She swept the card and the door hissed open.

As she burst into the room, she caught the glimmer of a laptop screen.

Late evening

Pål had spent the last two years in isolation, divided proportionally into two things, the booze and feeling sorry for himself. And he did everything in his power to uphold this holy balance.

But right now, as he supported one of the women whose foot was bleeding all over the snow, and eyed the children gushing with fear, he felt a pang of guilt. He couldn't quite understand what his holy balance had been about.

As they made their way to his car, Pål was worried sick. His tiny Fiat Cinquecento was the smallest tin can ever to be mass produced. The four people it was supposed to accommodate was just theory, and three was the more realistic limit.

So it wasn't without astonishment that Pål eyed the six women and their children as they squeezed into his minuscule vehicle. An unexplained but much-needed miracle.

Even the kids, who didn't quite understand what was happening, somehow sensed this was of great

281

consequence. Everyone kept silent, except an occasional whimper that begged their mums for just a little bit more elbow room.

Despite that everyone was crushed in the cramped space, everyone accepted the situation without as much as a single complaint.

The little one on his knees cuddled in for comfort, and for the first time in years, Pål felt a pang in his chest. The child found comfort in his arms, and he was the only one to provide it. His face glowed back to the kid, and this made all the difference in the world to the little one.

As he fired up the car, Pål's mind flashed back to his last two years. Here he was, still a man in his prime, someone who was more than capable of putting a dent in the sorry fabric of this reality. And the only thing he had managed was to drown himself in pity.

As he turned the car around, he knew he drove them off toward a place that would provide them with a more secure future. And hopefully less lies.

He began to feel good about himself. Maybe even good enough to upset his holy balance.

* * *

As she had lain cuddled into him, she had listened to his breath until it became an imperceptible whisper. And when it had become so subtle that she wasn't sure if she heard his inhalations or her own, her tears had come.

She never cried, never had the time nor the willingness to put a dent in her shell. It provided the much-needed security, something crucial for her everyday survival.

Yet this once, the very first time in a long while, she didn't try to stop the tears. And just this fact alone liberated some part of her that struggled with letting him be on his way.

Somewhere in the distance, swarming around her, she felt some movement. Maybe it was the police who had barged open the last of the doors. And as if to confirm this, she registered some faint movement from the corner of her eye. She realised the cops had made a circle around her, but despite their training and their procedures, none of them dared to speak a word. No one could explain what was going on, but everyone sensed this wasn't an ordinary patient.

Yet for Magda, this wasn't significant any longer. The only thing that was, were the few remaining moments with him.

* * *

Viola had found the files. But a simple delete wouldn't suffice. The first thing the cops would do, would be to run their recovery tools. This would dig up all the deleted files in a matter of hours, if not minutes. She had to initiate a low-level format, but this would require time. As she stared at the screen, she realised this would be about two hours. A lot more than she had at hand.

She heard a dull thud against the door. Had the police managed to locate her already? She knew that the last thing this man was about to wait for, would be for her to open the door. And as if to confirm this, several axes buried themselves into it. Her mind and body scrambled for another solution, one that she knew wasn't available.

Moments later, the team splintered the door out of its hinges, and the Chief Inspector locked onto Viola. The cop's eyes ran downward, to Viola's feet and stared at Magda's laptop.

But by now, the thing was one big mess, smashed to smithereens.

And although Viola had the sense to keep her mouth shut, her eyes sent the Chief Inspector a succinct message, telling him he could recover this junk as much as he wanted to.

Chapter 44

Night

Viola was dragged out of the clinic by the Chief Inspector himself. An IT expert from the force had taken extra care to pack up the laptop and he carried it now. Viola knew this was the only substantial evidence they had, or at least what remained of it.

But already, she noticed the cringes passing back and forth between the cops. They knew they had absolutely nothing. She had made sure she dug out the SSD and had pulverised it beyond recognition. Even the best recovery procedures wouldn't be able to deal with the thoroughness of her handiwork.

Couple that with the women being long gone, the lack of any substantial evidence inside the clinic, and Viola knew this case was about to explode in the Chief Inspector's face. He did everything to push away the simple facts, but Viola knew it was just as well as he did. He had failed on every level.

The only thing that remained was the question of Marianne. All the women had made use of the escape route, except for the blogger. This disaster-zone of a woman was bound to cause more trouble.

Maybe Marianne wasn't the only one with the knowledge of InviNordica's secret lab program, but she was certainly the one most willing to share it with the public. And after her disappearance had made her into a public figure, she was in the perfect position to snowball this case into a media circus seldom seen.

Viola was robbed of any illusions about the girl by now. After all, what more could she desire, especially someone as attention-starved as Marianne? Yet, there was a chance this whole thing could be kept under wraps. Not only for her sake, but for the women and their kids.

As Viola exited, her eyes were assaulted by an array of lights, all aimed at the clinic's entrance. It was the middle of the night, the brutal snow blizzard still blasted away at everyone, yet the police were far from the only ones parked outside. Viola realised there were two dozen reporters who gunned their flash-equipped cameras right in her face.

Viola eyed Stine's hawkish features, hungry for knowledge about her daughter's fate. Their gazes locked, Stine's face filled with a souped-up grin.

Viola felt her anger stir. She was handcuffed and dragged towards the police cars, but despite this, she jerked herself away from the cop's grip and grabbed Stine by the collar. She was about to trash the farmer's face to a pulp.

"Damn you, woman. You have any idea what you've...!" Viola lashed out at Stine. But the Chief Inspector's huge hands tugged at Viola's neck, twisted her elbow, then finally pulled her back.

"Not my doing, Miss. My mouth big, yes. But I'd not do that to my daughter." Viola didn't believe a word of it but then, behind Stine, a familiar face shimmered into view, her own mother, Anne.

Viola was struck by Anne's presence, her senses taking in the rest of her surroundings, the journalists, a couple of them familiar faces from *Aftenposten*, some favourable co-workers, and some bitter enemies. No matter the relation, each gaze stung at her chest. Being led out by the cops like a simple criminal, paraded to the world like some kind of spectacle, carried a finality to itself. This was all of her choices manifested. The only thing left for her to do was to shy away from their glances. Knowing all too well her life would never be the same.

Her mind raced to the inevitable conclusion as she realised who was actually behind the call. Stine was telling the truth; maybe they had been empty threats from the beginning. And the decision-making might have come from the person much closer to Viola.

And as her eyes swept to her mother, she realised her suspicion was more than justified. This simple fact left her reeling in devastation.

"You made a promise to me back at my office. Remember?" Here was a woman tired of her own daughter's reckless actions, far from prepared to accept what Viola had to say.

At some other time, Viola would have made an attempt to listen to her mother. If this was done for her, why all the reporters from *Aftenposten* at this site? Why were these bloodhounds gunning their gear at her? Was that for her own good, and she didn't know better?

Before Viola's thoughts could arrive at the inevitable conclusion, someone flew past her. Viola whipped her head around and realised it was Marianne, scuttling towards the reporters.

"Guys. Girls. You wouldn't believe what they made me do in there," she shrieked.

Viola tried to take in what was happening around her. Marianne about to launch into a story filled with her lies, not even giving a second thought to the consequences.

People are different in all sorts of uncanny ways, and sometimes one shouldn't expect too much of them. That had been her lesson a long time ago. She had tried to live by this plain fact. She had learnt to lower her expectations, way down to ground level, simply because her life was filled with so many difficult hurdles. As she grew older, this ground level kept getting even lower, and her assumptions with it. Yet at this moment, however much she tried to reconcile what she had before her, she simply couldn't.

And as Viola's eyes returned to her mother's, Anne moved closer to Viola.

"Viol, I always taught you that great journalism is supposed to provoke anger and inspire action while it batters our souls. But this place and what you've done here? This was done for your own good, girl. In time, you will learn to appreciate this, hon."

At this moment, everything snapped inside Viola and, irreversibly, a veil was lifted away from her eyes, one that filtered her whole life. Viola knew she would never find common ground with Anne. This would be the last time they saw each other.

So she ripped off her necklace containing the compass. And without any further comments, gave it back to Anne.

The next instant Viola felt her body swallowed by the crowd of police officers, as she was tugged and battered into submission, until she felt her face pushed against a police car's window.

Epilogue

The winter had gone, replaced by a touch of spring. Viola stared past the rain-soaked car window at one of the many suburban Oslo streets filled with endless brownish row-houses. Enough time had passed for the worst of the media carnage to die down. For the last couple of weeks, she was even able to go out of the house without being stalked by what used to be her own kind. The Chief Inspector's raid on InviNordica yielded him close to nothing, except disgracing the department for such a hasty action.

When the case got splashed all over the news headlines, everyone who was in some way involved with InviNordica, backpedalled on their stories, leaving the police department with table scraps of a case. The last she heard, the Chief Inspector was no longer stationed at Grønlandsleiret, and not surprisingly, there was never anyone available there to comment on his current status or whereabouts.

The women had either returned home or settled into a new life thanks to Pål's tenacity. Although there was little substantial proof found at the clinic, Magda had trouble explaining her fuzzy book-keeping and would see legal consequences of that. After the media attention, her partners at the clinic backed out and decided to close it down and sell off the property.

At first Marianne made a lot of noise, just the way she desired it, but Viola paid her a visit and reminded her that she was still in the possession of the recording which painted Marianne in a quite different light. The blogger quickly backed off with her news statements and blamed her inconsistency on a fictitious bipolar disease.

And herself, she felt lucky. Considering her stunts at InviNordica, and the potential legal repercussions hanging over her, she got off with barely a scratch. The most aggravating part was that she became an unwanted focus of the media for a while. But instead of concentrating on what had occurred at the clinic, she did her best to redirect the frenzy into something more constructive, a much-needed public debate on the current plight of childless women in Norway.

She returned her gaze towards the row of houses. They had never spent much time in his house, simply because Ronny always made arrangements that would accommodate her, sometimes even whimsical wishes.

She had attempted to forge a bond with several men over the course of the last twenty years. Each time it had crash-landed in an incessant battle of unfulfilled egos. She had cursed inside herself at their immaturity, their small-time pettiness, or whatever other reason she had for being dissatisfied with them.

Then she had concluded the last random quarrel with a daft smile, and left them without even the slightest explanation. At that time, she had thought it fortunate she had never looked back, and certainly didn't regret any of her actions. But now, she thought it unfortunate that she never reflected on her relationships. Never even considered reassigning some of the blame to her own ego.

And then, along came Ronny, a man who made it difficult to play out her own petty dramas. Instead of battling her, he listened, instead of forcing her, he gave in. And not because he didn't have his own views on matters, but simply because he cared, and rarely needed to be right. At first this emotional constellation was alien to her, it enraged her, then it baffled her, but with time, it melted into gratitude.

This was the fourth time she had come here, to his street, his home. She thought it would be simple, go up to the porch, pass through the cute knee-high gate, ring the doorbell that rarely worked, then just say hi.

Yet, she never made it that far. She didn't even make it out of her car. And now, as she sat there with her legs twisted in some unknown asana, her fingers twitching at her cell phone, she cursed at herself. What the hell was she thinking? Was she naive enough to think he would have her back, after what she had made him go through?

Damn. Damn. This was the last time she would come down here.

The tires screeched against the concrete as she stamped on the gas. But the impetus of her car ground to a halt. Before her, right in the middle of the street, a man's figure stood in her way.

Ronny.

Her first impulse was to step on the gas, drive past, pretend she wasn't here. Maybe he hadn't seen her and even if he had, it was not too late to flee. But he locked onto her gaze, confronted her with a smirk, then launched himself towards her car. And as he bent towards the window, she struggled to make sense of it all.

"I was just, you know, driving by," she said.

It was only a matter of seconds before he noticed she was pregnant. A longer pause followed. But instead of questions or discussions, he threw the door open and slid up to her.

"And I was just standing here. You know," he whispered, then grabbed her into his arms as she felt her spine bristle in panic. He just hugged her into himself. Her body loosened itself and folded into his chest. She squinted her eyes, then closed them as she felt a familiar warmth spread through her.

As it was now, the InviNordica incident still left a gushing wound inside her. But the bitter conclusion had also expunged the poison that had been inside her all her life.

And the last five months?

They had been different enough to have hope. She had felt a little bit lighter, less burdened by everything.

She remembered her shrink. He had told her that infertility and mitochondrial disease was a constant trauma. It was a ceaseless crisis on a physical and emotional level. He had explained to her how it bred negative emotions, and that her life energy would always be channelled towards reliving that fear. That her existence had been a constant anxiety zone from day one, the day she had learned about her condition. That she would find it hard to find joy and hope in her everyday life. Much less having a child. But if she tried hard enough, she would get stronger. And with time, daring, and perseverance, she would even find a way to enjoy the present.

At that time, this shrink's perspective only aggravated her. And why shouldn't it? She wasn't the one with the problem.

But as she thought about it now, she realised he might have had a point. Her worries hadn't disappeared, but at least they had settled into their usual everyday rhythms.

Was the baby too silent for too long? Was her morning sickness too terrible? And would the baby get enough to eat? Would she eat the wrong thing and hurt the baby? Was she too stressed? Would she be a bad parent?

All of that was still there. But for the first time in a long time, it also felt normal.

The child she was carrying, she knew exactly what it meant, the risks involved and the transience of it all. If she wanted guarantees, this was the worst idea she could have for a lasting happiness. The memory of Markus would always be there as a reminder of that.

No. This wasn't about any grand expectations of a perfect future. This was more about willing herself to put up a brave fight so she would enjoy this very moment. And the next. And the next. Miniscule steps.

And as she was prepared for the bad but yearned for the good, she expressed silent gratitude for each day they were given.

The three of them.

Vlog, 1ˢᵗ entry 9.7.2016

She felt far from ready for this. After twenty years, she couldn't imagine how she would ever be ready for this moment.

Her Vlog site "One in Eight" was prepared with the expert hands of a graphic and web designer. A service that cost her a small fortune. But more importantly, she had used all her spare time to prepare her message meticulously. Several weeks' worth of painful digging into her own psyche and even more rehearsals behind her. The endless training was necessary, as this was the only way she would gather enough courage to go through with this confrontation. So she had learnt to recite her first post walking, sleeping, and even in three languages, if need be.

Yet as everything merged into this moment of truth, and she was about to punch the "On Air" button, everything in her just froze.

She eyed her fingers, and realised they were cramped and twitchy. Useless again. And her mind was again drowned by all the reasons why this had been a bad idea in the first place.

What could she possibly have to say that was of real value to people? With the Internet swamped with so much information about infertility and personal struggles, would anyone listen, or even care? And even if she didn't focus on what other people would say about her, why was she a bag of nerves right now? Wasn't she an experienced journalist who had been in the firing line for half of her life? By now, these kinds of speeches should come naturally to her.

Maybe she wanted to do some good, but for all the wrong reasons? She would end up just like Marianne, enamoured more by being the centre of attention than actually building a supportive community for those in need.

But all of this was nonsense. This vlog was about something more important than the deep-seated layers of her neurosis. This wasn't about her needs or wants. Instead, here was a real opportunity to set things right after Marianne's mess. It was about what she could do for others.

And as she grabbed an extra deep breath, an electric jolt passed through her as she punched the record button on the webcam. Her body moved itself out of its own accord, and she saw her face reflected on her laptop.

A red lamp shimmered. She was live. And she felt herself step over the edge. Into nothingness.

"For the last twenty years I have been ashamed, terrified, and frustrated. All these years, I've run away, lied, and destroyed my life just so I could hide this from everyone. Today, I am changing it. And although I am expecting a child now, my struggle has made me into one in eight. That is how many we are. One woman out of eight will be touched by infertility at some point in her life and when it does, I intend to be here. To let you know that none of you are alone. Childlessness, that's me, but it could also be your friend, your neighbour, your sister. It could be you.

"I am Viola Voss, and I have a story to share with you."

If you enjoyed this book, please let others know by leaving a quick review on Amazon. Also, if you spot anything untoward in the paperback, get in touch. We strive for the best quality and appreciate reader feedback.

editor@thebookfolks.com

www.thebookfolks.com